Last Night and the Night Before

by

Patricia Popham Taylor

Copyright © 2007 by Patricia Popham Taylor

ISBN 0-7414-3860-7

Cover Art Designed and Created by Philip Shroyer.

Published by:

INFINITY
PUBLISHING.COM

1094 New DeHaven Street, Suite 100
West Conshohocken, PA 19428-2713
Info@buybooksontheweb.com
www.buybooksontheweb.com
Toll-free (877) BUY BOOK
Local Phone (610) 941-9999
Fax (610) 941-9959

Printed in the United States of America

Printed on Recycled Paper

Published April 2007

To Sandra Felix Shroyer
who always understood everything,

and

Christina Wong
who made this book happen.

Three

Last night and the night before
Twenty-four robbers came knockin' at my door.
I asked them what they wanted
And this is what they said:
Better run, little girl, or you'll be dead
I ran out as they ran in
Looking for the remnants of my next of kin.
Call for the doctor, call for the nurse
Call for the lady with the alligator purse.

Child's Jump Rope Rhyme

I went down to the sacred store
Where I'd heard the music years before
But the man there said the music
Wouldn't play.

Don McLean

But soon, too soon, the lover turns his eyes
Again she falls, again she dies!
How wilt thou now the fatal sisters move?
No crime was thine, if't is no crime to love.

Yet even in death Eurydice he sung
Eurydice still trembled on his tongue
Eurydice the woods
Eurydice the floods
Eurydice the rocks and hollow mountains rung!

Alexander Pope

Contents

Weather

It rained the afternoon Gard went looking for the Devil. And the Devil was open for business.

Return

She is sitting sideways in a large armchair, reading from the well of her lap. She doesn't know the time, isn't sure of the day of the week, has fallen so far down in the book she doesn't see his shadow filling the doorway, a massive silhouette.

"What's reading?"

She glances up. He can certainly enter houses quietly for so lumbering a man.

He comes into the room, looks for himself.

"*Le Fantôme de L'Opéra*? Don't they have this in English?"

"Uh huh."

"So?"

"Despite Andrew Lloyd Webber, the mind that produced this was not English."

"I live to learn. Research or recreation?"

"Rec. Accounts of hopeless love always amuse me."

She continues looking up at him, the book now closed and marked between her fingers.

"Maybe," he says, "I should have taken the part when it was offered."

"You're wrong for the role," she says easily. "Erik was skeletal."

"Which I am not."

She fixes her eyes upon his torso, carefully hidden beneath a leather jacket several deliberate sizes too big.

"Which you are not."

He notices she's lost her place in the book.

"And besides," she continues, "would you really have wanted to spend a year in Toronto?"

"Would you have come with me?"

"Certainly not. Canadians give me hives."

"Well, then." He touches her hand with his index finger.

She smiles, raises her eyes to his face, too broad and too beaten up to ever be considered handsome. He drops to her level, lays his forehead on her knees, flung over the arm of the chair.

"You've got me on your knees," he says quietly.

"Yours, too."

"Any help for it?"

She feels the words form against her kneecaps.

They have neither seen nor spoken to each other in three months.

"Which room," she asks, "of the *Hotel du Horreurs*?" Her voice reveals the very slightest of tremors.

He stands, excavates her from the shadowed depths of the chair.

"Any room. Third floor."

"Think your muscles have stayed intact? You eat too much on tour."

"I can take us both to the last room on the right, top of the house, without losing a breath."

"Will you kiss me when we get there, for God's sake?"

"Oh, yeah," he breathes. "And then some."

She lays her mouth against his carotid artery. The pulse accelerates. "Go," she says.

*   *   *

The afternoon faded, darkened, went to night.

Rest was in order. The sheets, ridden with perspiration, were hopeless.

"If you don't move, I can't untangle here."

"Move?" Gard said, his breath hitching.

"You lost your bet."

"Bet."

"That you could carry me up three flights without losing breath–have you forgotten your boast of only hours

3

ago?"

Gard lay on his back, dragging in air. His chest heaved.

"I did carry you and respiration was normal," he answered a minute later. "You didn't say a thing about regular breathing after that."

"This is true." She raised herself onto her left elbow. "Need food?"

"Need sleep."

"Wuss."

He tried to disentangle his right arm from the mess. He gave up.

"Been up thirty-six hours."

She snorted.

"You know what I mean," he coughed. "Have mercy."

She unwrapped the sheets from his arm. He closed his eyes. She smiled.

"Tolerance. I have tolerance." She ran her palm over his face. "Hey."

"Uh?" He didn't open his eyes.

"We cannot sleep in here."

"Not?"

"I do not like stewing in my own juices. And when you wake up, neither will you."

He opened his eyes without focusing. " 'Kay."

"Across the hall. Come on. Lean on me."

He made an unintelligible sound. "Lean on you, I'll break you."

"In your dreams, Band Man. C'mon."

In the facing bedroom, into laundered sheets and instant sleep they sank.

When the phone rang, it was dark still, or again, outside. She sat up straight, zombie from the grave. The phone rang again. She retrieved the handset, pushed "talk" and lay down on her side, facing her sleeper.

"Hello?

"It's me. Okay to call?

"Mm."

4

"Do you know what day it is?"

She considered. "Dark when we went to sleep. Still dark. Is it today?"

"Nope. Tomorrow."

"Really. I rather thought so." Now fully awake, she rubbed her face; color returned to it. "How were the Saxons and the Huns?"

"Looked a lot like Brits and Krauts to me. Sounded like, too."

She pushed her hair away from her face. "Too bad."

"Your standards are too high," he said, hovering over a laugh.

She shifted the phone. Gard was gone from the world. From the tide line of the sheets and bedcovers, she could see he had not moved since they'd changed rooms.

"Uh huh. So I'll assume the barbarians are just as properly versed in rock and roll as they were last year."

"Just as."

They smiled unseeingly at each other.

"Are you having us to dinner?"

She answered, "Of course. Thursday."

"For everybody?"

"Twice a year, like death and taxes. You know that."

"Even the new guy?"

"Even him."

"Will you marry me? I really want you to."

"No, you don't. You just want to eat Lily's cuisine and see if the new guy will piss me off."

He laughed. "I don't think it's gonna take this one too long."

"Because?"

"He wasn't even *born* when we did the first world tour. He's so wide-eyed he needs sunglasses at night. And he loves to ask stupid questions. Lots of 'em."

"Really. Has he any redeeming features?" She slid carefully up to a sitting position.

"Plays a hell of a sax. Burns up a Fender. Better than most. And percussion is his life. Maybe he's one of those

5

geniuses who can't do anything but count. Whaddya call 'em?"

"*Idiot savant*," she answered, amused.

"Right. You'll probably think he's just the idiot part, but the kid really can play."

"Then nothing else much matters."

"Not on tour. But dinner at your house may be more than he can handle."

"He may surprise us."

"Not as much as he's going to be surprised. He thinks you're Gard's cousin or something."

"Does he? Did he unravel that mystery himself?"

"Idiot, remember. And Gard's not telling him shit. You know how he is."

"Yes, I know. It has always been for my privacy."

"Probably Gard's gonna have to threaten him to make him keep his mouth shut."

"No, I'm sure not."

"Maybe so. Kid thinks he's friggin' died and gone to Heaven since he got this gig. He won't do anything to screw that up."

As the conversation grew longer, she dropped her voice until it was barely audible. Gard had not stirred. She hung up. Turned on a lamp. A half hour passed. Returned to lying on her side, watching him. At last she raised her head, arched her neck, and leaned over to his ear.

"Gard." Softly. "Gard." He did not stir.

"John."

Use of his first name was rare, and usually brought a response.

She rubbed his arm. For some time she spoke quietly in his ear, her hand on his shoulder.

He opened his eyes without seeing. She began massaging his neck.

"Who?" he said.

"Gard," she said. "Come back."

His eyes moved back and forth. She tracked them until they slowed. Stopped. Came to rest on hers.

"Deesh."

"Uh huh."

"It's you. Deesh?"

"Uh huh."

He moved, slid his arm over, reached for her hand. Raised it and kissed her knuckles. She nodded. He struggled up, sitting. Laid his head in his palms. Shook his head.

"Oh, man."

"What is it?"

"That was some dream."

She saw in his face tinges of gray around the skin.

"Jet lag or tour hangover?"

He shook his head. They sat in bed, she waiting for him to reply.

Finally, "Neither. Just a passing wave of weirdness."

"So long as it's passing." Her voice began to return to its customary irony.

He nodded. His hair stuck out around his head as if striking lightning had haloed it.

"Do you want to tell me?" She sounded quite calm, although she was not.

"No. S'okay. I don't remember. Not the pictures, I don't know."

She waited a moment before getting up and walking naked across the hall. His eyes followed.

"Every time I see you like that, it's like I've never seen you before. At all."

She returned, carrying his watch. "You're merely in post-nightmare nonsense. Wrestle yourself out of it." She got back in bed. Laid her head against his arm. "Looks to be about eight-thirty."

"Oh, great. Now we'll be awake all night."

She shrugged. "Okay with me."

"Come to think of it," he was grinning.

"Yeah, yeah. Time for you to take me out for an evening breakfast." She swung herself off the bed and walked to the doorway. "Come on down to my bathroom when you're steady. Oh, and your clothes aren't on this floor anymore."

7

For a half second what crossed his face was fear. She had her back to him and didn't see.

"Lily decided to oil the wardrobes up here, so I moved your stuff down a floor, lest you be in need of later fumigation."

"Uh," he said, returned to safety. "Do I need to know what day it actually is?"

"Not today. Maybe tomorrow."

He nodded. "Probably should go home and open some windows."

"You probably should." She turned back to him and passed him his watch. "Except that your truck is still at the airport."

He looked puzzled.

"Kas called."

"Kas?"

"Kaseem. Your bass guitarist?"

"I'm not following."

"That is apparent. You've left all your things, even your other woman, the Strat, and also the Gibson, the second Strat, your clothes, your wallet, and your passport in his van. You will now find said van in his garage. His account is that you demanded he bring you here as soon as the Fasten Seatbelt light went out."

"I did? Yes. I did. He slept on the plane and I didn't. Thought it wiser not to navigate alone."

"I wondered why you walked in with nothing but a key and pornographic fantasies."

He grinned as evilly as a sleep haze would allow. "When did you have time to wonder that?"

"My oh my aren't we pleased with ourselves this morning?"

"Yes, we are. And it's night."

As she rounded the doorway she threw back over her shoulder, "And to answer your question, just now."

She might have told him how her flesh and bones leapt when he walked through the door, how they were leaping still, but she didn't.

8

Aerial Photography

Imagine a house. See it as a hundred years old, a house the size of a hotel. Standing testament to former glory, when on this street there had been nothing but this house, its lawn, its fountains, its graveled drive, its carriage house, its glass-domed conservatory rising over a garden all the colors of love and pain.

A house alive.

Now see it, dead.

Take a cartographer's view. The roof repaired but the shingles thin. Clapboards gone gray in the rain and sun and heat and cold. Shutters gone, one left here or over there, dangling from a single hinge, equally grayed in relentless decomposition. And the heights of limestone, speckled with lichen and long-dead ivy. Why hurricane shutters on a stone house where no hurricanes will ever blow?

"Why not?" says Deesh. "They give the whole elevation that nice southern rot look."

"But we're not in the south," Gard reminds her.

"Not, praise Jazus, anymore."

Picture this mansion before, a kingdom unto itself, its lands sloping away for miles, fortified by its own acreage.

Stone walls rising higher and higher, two stories, three, four. A meticulous gravel drive trailing through the grounds, up to a porte-cochere, and through it to a mammoth stone carriage house, the child of the principal building. Surrounding all, the noises of life–clattering, laughing, calling, doors slamming, water spraying, the daylight hum of winged insects, the evening fall of crickets and mild night winds.

A house alive.

Now see it, dead. The walls themselves lonely and threatening, as if their purpose has been long decayed.

9

A house as corpse left in a pauper's grave, the grass subsumed by warehouses and train tracks; the warehouses closed, weathered, boarded up, no use, no reason left to be; the tracks deserted, wooden ties returning to earth, metal rails dulled by fifty years of dooryard dust, settling then scattering. Buildings, tracks, a withered tree, blowing brush, all sinking, this fashionless side of town its own Pompeii, collapsing under Vesuvian neglect.

A fortress so guarded by its solitude as to stand without witnesses.

Descend from the myriad of chimney stacks.

Stand close, your eyes level with paintless wood, the scarred and filthy stones, the mullioned windows releasing thin cold light, the gray buried silence of it all.

Inspect more closely.

Fancy you find yourself deceived. Examine the splintering wood and damaged stone, and see decay halted in mid-stride, a silent house sealed and resealed in polyeurathaned nakedness. The falling shutter secured tightly on its sagging angle, the crumbling roof not crumbling at all, but tight and weather-proofed under its illusion of mortality.

Notice the great front doors open quietly and at once on hinges decoupaged with decorative rust.

Look through a windowpane and stare. Inside see lush furniture, carpets, beautiful things collected from across the centuries, elaborate moldings, and within the walls fresh plumbing here and there, a growing matrix of new copper wiring creeping over the skeleton of the old. Elaborate draperies hang from walls seamlessly rising to barrel-vaulted ceilings many feet high, sheltering rounded door frames and rooms, as if this place cannot contain the sharpness of corners.

The house you find is not dead. It seems to be lying in a coma from an outer view.

Inside, details are old here, but they are clean, and astringently neat, beckoning, baroque, and whole.

Without access to its interior, to some the house appears dangerous, deserted, dying, a place to pass by quickly with eyes averted. Which suits its owner and sole occupant perfectly, unerringly, well. Why would anyone choose so splendid a homestead, only to pretend its splendor has vanished into time? A house no one wants, in neighborhood deserted by people, pets, and the corps of engineers. Why?

"So no one will come over unannounced to bring a plate of cookies or to borrow my garden hose," says Deesh.

"You have no garden hose," Gard tells her.

"Brilliantly to my point. Why squander time explaining that to the neighbors?"

"You have no neighbors." He is enjoying himself.

"Your powers of observation have sharpened with your months in Europe."

"Thank you." He bows. "Squandering. We could do that."

"Squander what?" Severity fails to mask her amusement.

"Time. Energy. Air." He shrugs. Her choice.

"What did you have in mind?" She runs her hand through the hair hanging over her forehead, pushing it back.

"We haven't been to the third floor in a while."

"I see."

He assumes a quizzical look.

"All right," she concedes, "As long as there is no sidebar, your honor, on the squanderous waste of one person living in a house with twelve bedrooms she rarely sleeps in."

"And one she does," he says fondly, as if recalling a priceless a work of art.

"And one she does," she agrees, kissing him briefly. "You could give up this gypsy life of wealth and world adoration, and just build rooms onto my house."

"Yes," he says, considering, knowing it's a fantasy. "But we're running out of dirt upon which to build. And you know you don't cotton to squatters. Would you be grateful if I re-carpentered the dormers in the back? Plumbed an outside faucet?"

"Why?"

"So you wouldn't have to carry buckets out to your

flowers."

"Then how would I water them?"

"Garden hose!"

She sighs. "And the next thing you know I'd have neighbors blundering over here to borrow it."

"God forbid."

She nods. "I continue to hope so."

He doesn't tell her that he has already bought every scrap of land around her; real estate is expensive here, but the land is zoned for commercial use, and no merchants would build where there are no people. The ghost neighborhood will remain undisturbed, as, he fervently wishes with all his soul, will she.

Nightfall

She looks up from the premeditated disorder of her desk.

He twirls what she believes to be a wrench.

"What are you making there?" He considers her writing black magic voodoo, impossible for those born without the knowledge.

"*Fin de siècle.* Poetics and culture in France and England. Late nineteenth century. *Symbolistes. Decadence.* Phantoms in opera houses. The usual."

"How come decadence sounds so much cooler when you speak it in French and it's a literary movement?"

"Because it's better when it's French and a literary movement." She smiles sweetly at him. Ducks her head into a stairstack of books.

He has tried to engage her in conversation, but she is unmistakably consumed with the nineteenth century, and he shouldn't wrest her away. She is working, after all. He endures no interruption when he is working, he knows the value of undisturbed concentration. Still, he wishes she would ask him what he's thinking, take off her reading glasses, and draw out of him the thing he wants to tell her. He doesn't even know what to say or how to say it, but the words form in him: "Help me." But help him how? About what? She would have to read his mind to know what's in it, and while she's consistently good at that, he has an idea that the unease he feels–brushing at him like the whispered wing of a bat–arises from a source completely unknown to her experience.

So he says nothing. He forces a grin at her, and assumes a facade of nonchalance as he leaves the library, certain he has somehow re-validated a death sentence pronounced on him by an unknown judge for an undisclosed crime.

A Party for Dinner

"Are you certain this is all right with you?" he asked.

"I am reclusive, not misanthropic," she answered. "Lily cooks. Lily cleans up." She shrugged. "What's the big deal?"

"When," he asked, stroking the inside of her elbow, "did you last have anyone but me to dinner?"

"Long enough that Lily probably doesn't remember the kitchen. But it will come back to her."

"And anyway," he said casually, "she has laundry to do, hasn't she?"

"She has. And quite a lot of it, too."

"I'm proud."

"Uh huh. As soon as she remakes all the beds, you'll have to start over."

"All twelve?

She nodded. "And I should think my room as well."

He looked across the library to the doors leading there.

"Thirteen's a good even number."

She looked sternly at him. "It is fortunate that you possess one or two life skills to compensate for your pitiable grasp of mathematics."

He played a little air guitar and hummed. "I have an errand. Back later."

Returned to her book, she waved without looking up.

*   *   *

He came back hefting a crate from the liquor store.

"What's The Queen reading?" he asked.

"Herodotus."

"Doing the ancients next book after this one?"

"No. I am calming myself."

"Do you need–er–calming?"

"Not from you when," she looked up, raising her eyes in surprise at the stamp on the crate, "you've a case of champagne in your arms. Dom Perignon is a jealous mistress. And the guys would have been just as happy with Krug and beer. What possessed you?"

"I'm rich, remember?"

"Ah. I had forgotten. Can six people drink twelve bottles of such costly stuff?" She smiled indulgently.

"Seven people. One of these is for Lily. *After* she finishes cooking." He smiled indulgently back.

"So where's your white horse?"

"Don't need one. Hero on a bike, that's me."

"Motorcycles. When was it you were supposed to have grown up?"

He shifted the champagne to one arm. "Day I met you, wasn't it?"

"I wasn't much help, I see."

He shrugged. "It is rumored you have other gifts."

She raised an eyebrow at him. The book was still open.

"Come on, babe. Cheer up. I think your dinner parties are the only thing in life Cleve looks forward to."

"Cleve thrives on melancholy."

"That's why he composes and lyricizes so well."

"*Lyricizes*?" She blew out her breath. "Go to the kitchen. Isn't the crate getting heavy?"

"Not yet." He shifted it to the other arm. "See?"

She watched him stand in the doorway. Finally, "Boxer's body, depreciated face, voice of a god. Spends a fortune on champagne he won't drink. Strange man," she said affectionately.

"But you crave me to distraction despite my mis-shapen parts?" He was laughing at her now.

"Of course. It only got worse after you sang with Pavarotti. I was never the same after."

"Neither was Pavarotti, I'm afraid."

"I'm not going to have this conversation with you again. I have pointed out some dozen or sixteen times that you could have sung opera if you'd wanted to."

"Did you want me to?"

"No," she said.

"Why not?"

"I do not want ever to have to have Pavarotti to dinner."

He snickered and blew a kiss at her.

"I will now schlep the jealous mistress off to the kitchen, and see what I can find to eat before dinner," he said.

"Good luck," she said absently, returning to her book.

*   *   *

Later, he wandered back into the library. She sat, staring into the fire.

"Thinking?"

"Mm."

He waited. Walked down the lines of bookcases, dragging his hand along, fingering spines, smelling leather and yellowing paper. It was good to do nothing.

"Lily here?" she called to him.

He strolled back down the room. "She is that." He threw himself on the sofa facing the fireplace, propped his feet on the table before it.

"Been looking into Homer," he said, endeavoring casualness.

"You must be desperate," she said, rising and sitting on the table to face him.

"In English," he amended apologetically.

"I supposed so," she said, dryly.

"It's different in Greek, huh?"

"Yes. It's in Greek."

He took in air, blew it out.

She relented. "The poetics are completely different. Do you remember which translation you have?"

"Oh, is that who that guy is? I thought he was the writer, that Homer was the publisher or something." He grinned. Back on even ground.

"Uh huh."

"Um. Fitzgerald, I think."

"Then you're reading it in iambic pentameter. English usually works best in that."

"That why there's so many poems in it?"

"You're a very quick learner, did you know that?"

He bowed slightly. "So why is it different in Greek?"

"Because its construction is best suited to dactylic hexameter, which usually sounds pretty flat in English. A different poetic language, you might say." She drew her knees up, wrapped her arms around them. The fireplace smackled just behind her.

"You know, I'd feel more like the student and you the professor if you'd get up here with me instead of sitting on the table at my feet." He moved over, offering a narrow space between himself and the sofa's arm.

"I'm sure," she muttered. In a few moments, she took the space. "Please don't assault me. I don't want to looked mussed when the company comes."

"Good Lord, woman. Who'd want to assault you? A man'd have to be blind."

"Silly me not to have thought of that," she smiled sweetly. She opened a few buttons on her shirt and ran her hands through her hair. And waited.

His color changed slightly. "Okay, okay. I was mistaken."

"Very mistaken."

"Yeah, very, very, very mistaken in very many ways."

She rebuttoned. "Now, where were we?"

"Homer."

"Yes. In Fitzgerald."

"Yeah. It bothers me."

"Why?"

"I don't know. It's like Odysseus is . . . *familiar*

17

somehow."

"He should be," she said. "He could be your brother. Considerably older brother."

"Misshapen."

"You are not misshapen."

"Well, disproportionate, then."

"Stop bellying up to the barbell and hoisting a few hundred, then."

"Gotta hoist."

"The defense rests."

"So what reminds you? Of him and me?"

She looked at him intently. "Courage, I think. The guts to never give up. And you could charm the scales off a snake, if necessity beckoned."

He glanced away. He was never confident of his own steadiness when she spoke to him of heroics in so matter-of-fact a tone.

"Yeah?"

"Yes," she said, so softly he could hardly hear.

"You know what I like about him? Penelope was smarter than he was. And she stayed for him, all that time he was on the road. Twenty years." He shook his head, wondering at it all.

"Maybe," she said, smoothing his hair, "she liked the way he wore his flowing locks."

Whatever answer he was reaching for was interrupted.

Lily knocked on the open door. "How many this time?"

Gard and Deesh counted on their fingers. Lily rolled her eyes.

"Well," he said, appearing to be deep in thought. "There's Cleve, Leslie, Kaseem, Vlad, Shiv, that's five, plus us, that's eight."

"That's seven," warned Lily.

"Oh, come on–"

She interrupted him. "I am not eating with that tribe

18

of wild Indians."

"Band, Lily, *band* of wild Indians," he interrupted back with as straight a face as he could muster.

"I'll just put them off," she replied, ignoring him, "and likely as not, they'll put me off. Why don't you remember the help don't eat with the master?"

Deesh looked up sharply. "One more white slave/master remark, Lily, and we'll all follow you around with our plates full, waiting for you to land."

Her tone was one of a point long debated and never resolved.

"Lord have mercy," shivered Lily. "All right, I will eat in the kitchen because it will be more civilized than your dining room tonight."

"You're certain?" She gave Lily a surrendering look. "But don't stay after, cleaning up. Come tomorrow. I can give you a hand then."

Lily acquiesced. "And it will be seven?"

Deesh glanced at Gard. "Unless this Shiv has two heads and requires two places."

Gard said with absolute assurance, "One head. Just one."

Lily withdrew.

"*Shiv?*" she asked.

"I know, it's awful, isn't it?" He shifted, locked his arm around her shoulders. "But he's nineteen, and he thinks it's a cool name for a renegade musician."

"He's a renegade?"

"Not nearly as much as he thinks." He laughed. "He's so local, it's all he can do to keep from saying 'Gahh-leeee' most of the time. He's right out of Michigan–played with a band called Bagel Creek, for God's sake, and he wasn't born when we did our first world tour."

"Yes, Kas told me."

"So be warned, he's likely to ask you all kinds of questions you're not going to answer, and all kinds of questions that you'd surely reckon he already has answers for." Gard sighed. "But he doesn't, so just ignore him. I'm sure Leslie and Cleve have already explained the house rules to him."

"I don't know the child sufficiently well to dislike him enough to invite him for dinner and ignore him." She stretched her legs out next to his. "And isn't Michigan where you started when you didn't have any answers?"

"Don't remind me."

"So, if he's so annoying, why hire him?"

"Because," he answered, "he's madman on a guitar, and he plays the saxophone like fire burning on gunpowder. Also, he's the best drummer we heard."

"Ah. Kas suggested he was a savant."

"Idiot, yes. I won't let him get too close to you."

"If you didn't tour like a bat blown out of hell, you might not have to shop for drummers as often as you do."

"Want me home more often?" he smiled smugly.

"No. Nor do I want you home less often. If the rest of them could take it, you'd be on the road ten months a year instead of six."

"If the rest of them could take it, then you'd have to come with me, so we'd fight about that all the time, and there you are."

"Really, don't you think about booking more venues?"

"Yeah. I think about it. That's all. Six months a year is enough. Now, if the kid can just adjust to the pace. By the way, the guys call him Yewit sometimes; he doesn't get it, but he thinks it's some kind of club password or something, and he's in."

"Yewit?"

"You Idiot."

"Ah. The lilt of the southern accent." She wrinkled her nose, as if southern accents summoned allergies. "I'm sure," she said kindly, "that Leslie will keep a leash on him."

"Just like she does with the rest of us, you mean."

"I mean."

*   *   *

Still later they were back to Odysseus when the first knock came.

"'What fresh hell is this?'" she mocked.

He looked pleased with himself. "Probably those who burn their candles at both ends."

"Very good. You surprise me. I wouldn't have thought you'd remember."

"I remember everything."

"Sure you do."

Again the frustration when he was serious and she wasn't and he wanted her to be.

"C'mon, Deesh."

"Okay, I'll stop. But don't you think, Sweet Potato, that we'd best let the hell hounds in?"

Out of the library they went, as one, to answer the door.

The musicians who made up Evermore were largely unchanged since the six months last she had provided them dinner. Leslie came in first, her hair a black cloud. She was so surprisingly beautiful that once upon a long time ago Deesh was of the private opinion she must be faking it somewhere.

"No one can look like that and be such a good person, too."

Gard had teased her that she must be jealous, and she had told him he was quite right. "I can't imagine what it's like to have a face so perfect."

"Funny," Gard had remarked. "She sort of said the same thing about you."

"Just flattering your vanity," she snorted.

But the time had come, and the time had gone, and the time had come round again, and she knew that Leslie had no falsehoods about her. A close alliance had slowly soaked through time and geographical division, and she marveled at Leslie's patience with them all. Her voice could match Gard's any note he chose, and so it was her job to sing

21

anything he could sing, and to protect everyone in the band each from all the others. She had no illusions, and she never told everything she knew.

Behind her, eyes and eagerness, was Shiv. Bony, with thin blond hair straggling weedily around his shoulders, a pack of cigarettes outlined in his back pocket. Decked out in an old blazer and thrift store tie, he had missed the word that dressing for dinner meant jeans and clean socks. He ditched the tie immediately, and looked baffled as to what he should do with the jacket. No one told him. There were some things, Vlad had noted, the kid would just have to learn for himself.

Then Kas, shaking his head and laughing at something (Gard guessed Shiv), came in and hugged Deesh, whispered something in her ear, and looked plain-faced as she laughed outright. Kas, Cleve, and Gard were the only members from the beginning. It had been a thousand years, Cleve insisted, even if a mere thirty had passed on the calendar. Leslie had been with them around nine hundred.

Cleve followed. The only person in the room who had his complete respect was Deesh, and why she could never fathom. Rock Star from the River Styx, she called him. Had anyone else so said, Cleve would likely have broken sundry arms and legs. He did not look the brawler; rather, he might have been the Archangel Michael, with yellow hair graying and haloing around his head, dropping in a curling mass down the length of his back. Thin nose, wide mouth, sharp-edged cheekbones rising against eyelashes long as spiders. Not so very tall, but very slender, and day or night he saw the world behind aviator sunglasses so black the world could not see his eyes. There was little else to see of him, as well, covered as he was always in black leather. How he played piano in leather gloves, Gard had yet to figure out. But he wrote music no one else could imagine, and Gard sang it accordingly. Theirs was a love-hate relationship only they understood. If opposites made music, they were born to it. As it happened, Cleve the heavenly being could be a very frightening man, particularly given his motto: "Give me a bottle and a good-looking woman and get out of my way."

Gard, the scary-looking one, never went looking for a fight. Anymore.

Cleve, the classically trained pianist, the *ne plus ultra* of rock singers' composers, sang like a mad cat.

Gard, who couldn't organize a single measure or lyric, had the voice of the rock and roll ages.

Apart, they limped. Together, they could sell out a trans-Atlantic concert in forty-five minutes. They rarely agreed about anything; Cleve thought Gard a creative idiot, and Gard saw Cleve as a ridiculous prima donna. When their fights escalated about Cleve's writing, or Gard's interpretation therein, catastrophic professional consequences followed. Their third album had been delayed four years because Gard hated the songs, and Cleve hated Gard for hating them. The latest album had taken three years of their warfare to get in and out of the studio. Cleve allowed no one to cover the material he wrote for Gard, and Gard would not cover another composer without Cleve's approval.

Vladimir—edging through the door to see Deesh looking closely at Cleve's gloves and asking, "Hands bad again?"—was always the last one in and the last one out.

"He was bleeding on the keys the last two shows." Vlad, giving himself over to an uncharacteristically long sentence, thought the blood-letting pretty cool.

"Don't look so pleased about it," Deesh said to him in his native language.

"Ah," he approved. "Your accent gets better."

She patted his shoulder as if he were a great raggy dog. He missed Gard's company in raising black and mighty hell after performances, but then, he'd never been clutched by a Chicago hotel ledge. After Chicago, Vlad spoke even less than before. Whether he blamed himself, or fostered angry disappointment that Gard couldn't keep up with him, Deesh wasn't sure, but she knew it was one or the other. Whether he'd washed his hair in weeks or months she also wasn't sure, but knew that, too, was one or the other. He enjoyed the look of the mad monk, and had perfected a

23

chilling stare to go with it. Not likely anyone would guess he had more education than the rest of the band put together, and spoke nearly as many languages as Deesh could read.

It was time to shrug off the mantle of infamy, even if temporarily, and cease to exist as performers first, last, and always.

Lily appeared, wordlessly. Deesh arched her neck in the direction of her dining hall.

Dinner, it seemed, was served.

*   *   *

They ate and drank in the manner usually associated with people at county fair all-you-can-eat contests. Deesh and Leslie watched and looked with accepting disgust at each other. Certain traditions must be, they said silently across the table, unkillable. When hungry, men were indeed pigs.

Later plunking themselves about like so many spineless squids in the living room, they sprawled, clanking champagne bottles. The furniture, not meant for guests, was comfortably enveloping. Vlad and Deesh sat with their heads together over a Russian critic's article about the latest tour. Shiv watched them, apparently not understanding that they were actually reading it. Then Deesh pointed to a word, raised her eyebrows.

"Hmm." Vlad thought for a moment. "Slang for . . . mm . . . cardiac arrest."

Gard looked over from across the room. "Good or bad?"

"I believe you have been lauded," Vlad answered, in a tone suggesting it must be a mistake.

Gard nodded. "Would you read it to me later?"

"Would I be your nanny?" Vlad snarled. "I read to no one."

Gard nodded again. "You keep to your principles, V. It's what we all love you for."

Shiv was looking about the room the way he would a museum. "I don't get it," he said to Cleve.

"I'm sure," Cleve answered. "Whatever you're talking about."

He had taken as much notice of the kid as he would a freckle on his arm; that the freckle would speak was an annoyance.

"I mean, look!" Shiv swivelled his head. "All this furniture, all these rugs and chairs and sofas and stuff, and there's nothing on the walls. Not anywhere. No photos anywhere, nothing.

Cleve sighed. "Yeah? So?"

"Why don't she have any paintings or something? Or pictures? There's not even any pics of Gard, or the band, or nothing."

"Shut up, Shiv," Cleve sighed.

Leslie got up and went over to sit between them.

"Ssh," she threw a look at Cleve. To the group's freshman member, she said quietly, "Deesh is a writer. I think she prefers bare walls," she lied, "because she doesn't want to be distracted when she's working."

"Oh," Shiv said, as if he understood. "What's she write?"

"Histories. Cultural studies of certain times in certain societies."

"Oh," he repeated. "I never heard of 'em."

"No shit," said Cleve.

Leslie tossed him another look. "Lots of universities use her stuff as textbooks. Sometimes kids sign up for courses just because her books are the required reading."

Here was a notion Shiv could understand even more poorly than naked wall space.

He said, "Oh," a third time.

"And she doesn't talk about it, so don't ask her anything. I've got a couple of her books if you want to read one."

"Uh, yeah."

Cleve opened his mouth.

Leslie's eyes bored into his, and he closed it. There was nothing to do but endure this, her face informed him.

25

They had already explained the deserted neighborhood, the crumbling appearance of the house, the faux decline of everything exterior.

The brain in Shiv's head almost asked "Is she crazy, or what?" but before the words could take shape, Leslie shook her head at him. Fine. He would, he thought, just figure she was crazy and say no more about it. If Gard wanted a nutcase for a girlfriend, okay with him. He'd had a mental case once, himself. Total crackerbox, but she'd had other talents. In a rare moment of introspection, Shiv decided maybe at present it would be best not to recount them. Still, what was the deal with no pictures? Everybody had pictures, especially if they were making it with a fame-name. There was something too fucking weird about this joint, even if it was the biggest house he'd ever seen in his life.

In a few moments his ruminations began to bore him, and he shifted his attention to Leslie. This was a major babe, even if she was old. He wondered if she liked younger men.

*   *   *

It is ritual. They know when it's time to suspend the several conversations going on around the room, when it is time to play the game.

"Okay, ready? Set?" Gard alone sits next to Deesh. No one jockeys for a place there. This is Gard's three months off, and they know better.

He is always the moderator. Everyone but Deesh has to play. "One point for the country, two points for the city, three points for the venue. You stop at any point, anyone who can hit more than you can take your points." He pretends gravity while consulting a travel notebook.

"May 16," he calls.

"Aberdeen!" Vlad is as drunk as is possible for him to be, but he always remembers the first night of every tour. "Scotland!"

"Three points. Anyone want to take them?"

Shiv is trying to catch on. He has learned this is one of his responsibilities in belonging to Evermore.

"Exhibition Center," says Cleve quietly.

"Yep. Cleve wins the first round."

"Is a draw," Vlad mumbles, proud he can still add this late in the night.

Their hostess says nothing. Her eyes move from player to player, wondering if she should give a damn who wins. Unless it's Leslie. She suspects Leslie doesn't give a damn, either.

"June 10."

"England! Manchester," says Shiv, trying to seem modest.

"Nope. Country right only."

"Sheffield. Sheffield Arena."

"Five for Kaseem."

Bottles emptying, there is groaning and laughing. She sees that Gard is much amused.

"May 25."

"England, Sheffield, NEC."

"Leslie wins the round in one."

Leslie smiles at Gard, as if to say, "okay, I played, now leave me out of this."

"June 16."

"Scotland," says Vlad.

"No."

Another voice. "Germany. Hanover."

"Right. Venue? Anyone?"

No one remembers. Or no one is willing to risk pronunciation. The room becomes too quiet. Leslie hums a bit, then sings "Hitler's Bunker is Where We Hunker." The rest follow her lead, creating German towns, many named after mid-century war criminals.

Gard insists on the game after every tour, and ignores the truth that for some unknown reason, he is beginning to feel dislocated from the fun. He looks tired. Still, the evening will not move on until the game is over, and Deesh doesn't like the ashen patches spreading around his eyes.

Amid the rising spiral of voices, she says in only slightly accented German, "Eilentiedehalle."

They look at her in amazement. They know she removes herself from all details of their tours.

But she is staring into Gard's face, now less than a foot apart from hers. He knows she has just done that which she is loath to do, indeed has never done. And why? No answer occurs to him.

"June 24," he says into her eyes.

"Germany. Dusseldorf. Philipshalle."

"June 25."

"Germany. Magdeburg. Stadthalle."

"June 18," his voice emotionless.

"Ireland. Belfast. King's Hall." Likewise, her voice betrays nothing. The others are watching.

"Well. I guess this gig's up," says Leslie. Her speaking voice is of the same clarified strength as her singing. Gard appears not to have heard.

"June 5."

"Wales. Cardiff. Cardiff Arena."

The room has receded, there is no one else in it. At length, he runs out of dates and times, and someone far away seems to be speaking. His expressionless face still locks on Deesh. He will never be able to ask her how she knows all this. She would not forgive him if he later reminded her she had so exposed herself in front of the band, in front of him.

Suddenly Leslie's voice seems to have registered. He looks up, startled. "Oh. Yeah. Okay. Tour videos. Everybody change rooms."

The final part of the evening. They have had audiences in the tens of thousands, but they won't go home until one more person sits rapt. Deesh reminds silently herself to be rapt. Gard still looks tired.

They adjourn to the library.

"Sort of like football film after the game, huh?" Shiv inquires of Vlad.

"No," Vlad replies, and walks away without further explanation.

"Now I see why you insisted on this vulgarity," Deesh says from the doorway. Gard is pushing buttons by the fireplace.

"I knew you wouldn't want to miss a single screw-up," he answers.

Shiv looks confused.

"It's a joke," Kas says to him.

"It is?"

"Trust me."

Shiv appears relieved.

"Anything usable for a video?" Deesh says.

"Maybe," Gard says in an odd tone of voice. "Find a good seat and cast your vote." Something, she thinks, must be up.

A screen of mammoth dimensions descends. She assumes an air of disgust.

Shiv looks confused again. Kas heads him off. "Gard put the screen in himself. She says it's his and she hates it, but she's never made him take it out. Don't ask any questions."

"But the bookcases that opened up. I thought they were real."

"They are."

"Books, too?"

"Yewit," Kas loses patience. "Try and remember where you are."

"We sit," says Vlad sternly. Everyone sits. The library lamps click off.

The screen darkens, lightens, and she watches. Anyone's guess what country they are in now.

Gard on a stage, slumped on a stool, band silent in the blackened background. He plucks a few notes.

"This is so cool. Acoustic, you know."

She knows whose voice has volunteered, and declines to speak the truth that she does not need the term "acoustic" or its value explained to her.

She sits upright, alone in a straight-backed chair, off to the side of the others plopped like throw pillows on sofas and settees. The room is dark, but from the screen comes what seems a protective light slanting directly on her chair.

This is what she hears Gard sing:

Longing unto the unbearable.

Clawing hopelessness.

Grief unto death.

Pain.

A nameless woman is gone from him. Which to choose, then? To live? Longing, hopelessness, grief, pain?

Death.

A man so much in love with a woman for so long, he would choose damnation rather than be without her.

The words are simple, the melody a raft in a hurricane. His voice is controlled, his eyes on his Gibson. His head drops lower; he does not meet the eyes of his audience. There is no rock and roll here. There is only sorrow so great, confusion so irreversible that when he is done, the unseen audience makes no sound. Then, a catapultive, screaming, whistling wind sweeps over the stage. The ovation is still going on when he sets his guitar aside and walks, unacknowledging of the uproar, off stage.

There is silence, too, in the library, as if a collective group of breaths is being held.

"Lights," someone finally says.

Lamps go on.

She turns in her chair, stares at Cleve with something unreadable in her eyes.

"How," she asks him, "did you do that?"

Without inflection Cleve answers: "I didn't."

She stares. "Cleveland."

"I didn't write it. Lyric or tune."

"Don't be stupid, Cleve." Her voice is sharp.

"Really, I swear. I didn't write it." He looks around as if for corroboration.

"Who, then? And how did you get it? Who gave it to you?"

"Uh." Cleve hesitates as if he's not sure it's not a treasonable action to tell her. The room waits. "Uh. Gard."

Gard has not written a song since high school.

She loses enough composure to allow an expression of shock to pass over her face. No one moves to a different seat. No one says a thing until Kaseem. "So? How was it?"

"Not bad," she says, barely moving her lips.

"That all?

She nods. She looks at Gard. "You wrote that? You did?" She pauses, passing her hand through her hair. "I doubt it will sell more than twenty or thirty million copies."

There is a noise of relief. It sounds like applauding, of hooting, of cab whistles.

"You know more about poetry than I thought," she says to Gard, sitting and sheepish across the room. He shrugs.

"It's not that much."

"Possibly not. I doubt Cleve need give over his day job to you. Still, it's . . . it's, I don't know. I've never heard anything like it. It is," she pauses, blinking, "extraordinary." Her voice trails away, and once again, there are only two of them in this fully-peopled room.

*   *   *

"So what's it called, Gard? You never told us." Leslie's voice rose over the general conversation, which Leslie's voice would do.

Silence waiting.

"Yeah, what?" said Shiv. Leslie elbowed his ribs without subtlety.

"It's called," Gard said.

Deesh leaned back against her chair, watching with the rest. She couldn't detect if he was hedging from shyness, or melodrama. She turned around, her 'yes, let's get on with it' expression aimed at Leslie. Leslie shrugged her shoulders, indicating 'You know how he is. Can't change him now.'

Shiv pretended he could decode the signals. Deesh

turned back around in her chair, drew her knees up to her chin. If there were a beast of divine inspiration, she thought, it must have hit Gard long and violently. She looked as if she still didn't believe that Cleve hadn't written it.

"Come on, Gard. What's it called, 'Love Song to Make a Million Dollars With'?" There was only a shred of jealousy in Cleve's voice.

"It's called," Gard hesitated a moment, "'Eurydice.'"

"What's that?" asked Shiv, catching neither significance of the title.

She dropped her feet to the floor. Allowed her shoulders to fold. Dropped her head to protect her face. Gard got out of his chair. She put her hands up, looking down into them as if she could right there and then disappear into their midst.

This was, he thought, not the way it was supposed to turn out. Her disappointment had shaken him. He sat down at her feet and waited until enough was enough.

"Come on, Deesh. I can change the name if you hate it that much."

Her shoulders had begun, a little, to shake.

So she was going to laugh at him to hide her worry that he had taken very public liberties with the most private word in her existence. She even published as simply 'E. Calder.' An odd sound issued from her throat. She was trying to do the right thing and keep her hilarity at just the right temperature for the occasion.

He gently pulled her hands from her face. She was not laughing.

"Deesh?"

No answer.

"Is it so bad? I can call it Homer's Classic Comics Illustrated for all I care." He waited for her to remind him that Homer had not composed the particular tale to which his song alluded.

She wouldn't look at him.

"I . . . can't," she croaked.

"What?"

32

"I can't. I can't."

He put an arm around her, took her from the chair. She turned her face into his chest. "I can't. I can't."

"'Scuse us," Gard said to the room, and gently took Deesh out of it.

"Hey! Wait!" said Shiv, who thought the whole thing was some traditional ceremony everyone in the room knew about but him. As Gard and Deesh disappeared into other reaches of the house, he petitioned the others. "Is he mad at her?"

"Yewit, don't be a retard," Cleve said, tiredly.

"Whas'is about?" Shiv sounded as if he were going to be branded guilty of something he didn't know he'd done.

"What this is about," said Kas, "is we lock up as we let ourselves out."

"But . . ."

"The party is over," said Leslie, in a careful voice, as if explaining to a distraught third-grader why he had to come back in from recess.

They steered him out of the room, out of the house.

Outside, Shiv decided to assert himself. "Jesus H. Christ, what the hell was that? And what was all that before when we were playing the game?"

"Mm?" Leslie answered.

"I mean, it was kinda creepy–like they just–you know–were *doing* it right there in front of us."

"They were," said Leslie. "It happens sometimes. You never know. I don't think *they* ever know."

"Huh?"

"Metaphor, Shiv, metaphor."

"Uh, yeah. And what kind of weirdo house IS this?" His eyes swept the gables, the turrets, the black diamond shine of mullioned windows. "I mean, Gard lives HERE?"

"No," said Kaseem, taking over for Leslie, who had begun to roll her eyes. "He doesn't live here. His house is in the Colony, on the beach. He spends lots of the time here when we're home, though."

"Then why don't he just live here?" Shiv's puzzlement was taking on an exasperated edge.

"Because they have this autonomy thing. You know."

Shiv had no idea what Kas meant, and so took a different tact. "Still weird. And man, that book room of hers. It looks bigger than the public library."

"Like you've ever been in one," said Cleve, flipping his key ring around his thumb.

"And those books are hers? She's read them? There's stuff in there ain't even in English."

"Yes, they're hers," said Leslie, taking him by the arm, leading him away from the house, "and, yes, she's read them."

Shiv gazed at the small windows fronting the fourth floor. His neck protested. He dropped his head and continued, "and wha'd she get out all the silver and stuff for dinner for? And how come she hardly talked all night?"

They looked back at the house, dark and deserted looking, wrapped in its own shadows.

"Yewit, Yewit, Yewit," Kas growled, in the manner of an elder repeating to a dullard the multiplication tables one more weary time, "try to remember where you are."

They were tired of talking to him, and they all went home.

It was always tough, breaking in the new kid.

Meanwhile

He ushered her across two rooms, then another, then into the dining room. Kicked the door shut. Bones and scraps of their dinner sat dead on the table. Someone had dropped a napkin under a chair. The E and C embroidered there were crumpled.

He sat her down on the overstuffed monstrosity stretching the width of one end of the room. The draperies were open. Starlight blurred through the hundred-year-old panes. Vague shadows crossed the grounds; had the house been a lesser fortress he would have heard footsteps, car doors opening and shutting, bike motors revving, his friends fading into the evening. But no sounds entered. He left the curtains open.

The room might contract around them, it might do that if he shut out the last of the light. He held her in his lap, something she rarely permitted him.

"Tell me," he said into her hair. "Tell me, honey. Tell me."

She shook her head against him.

She had every appearance of a woman sobbing, if one could do such a thing without tears.

"Can't what? What can't you do?"

She put her arms around his neck. "It's yours." Her voice broke. "I can't take that from you. It's you, not me."

He raised his face to the ceiling and closed his eyes. "It's you."

"I can't take it, don't you see? It's–there's too much."

"Deesh," he said in one tone over a whisper. "Come on, Deeshee. You know I can't write. Never comes out the way I want. I know what I want to say but it just never comes out right. Except this time, somehow, it did. You have to take it because it is yours. Deesh? Honey? You breathing

35

all right?"

She nodded into his collar bone. Perspiration was drying at her hairline.

"Don't worry about the guys. They'll pretend they never saw a thing. They'll explain to Shiv that he never saw a thing either." There was nothing but the serious and the certain in his voice.

She was still, as if deciding whether or not to believe him.

"Deeshee, baby."

She tried again. "Really," she croaked, "I can't. I don't think I can."

"Shsh," he said, lifting her hair, brushing it one-handedly away from her eyes. Smoothing it back from her forehead. "You can, too. You already have." He kissed her temple.

Clouds, small and flimsy, moved over the moon. He kissed her forehead. She sagged against him. He bent his head and kissed her slightly on the mouth. They slipped to the floor.

She opened her eyes.

No irony. No amusement. Just watching his face, in and out of passing shadows. He kissed her again, and she opened her mouth. He took her lower lip between his teeth, dragged his tongue over it.

She lay absolutely still and waited. He slid one hand under her head, holding it off the floor, the other against her ribs as his arm crossed under her back.

Kissing again, careful as if to keep violence at bay, as if he could take no chances with her, take no risks with her body. The moon rose, past the top of the window casement.

He reached up, blindly dragged a cushion from the settee, lowered her head to it. He opened a button on her shirt. She reached at him to do the same, but he drew her hand away, held her wrist at her side. Shook his head, said the last words of the night. Carefully.

"Let me."

He ran his tongue in the hollow between her collar-

36

bone and shoulder, trailed his mouth over it, feeling her back stiffen. Her shirt was off. She looked at it as if it were some odd foreign object, finding its way inexplicably to the floor of her dining room. Felt his hand sliding her jeans away without sound or effort.

Details began escaping her. She felt his mouth at her neck, moving with the pulse. The hair on her arms began to stand, showing white in the moonlight. His hand barely touching the inside of her thigh, hovering up and down, smoothing her legs a small space apart. He'd shucked his own clothes, but when?

His breathing had not changed. His eyes on her remained open and steady. No usual signs he was beginning to forget her, forget himself, hurtling toward pleasure with such force that it would seem if there were even a moment's pause the pump of his heart would burn out, metal on metal screeching and he would die at once. And she would die with him. No, the usual signs were not appearing, yet she could feel him moving over her, felt his mouth pulling at her, but without greed. Rather, he seemed–what? Every fuse she had was going into overload, and he always knew when, fighting her, daring her as if they were well-matched opponents, wresting a rough control by displaying their skills. But not now. He knew. She knew he did, but his touch did not change. No fight to the death, just the careful quiet. The word came to her, recognition more than memory. He was not consuming her. He was–worshipful.

She knew this sort of restraint was not meant to last, that soon he would cease all this tenderness and drive her backbone into the floorboards.

But no such velocity. Without resistance he was in, and slowly out. Exerting careful control, silk in slow regular rhythm. Holding her slightly at an angle in one arm, on his knees, keeping her between the floorboards and his body. His hand flat on the small of her back, lifting and lowering. Joined at a solitary intersection, he did not take his eyes from her face. His movement constant, even, on and on unchanging, not taking her as if he could not help himself, but smoothly, slipping in and out without worry. What was in his eyes she had not seen before. But no danger, and danger was always there, where had it gone?

Her function for coherent thinking slowed to near nothing. He could make it good, make it right. She could float here indefinitely in this narrow space where time was only time and therefore useless and night was only night and could come and go as it pleased, she would never be like this again, weightless.

The shock of coming was so great as to feel like a sudden, unnatural awakening. She arched her back and moaned as her body locked, then slumped back into his hands, knowing now what he would do.

But he did not. Just kept on and on, whispering soothingly, inaudibly in her ear. No words decoded in her head, but whatever he was barely saying must have meant something because she came again without warning. Still he went on and she continued to shudder against him, get her breath back, lose it again.

Until he felt her ready to concede, give out, give up. Then he laid her down, dropped his head against her breasts, plunged, and seeing it was himself in concession, began without voice to quake.

So it was twice this night, she thought, that he had made love to her in ways she had never known.

Slumlord

It was good to be home; good as on the road. He mused. Better check with his business manager, make sure all the property taxes were paid. His own house he never worried about, but his acreage across town was another matter. Nothing must ever open the door to foreclosure on that land for back taxes. No investigations, no appraisers. It must remain exactly as it was, as it had been for so many years. He was losing track of how many.

'Course, his business manager, the one he'd had so long ago, the bastard, had given him much too hard a time about the investment. Why, he kept asking. Why why why?

Because, Gard had answered, because because because.

But if he wadn't gonna develop it, his manager whined, then what for?

Land might be worth something, someday.

Oh, yeah, sure. Place is a shit pile, nothing down there but blocks of falling-down warehouses, and that giant old house that's gotta be falling down, too. Not enough to sell for scrap, even. And the cost to tear it down, Jeez!

Not the house–what, you ever listen? Not the house; just everything around it, everything else. Got that?

Well for Chrissake, what're ya wanting with a buncha shit buildings, then? Nothing but dust and rot out there; I'm 'sposed to advise you, so listen, man. It's way too many bucks for the bang.

Gard had looked at him quickly, then, but saw no double meaning in the man's words.

Okay, you've advised me, now shut up and buy it. And remember, no one is to know. Ever. You so much as mention it, I'll have to hurt you.

Fuck it man, whaddaya take me for? Who the hell

cares about it?

I do.

Then, okay already. Don't be so jumpy. I'll take care of it.

You'll take care of it today.

Yeah, yeah. Jeez. Rockers. Got rocks for brains.

Whatever–just buy it. Put it in a corporation name–all that slippery stuff you're so good at.

Yeah, okay. But if ya don't wanna develop it, can't you tell me what you do want to do with it?

Yeah. I'll tell you. I want to make sure no one ever develops it, no one even moves into the neighborhood. Ask me anything else, I'll take you down right now.

Okay, man, okay. I'll get it. Then what?

Shut the hell up about it.

He smiled to himself, thinking on it. He wouldn't, but he'd love to tell her what a good deal he'd gotten. That had been a long time ago, and two or three business managers ago, but he still owned the land, and she still didn't know. Life was good.

Another Argument Lost

"I think you should marry me."

"I think not." She licked ice cream off her lips.

"Will it help if I wheedle?" He crunched a bite from his cone.

"Doubtful. Why has the idea occurred to you this time?"

"No official title. It's awkward when I talk about you, anonymously, of course."

"You mean label, not title," she said. "I can't stop you from speaking of me, but I wish you wouldn't, and I thought I was your Dearest Friend."

"No, I don't mean label. I can't help it if I slip every now and then about mentioning you, you're just so dishy, and 'friend' is fine, but not wholly accurate, is it?"

He ran a little short of breath.

"Hm. I see your point. Well, you'll just have to settle for 'sex slave.'" She smiled sweetly, and took another swipe at her ice cream.

No! He thought, *No! I want more. I want more of you. I want all of you there is to want. I want all your heart, all your soul, all your mind. I want all of your bones, all of your flesh, all of your fears and longings and joys and love. All. And more. More. More.*

But, of course, he said nothing. He sounded like a five-year-old, even to himself. Wanting more ice cream, more more more. She looked as if she knew what he was thinking. Hell, she probably did. But she smiled gently at him, and offered him the rest of her cone, seeing that he'd already consumed all of his.

The Price of the Past

"What do you think you'd be," he asked, "if you weren't a writer?"

He observed that the library was an excellent place for an afternoon snack. Maybe he could convince her after they finished their *hors' d'œuvres*.

Licking marinade off an artichoke heart, she looked at him over the tines of her fork.

"On welfare."

"Yeah, right. Come on, what would you have become?"

"Oh, who knows. What do you imagine?"

"Painter," he said, promptly.

"I don't," she said very quietly, "think so."

"Why the hell not?"

She laid the artichoke heart, still impaled on the fork, down on a plain, faintly stained plate.

Did she want to tell him? He thought not. But once he discovered she had had a major in painting as a long-ago undergraduate, the subject intermittently dragged at his curiosity. He thought eight years together was enough time for her to give him a hint. He expected the delaying tactic of conversational redirection. He was not disappointed.

"Would you be an accountant?" she asked.

"God, no." His face squinched in disgust.

"You studied to be one, as I recall."

"Yeah. And you can also recall I dropped out after four semesters."

"Seduced by an unscrupulous guitar."

He smiled into years past. "Yes, I was. And it was great."

"So, what other else would you have chosen, had the choice been yours?"

"You saying it wasn't?"

"Yes," she said in mild surprise at herself. "I *am* saying that.

He was interested in the turn of her tone, but had the feeling that elaboration would not be forthcoming.

"Jeez, Deesh," he said, mildly. What *would* he have become? "Maybe a lower echelon Hell's Angel? You have to take an oath you'd kill for them, didja know that?"

She did not say she knew a great deal about the club, as they were most of the third chapter in her fourth book.

"In those days," he went on, "I for sure could have beat the living shit out of someone and been proud of it. Good personality for an accountant." He grinned. "But tearing up the freeways on a Harley all day, getting wasted all night, being scary just because I could be? I hate to say it, but I'da been really good at that."

She laughed softly. "And you would have liked it, too."

"Yeah." His eyes looked away into a life unlived. "For awhile. Then."

She nodded. Silence lengthened. At last she said, capitulating, "I don't know there was anything else I could ever have been."

"You could have been a painter."

"All right. Yes."

"So why didn't you?"

"If I tell you," her voice hardened slightly, "you won't ask me about it. Again. Anymore."

He shrugged in careless agreement.

So she told him. Her voice expressionless, she recounted at length, as if she were speaking of nothing more than the contents of a phone book.

Then there was so much quiet for so long after she stopped he could almost hear her books creaking in their spines. The room seemed to lose focus.

He steadied his sight on the congealing artichokes. "Where'd you get that plate? Don't look like that stuff of yours I can break by breathing too hard on it."

43

"It's a take-home from Pearl's. From last week, re-member? I'm reminding myself to take it back to her."

"Nothing special?"

"Just pedestrian institutional crockery. Probably ten dollars a case."

"Good," he said, standing abruptly. Handing her the fork, he picked up the plate and took it out to the back garden where he stood stock still before hurling it. Shards of white pottery crashed in all directions against the stones of the carriage house. Artichokes left slug trails down the walls. He leaped on his bike, revved til the engine shrilled in pain.

He tore home then, destroying speed limits, consider-ing what else he could throw, crack, smash, and ruin at his own house.

She knew he would go. He always took himself away when rage overcame him many too years too late. It was pointless to tell him that even had he known her so long ago he could not have saved her, not from any of it.

With a Bullet

"How's the *fin de siècle* coming?" he asks, appearing early in her doorway. She is roosting in one of the bigger chairs, dressed, making notes in the margin of a large, yellowing book. The morning is so quiet he can hear her pen scratching. She looks up.

"Would you close the door? Thank you. The manuscript is just about finned, thank God. This is the last," she says hefting the tome in her lap, "of the research for the last chapter. The *siècle* awaits."

"Getting bored already?" he teases.

"Bored with worrying slightly about the deadline. Time to finish the writing, so I can start thinking about the next one." She peers at him quizzically. "You never get up this early. What brings you around in the ungodly hours of the a. m.?"

"'Eurydice' is going to buy us the house in the Bahamas."

She lets the book fall flat into her lap. "Buy *you* the house."

He sighs. "Must you?"

She caps her pen, lays it in the valley of the book's spine. "I must. Your money. Your house." She moves the book aside, parks her elbows on the desk, and leans her chin against her folded hands. "But never mind that. 'The Only Song You'll Ever Write' is picking up?"

"Charted." He is not skilled in containing his glee. "Twenty-six. Moving fast. In America." He wears the expression of a child hiding a stray puppy behind its back.

"Yes? Really yes?" She allows her voice to rise a half-step. "How long?"

"Today. One day, it's twenty-six." He bows.

"Well. Think of that. And how many copies have you

peddled in Europe?"

"The quantity is so vast it would embarrass me to mention. We're thinking it'll be charted in the UK this week. At one, maybe."

"Why don't you sit?" She motions to the chair nearest the desk.

He sits.

"It's been some time since you all had a hit single."

"Three years." His expression suggests it might have been three hundred.

She pushed her chair back, rose, and walked to him. On her knees she laid her head in his lap and kissed his hand. Smiling when she thought he could not see her face.

"I suppose I'll have to take you out for an obscenely costly dinner," he said, his free hand fingering her hair.

"Why not? Aren't you the poster boy for the Stinking Rich now?"

"For now."

"Good enough for me." She stood up, hooked his arm. "Let's go."

"Uh, isn't it too early for dinner?"

"Yes," she answered. "We'll start with breakfast. Then we can make it up as we go along. Til dinner."

His grin lengthened. "And after, what say we go back to my house and do bad things to each other?"

"Only if at dinner you ply me with liquor and watch me get solitarily tipsy."

"No problem, little lady. No problem *atall.*"

Unable to help herself, she grinned back at him.

"What about your finiecle?"

"You want to sit here and watch me work on it? Or do you want to go home and be alone? Or have you got a studio booked so early this morning?"

"Yes. No. No."

"Thank you for the compliment. I think today I will sit and watch *you.*"

"For sure?" he asked, uncertain she meant it.

"Certainly," she said crisply. "Come on. How 'bout

it?"

Suddenly, he was washed over with the urge to tell her he loved her. But, ever mindful of their rules, he did not. Rather, as she rose and took his arm, he silently acknowledged his gratitude for Eurydice, in the flesh and on the charts.

Shrike

The landscape is the colorlessness of ash. Ground and sky insubstantial, unstable. Gard feels a familiar sickening, though familiar from where he cannot tell. He does not want to be here. But he is here and he has been here before. This he knows, though he can't remember.

The Voice rises, or it falls; hard to get one's bearing in this place. If it is a place.

"Not a place in the conventional sense," the Voice says. Reassuring it is, even rescuing. "Actually no place is any place in the grander scheme of things."

Gard's throat feels hollow, as if flesh and vocal cords have been scooped out smooth. He is surprised when he hears himself.

"Where are you?"

"Need you ask?"

"Yes. Show yourself."

This is not sentence structure typical of Gard, and he thinks of it flashingly, then loses the thought.

"Show myself? As what?"

"What you are." Gard closes his eyes–inside his lids he sees the same peculiar ashy color.

"I Am What I Am."

Gard puzzles.

"Need you more? Then, I am a good many things to a good many people, but for your purposes one will do."

"My purposes?"

Silence. Gard thinks over his purposes. He finds himself without one. A vague nausea passes over him. Still, he does not wish to go. Yet. Something, someone is plucking at him, as if his ribs were heartstrings. Heartstrings, he thinks.

The Voice laughs.

Pleasantly, with well-modulated tones. "*Heart*strings?

Oh, Gard, you have been singing drivel too long."

Has he? He hadn't thought so before; now he wonders. He can't recall a word or a single note. Odd; where is his mind?

Again the unusual comfort in the Voice. "You don't need one here. Or you don't have to keep yours on so tight a leash."

"I didn't speak. Are you reading my mind?"

A jovial chuckle, as if Gard has turned in his homework early. "Just as you're reading mine.

"Cool."

"Isn't it?"

"But I want to see. You."

"Oh, all right, but just a little." The Voice speaks as a generous parent's indulging a child's whim. "Look!"

Gard wonders why he doesn't say 'behold!' Isn't that how it goes?

"It may surprise you to know the Queen's English went out when she did. About 1603, wasn't it?"

Well, that would be true, wouldn't it? Gard chides himself for expecting Charleton Heston.

The Voice chuckles again. "Open your eyes."

Gard opens his eyes. The horizon, so tiny it must be a thousand miles away. The ashes there shift, run down in little mud slides, reform. The horizon comes closer. The indefinable shapes begin glowing, pale and pink at first, then deeper to red and deeper. Purple bands appear, the sky turns midnight blue. A violet fault runs through the line of ashy dunes and as it does, the landscape gives off an intermittent glitter, a spray of blinking gold.

It is beautiful, Gard thinks. Softly. Still, he is heard.

"You wanted to see. Beautiful? Yes, I suppose." A note of sadness appears, vanishes. "There. I've shown myself."

Perhaps, Gard thinks, he should not have asked. Sadness should have no place here.

"But are there not so many things to be sad about? The world is very difficult, even when it is far from us, is it

49

not?"

Yeah. And Gard should know.

The Voice understands, speaks soothingly, the past is dead, let the dead bury the dead.

Gard nods. He's not really listening now. He's watching cobalt blue clouds float down, yellow and orange ash particles attaching themselves, then blowing upward with the clouds. They leave a blue-green exhaust beneath and behind, which circles around itself and fades.

He could stay here, he muses. Just watch the wonders rising before him, be lost in the coloring clouds, thinking nothing. Yes, he could do that. Couldn't he?

No answer. The Voice is departed, leaving Gard to ponder in privacy. Somehow, though, it's not as lovely now.

Come back, he calls. *Come back*. There is no response. *Come back.*

There is such emptiness resonating, for a moment, and one moment only, he is struck though with an unbearable loneliness–the empty, queasy fear that he is where he is alone and forever, and he closes his eyes, trying to quell the bile climbing up his throat.

When the Voice goes, it takes it all. Gard understands, wonders why he ever had doubts, much less disbelief.

A second, and there is nothing the matter.

Except the ashen color is creeping back across the land, if land this is. Smothering the liquid colors as if killing the oxygen in a spreading sepia fire.

Gard feels a lightning strike of hopelessness, and it is the worst, he knows, the very worst moment of his life.

Come back, he calls, weakly. I want to see more.

I want more! But there is nothing and the feeling is dragging the life out of him. He closes his eyes again, yells mutely over the greying grounds,

"I want out of here!"

And his wish is a command obeyed.

*   *   *

The sun is through the windows and it is a sun with sharp edges, cutting across his face. Gard drags his eyelids open, finds himself nowhere he knows. A shot of panic. Then–something moves. Slowly he comes to see it is his foot, making a little moving mountain of the sheet and blanket.

There is his hand, moving to shield his face. The sunlight is harsh as lye. Piece by piece he recognizes himself. Object by object, the room clarifies. Fireplace, cold and dead. Chair, love seat, wardrobe, bed, tables, lamps.

Yes, he's got it all in one picture now, and he irritates himself it's taking so long. The molding around the a high ceiling–too high. The room seems a cavern.

Deesh.

He is in Deesh's house, it is morning, and everything is as it should be.

Except he doesn't recognize which room he's in, or what floor, or how long he's been here.

Interlude

"Do you believe in God?" he said.

"Are you so parched for conversation that explora-
tory theology will serve to entertain you?"

His eyes level on her face, he asked with no inter-
rogative inflection, "Do you?"

"Oh. It's like that."

"It is."

"Have some more bacon." She pushed the tray across
the dining room table. He took it.

"Where's Lily?" he asked.

"I don't know. Not here."

"What, she came in just to cook breakfast?"

"Just to cook breakfast for you, Moosie."

"You shouldn't let her."

"I know, but you try stopping her. I can't. You're
home from tour, and therefore you get one breakfast we
don't go out for. Doesn't trust me to cook it."

"Thank God," he grinned.

"So to speak." A moment or two passes. "Yes," she
said, returning to his first question.

The neutral expression on his face returned. He
pushed the bacon platter back to her.

"Why?"

"For no reason you would understand."

He laid his knife and fork parallel across the breakfast plate. She folded her napkin and put it down.

"That's not the reason."

She nodded, stood, waited for him, left the room,
crossed two more, pushed open French doors, and walked
across the library. He followed without remark.

She pushed her sleeves to her elbows. Footed the
library staircase and spiraled up about fifteen feet. He stood,

eyes tracking her. She followed the bookcases down the length of the room, turned at the corner. Walked farther. Where the shelving came to interruption by a Palladium window the height of the room, she stopped.

Pulled a book from the fourth shelf up, six volumes into the row. Walked the catwalk back and around to the ladder and stepped down its open funnel.

"Are you going to read me Thomas Aquinas?" He thought he was smiling.

"No."

She crossed the room, stood toward him, opened the book. Flipped to page 35. Looked at him silently–one chance to retract the question. He waited.

" ' . . . and I remembered the question,' " she read, " ' . . . as to whether I hated my father for his ill use of me . . .

" 'I believe to hate my father would be to give in and make small my real feeling which is strong, but not hate, as that seems simple, pure, and clean. Yet I feel that my father put this dark place in me that brings sadness on me unawares, when I should be happy to have my good place and such friends as I have. But for me, though I can get past it, there's often this darkness and sadness, unexpected and coming from things that should bring happiness . . .but then it rises up inside like a blackness,' " she turned the page, " 'and I really am in that blackness where my father left me, with no way out and nothing to do but wait until somehow there's merciful release and I come to myself again.

" 'So I feel my father made me thus, or left me thus, with this sadness that has been hard to bear and will never likely leave me no matter what fortune I have, and it sets me apart from my fellows who never seem to know it . . . neither can I regret what I am, and there are times when I would not give up the sadness and darkness . . . it has to do without being alone and dying alone, which we all [must] do. I see I have this patience to wait it out, and the truth is no matter how dark I feel I would never take my own life, because when the darkness is over, what a blessing is the feeblest ray of light. Because we are,' she paused to interject, "she's

53

talking about the doctor here, not her father," and resumed *" 'both souls who know this sadness and darkness inside and we have both of us have learned to wait.' "*

She closed the book.

"A gift for writing such as this does not rise out of primordial slime and slowly grow feet and walk. I've no idea where it comes from, so I think of language genius as visitation from something not visible, and that invisibility must be, for lack of better choices, God.

"Who did the writing?" His voice had lost its clarity.

She held up the book. *Mary Reilly*. He nodded.

"She–that writer–could have been someone who knew us better than we know us," he said slowly.

She nodded.

Turning, she walked back to the stair risers, climbed, and made the return path to where she had been before.

She leaned slightly over the railing and said down to him,

"And we do not hate, do we?"

"No," he answered.

"And we have both of us have learned to wait."

"Yes."

"And we do not regret what we are."

"No," he agreed.

"And you were alone when you were made thus or left thus?"

"Yes. And you."

"Yes. And you don't think either of us got to who we are, or to each other, through a series of natural selection of wild coincidence, do you?"

She uncharacteristically slammed the book in returning it to its place.

"Are you angry?" he asked when she came back down.

"No. I just really do not like explaining myself on this particular subject. Is there a God? Is there not? Such a discussion is not recreational speculation to me." She sighed, softened her tone. "What difference does anyone's belief make?"

"But you talked to me."

A look of impatience passed over her.

"Yes."

"Why?"

"Oh, come on. Time to come in out of the rain."

He waited.

"Because," she said in a tone suggesting she had broken a fatal law because she'd had no choice not to, "it was you who asked."

Golden Idols in Sheep's Clothing

Looking for a copy of his latest contract, his Sacred Objects came into view. The misplaced paperwork was forgotten. From another room, she called, "Have you found it yet?"

When he made no answer, she appeared in the doorway. "Gard?" She repeated herself. He jerked as if she had awakened him unexpectedly and too soon. "You seem to be deep in thought; shall I excuse myself from the search until later?"

His back was to her. "Uh, yes. No. I don't know."

The room glinting from sun-struck walls lay between them. She crossed it rapidly. Laying her hand against his back, she had a feeling she already knew what this was about and wished she didn't.

"What should I do with these?" His hand swept angrily across the shelf. "They're nothing now but bookends."

"Gard, stop it. They are *your* Grammys."

"They're getting old. So am I." He looked disconsolate and angry at once.

"What do you care? You won them, for God's sake. You want more?"

"Yes." He spoke slowly as if struck with a revelation. "I do. I want more."

"What would you do with a third one? Use it as a doorstop?"

He opened the sliding doors and walked out to the veranda. His hair blew out behind him, and he gripped the railing as if to pull it from the ground. She followed. The air rose through the enclave, smelling, she thought, of saltwater and money. She laid her fingers over his knuckles, whitening in the wind. She saw the muscle in his lower jaw contract, expand, contract.

"Deesh. I'm tired of being a ghost in my own country."

"Nathan Hale. Poor boy."

"What?"

"Nothing. Just a little fret action in Historyville."

"You don't take this seriously?"

"What for?" She seemed surprised. "If you don't know that recording prizes are worth a little less than the gold plate they're painted with, who am I to correct your misconceptions?"

He stared at her, his eyes narrowing against more than the wind.

"You know the award stuff isn't the point, not for you. They don't increase your gift, your powers, anymore than they can give talent to those without it."

Come on, said her face, come in out of the raining self-pity.

"Exactly." His voice was tinged with the all the signals of rage multiplying. "That IS the point."

He was at the edge of shouting.

"Who the hell are these one-hit wonders, and these jackasses who can't sing their way through a plowed pasture, much less read music? They win, I'm not even nominated. What does that say about me?" He shook her hands away. "We've sold nine million copies of 'Eurydice', and it hasn't been on the charts but three weeks! Nine million *nationally*. The global sales are going to exceed that, if you believe the buzz. And I can't get even one goddamned nomination. WHAT DOES THAT SAY ABOUT ME?"

"Nothing," she answered so quietly he barely heard.

His shoulders slumped, the sulphuric danger went out of him.

"Let's just drop it, okay?"

She nodded.

"And will you forgive me for the next couple of hours?"

"Am I involved?" she asked calmly.

"No."

"Then you are forgiven."

He pushed himself back into the house. Shortly, she heard his bike motor flexing into high rev, heard it down the driveway, down the street, turning the corner. She made a brief and silent plea to the Gods of Motorcyclists and Other Fools that he not kill himself before coming to his senses.

She sighed heavily. Then she went home.

Time to Connect

He was watching her television, some educational program on life after life; why he had paused here in his surfing there was no figuring. He was not in an introspective mood.

When Deesh came through the doors, lost in opaque thought, he pulled her out. "Waddya think?" He turned the picture off. "Think there's a better deal after we're dead than we have now?"

She shrugged. "All in due time, my pretty, all in due time."

"You think," he asked carelessly, "it's possible the Mad Russian will get into Heaven?"

She chortled. "Vlad? Sure. He grew up in Detroit. The universe owes him something."

"Ah," he said.

"Enough eschatology. Let's go to the movies."

"When we get there, will you tell me the definition of 'eschatology'?"

She slid on his jacket, black, leather, and miles too big for her. He liked that she would wear it, liked the look of her swallowed in it.

"It might happen," she answered. "If I decide you're old enough to be promoted to fifth grade."

To demonstrate his maturity, he remarked on someone playing dress-up in his clothes.

"Ooh," she said, as they left through the garden, "maybe even sixth grade."

"Sixth grade–ugh. So what do you want to see?"

"Have you a preference?"

"Is there a movie out about Odysseus?"

"Not for a long time." She eyed him curiously. "You are still thinking on that?"

He handed her into his truck. As he switched on the ignition, he said, puzzled, "Yeah."

He shook his head.

"It's like–look at everything. All the years, all the monsters, gods, dangerous women, greedy men, the splintered ships, *twenty years*, just to wake up one evening alive and at home. On the beach."

"Kind of like you, remember?" She was recalling, not teasing.

They drove through shadowing streets. "Even to the part about the beach."

She kicked off her shoes, put her feet on the dashboard. He steered around a corner, came into another part of town.

"Doesn't seem like much reward for the fight, except that it was everything."

"Yes," she said.

"Penelope." He looked straight at her, returned his eyes to the road.

"Don't go taking the comparison too far," she warned. She wiggled her toes against the dash.

"Penelope was everything," he said, stopping at a light.

"I am not Penelope," she said levelly. "And pay attention. Your light is green."

He turned back to the windshield. "Yes, you are," he said, accelerating.

He was coming dangerously close to the forbidden zone. The proximity hung between them, and he knew it. Better to steer into safer waters. "So you wanna see a chick flick? Lots of gooshy stuff? You know how I love 'em."

She laughed softly, slipped her feet back into her shoes. "Odysseus was a prize-winning liar, too."

"Yeah," he agreed, "but he got Penelope in the end."

She looked at him oddly. "Did you think he wouldn't?"

Like hell he was going to tell her that he doubted the hero's ability to regain his wife with every page he read.

Sleep A Dream with the Devil

"Well?" says the Voice.

"Well, what?" Gard stumbles a little.

"You're back. So what'll it be? Earthquakes, fire, and rock and roll? What's in space a trillion miles from here? Name your colors."

"I . . ."

"You . . .?"

"I didn't really come here on purpose. It just sort of *happens.* I'm not here to beg favors or anything."

"Then what are you here for?" The Voice hasn't lost its slight timbre of omniscience and cool amusement.

Gard surveys the landscape, shaking his head.

He has no answer.

But he remains.

"Do you have a name?"

"Call me Shrike."

"Shrike?"

"Yes. It's an ancient Arabic word for "Guardian.""

"Yeah?"

"Quite so."

Gard is awash in relief. "Then it is safe here. With you."

The Voice drips the honey of reassurance. "Well, of course it is. Gard, if you want to see truth, you really must learn to be more trusting."

That must be so. Gard feels ashamed. Shrike wouldn't lie to him. Would he?

The Dream Remembers When

He was not a monogamous man. Not expected or even preferred in his profession, and she knew it.

"Just don't tell me," she said. "I'm weak enough to be jealous, and I've no time for that sort of idiocy."

"My, uh–straying?" He wasn't sure where they were going with this, and he suspected he shouldn't have hinted at the subject in the first place.

"No. Don't be stupid."

"Oh. Jealousy."

She gave him a half-nod, and he should have been satisfied. So why wasn't he?

"I'm jealous," he blurted.

"I dare say," she said wryly.

"I mean, I would be if you–"

"I know what you mean."

How could she sound amused? He decided she must be a fool or faking it, and Deesh never faked anything. Then–what?

"You think I must be a fool," she said. In those days he hated it when she did that. Reading him like a street sign.

"And," she went on, "you know better. You've no reason to keep company with the green-eyed monster."

"That doth mock the meat it feeds on," he muttered.

"Now you're just showing off. Give me the act and scene, and teacher will be gratified." She sat on the arm of one of the library's deep sofas, casually swinging her legs.

They might have been discussing which color not to paint the front porch.

He turned away, the better to send his rising anger in a far direction. She could see the muscles of his back tense beneath the thick fabric of his shirt. She relented.

"You really don't get it, do you?"

He did not turn around. She did not ask him to.

"I jump the bones of no man but you," she said levelly. "My choice. Your choice is your choice. No martyrs, no villains. If I change my mind, I'll change it." She shrugged. "If you change yours, it's yours to change."

He turned back to her, seemed doubtful.

"But . . ." he trailed away.

"We don't even live in the same country six months of the year. I won't make your decisions for you when you're not here."

"Or when I am here," he said sadly.

"And you wouldn't want me to," she answered gently.

"Maybe not. And okay you don't want to know if I . . . mm, get randy on tour." He pointed a finger at her. "But *I* sure as hell want to know if there's been something to know while I was away."

She laughed.

His anger trembled again.

"Oh, stop," she said. "I've already told you I have no desires for anyone but you.

He considered. "But WHY?"

"You mean other than in the three years we've been together, the whoopie we are so perfectly suited to make?"

He shrugged.

She stilled her legs. She looked at him strangely. "Surely," she said without any inflection at all, "you can figure that out."

He could. And having done so, he had the grace to be ashamed.

*   *   *

Seven months later his leniency towards his wandering dick came to an end. He said nothing, but she suspected. And one late night, she knew.

Her dreams were never, since childhood, only dreams. She understood this about herself as easily as she understood it about him. That he did not perceive the truth of it about either of them was his business. As he had not sought to seek her opinion, she had not enlightened him.

He had left on tour only the week before. She was in one of the larger bedrooms on the third floor, thinking herself to sleep. Closing her eyes, she dropped straight into dreams. She saw him in Bristol. With the rest of the band, crowded into a small control room. A deejay named Nigel was interviewing them for his Gard-worshiping listeners. Nigel had wound them up with a question about who was most important to their performances.

"They are," said Gard, jerking his head at the band sardined in with him. Simultaneously, they each pointed at Gard and said,

"He is."

Everyone laughed, because what the hell was there to do in a tiny room with someone as earnest as Nigel? His next launch to get them flying, perhaps at each other, was introducing the topic of legendary singers who didn't write their own material.

Deesh moved in her sleep, knowing what would be coming.

"Rumor has it you fight rather a lot," Nigel said into his microphone.

"All the time," Cleve chuckled.

"Yes?"

"Sure," said Gard, "he thinks he knows everything, which is too dumb for a tree to believe."

He glanced up at the studio clock, having come to the end of his breath on the matter. Why, he wondered, did British speaking voices always sound like they were on the verge of a bad cold?

"Cleve?" invited Nigel.

"*He's* the one who thinks he's master of the universe," said Cleve, jerking his head toward Gard, "always telling me how to write. Hell, I don't tell him how to sing, even when he's really fucking it up."

"I never fuck up singing. You fuck up getting all

twisted about whether or not I'm expressing your 'vision' or whatever crap you call it." He glanced at Nigel. "Hey, can I say that on the radio?"

"Say what?" Nigel looked disconcerted.

"You know. Fuck."

"Eh? Yeh, in England there's no problem with 'youknowfuck.'"

Hooting and more laughter.

"Hm," said Nigel, pretending to consider his next question, "if you both hate each other so greatly, how does one account for your working relationship continuing so many years?"

"Yes, how does one?" said Leslie, in perfect imitation of the hapless Nigel.

Cleve and Gard each nodded at the other and, unrehearsed, spoke as one.

"He's a genius."

Leslie's giggling was audible in the background.

"Ah," from Nigel. "Well, there you have it. No one would argue with that."

"Yeah, *they* would," said Leslie, leaning over Gard, who fidgeted in the small and ill-fitting chair they had pulled up to the control board. "They can argue about ANYTHING." She sputtered, still laughing.

Nigel was now directionless, so leapt into another, safer (he thought) topic.

"So how do your girlfriends, and"–he nodded at Leslie–"boyfriend, fare when you're away so often? What do you like to do when back in the States?"

Gard said, "I don't have any particular girl, but if I did, I know exactly what we would do."

"Yeh?" answered Nigel, who ought to have known better, but didn't expect what was coming.

"Yeah," said Gard. "We would eat lots of American food," more laughter from the band, "and she would read to me, and I could rest my voice. And, let's see. Oh, yeah. We'd occupy most of the time by youknowfucking each other into oblivion."

It took Nigel a moment to quiet the band's response. He was not so sure his next query would be at all what he should make, but the producer had insisted, and Nigel was too craven to ignore him.

"Any truth to the rumor that there have been–orgies on the road?"

Now none of them could stop howling with hilarity, even Vlad, who generally worked on his glower during interviews.

"Yeah," said Gard. "Cleve has orgies with himself."

More laughing, enough that Nigel became aware he had lost control (or his illusion of it) of the interview.

"Man, you're kidding, right?" Kaseem skirted Gard to aim at the mike. "My girlfriend would murder me, dig up my grave, and murder me again if I did anything like that."

"You mean if you got *caught* doing anything like that, don't you Kas?" Cleve asked casually.

"She'd torture and kill me either way."

"How about the rest of you? Would your women do dastardly deeds to you under such circumstances?"

"Mine wouldn't," opined Vladimir.

"Oh? You're into girls?" snorted Cleve.

"Oh, he is, yes indeedy doody, he is waaay into girls," said somebody in falsetto *sotto voce*. Nigel got no word in edgewise, shrugged, and gave up trying for serious answers.

"Of course, Gard's old lady ain't so understanding," said the Drummer of the Month.

Deesh shivered under the bedclothes. Poor drummer. Her existence, much less her name, was off-limits in any interview. Always. To violate Gard's orders of silence on the subject was to buy one's own ticket back stateside, there to hustle hopelessly as a pickup studio musician paid just enough to starve genteelly.

The tiny room was struck silent and, as happens in dreams, emptied instantly.

Cleve dragged the drummer down the hallway, tearing his collar from his gray tee shirt. "Hey, man!" Drummer yelled, "You're wrecking my threads–hey, man! Quit!"

Cleve pulled him around the corner, said in his dangerous, pitying voice, "You don't get shit, do you?"

"Huh? Nyuh?"

"You don't make stupid jokes, or anything else about her to anyone."

"Her?"

"Gard's girlfriend, asshole. And she's private. Period."

"Hey, man–okay. Hey, let go, willya? Hey! I'm not the one cracking wise about his singing. Why's that okay? You said way worse shit about *him*. How come he don't kill you for that?"

Cleve released the kid's collar. Saw he really did have to explain it to him. Hell, the guy was new, hadn't been around long enough to learn the obvious, much less anything else.

"Pay attention. Music is only his life," said Cleve, gently pushing the kid against the wall. "Deesh is his religion."

*　　　　　　　　　*　　　　　　　　　*

Her eyes open suddenly, adjusting to dark of night. Where is he? She has not looked at the itinerary yet, too early to start thinking about it. But downstairs at her desk, barefoot and chilled, she pulls the schedule from the back of a drawer, and checks. It is afternoon there; he is scheduled for an interview, and he is in Bristol.

Dictionary Prison

Words That Will Not Pass Between Them

1. Why can't you . . . ?
2. Why didn't you . . . ?
3. Where have you been?
4. I love you.

Morphine

His dreams have become so real that waking seems to be the dream. The past is dragging at him, as it sometimes does. His house is closing in on him, and it's still six weeks before the winter tour begins. If only she would come. But she won't. She has never seen him perform.

He won't make it.

He is backing away from the prospect when the telephone rings. He answers.

"Want to go to the circus?" she asks.

I am the circus, he thinks, dizzy and sick, one ring right after another. "No."

"Didn't think you did." She drops her voice, asks in the tone that always makes him think she's behind him, speaking directly into his ear. "What say," she goes on, "you meet me at Pearl's? We'll order one of everything, and I'll read you a nice American writer. In English."

Rummaging around his brain, he's looking for the word to agree.

"I know a way to make the day even more a festival of poor nutrition."

Silence echoes down the line.

"Drag your chopper out of the garage, ride over here, and pick me up. I'm in the mood for a death wish."

His voice lurches out. "You can't be serious."

"Oh, but I am. Come on, here's a once-in-a-lifetime opportunity for you put my life in your hands. Getting me onto that thing."

This he can do. Roll the bike onto the driveway, rev and roar. He can feel her arms around his waist, see her hair flagging out behind her. He can do this; get out, get over, and get on with this day. The can eat themselves sick on Pearl's pies.

In a back booth, the sit across from each other. Under the table, she puts her feet up on his seat; they eat pie until they are cross-eyed, and she props open the book and reads between mouthfuls.

"What's it called?" he asks, searching the blank, jacketless cover.

"*The Valley of Decision.*" A smile pushes at the corners of her mouth.

He makes a face. "How appropriate."

"Isn't it."

He leans back, closes his eyes. She reads.

They stay all day. No one minds them; Pearl is nothing if not discretion in an apron. Deesh's low voice remains at the table.

He may sleep. She can't be sure, listens to herself, keeps reading.

"Good story," he says abruptly, eyes closed.

"Yes," she says.

"Funny sometimes. Funny like us." He fiddles with a fork encrusted with dead blueberries. "What part do you like best?"

She closes the book, cocks her head. "Mm. 'Choose your enemies with discretion; otherwise there's no sport in the slaughter.'"

He laughs.

"Don't you agree?"

"Hell, yes. We chose each other, didn't we?"

"Slaughter every night," she says contentedly.

"Come home with me," he says.

"All right."

"Sleep on the beach."

"Ugh."

"Please?"

"Oh, all right. You're such a child."

He pushes away a pile of plates, winks at Pearl behind the counter, and pulls himself out of the booth. "By the way," he says casually, "how did you know?"

"That you needed someone to call and ask you out

for pie?"

     "Yeah."

     She shrugs.

     "Well, anyway. Thanks."

*   *   *

     In his big sleeping bag, they are dreamless, spooned together under the noise of the surf. In the morning, when he awakes, he is unafraid to go back inside his house.

Mad, Bad, and Dangerous to Know
(Third Row Subterfuge)

But she had seen him. Years ago, in Berlin. Gard, restless with a throat infection, would not remain in bed, and the entire tour was threatened. Leslie had called her; she had booked the next overseas flight the same afternoon.

She sat in his hotel room with her legs propped on his bed, reading Dante to him. *Nel mezzo del cammin di nostra vita/mi ritrovai per una selva oscura/che' la diritta via era smarrita.* He heard it as singing; if she ceased, he begged her to continue. At the end of ten days, his throat was clear, and hers was raw. She remained, unknown to him, for one performance.

From the third row near the exit aisle, she was partially hidden in shadows, and he never saw her. Risky to be so close, but she wanted to know, wanted to witness in detail what made him what he was. Is. The witness swears to remember the truth, the whole truth, and nothing but the truth. Just this once.

As soon as his head emerged from the wings, the noise was nothing like anything she had ever heard. It was painful, nearly sickening, hypnotic and compelling. She glanced about her, at the crowds of faces all wearing the same gasping expression. Fish denied water. To evoke that, she decided, must be real power, and for a moment she trembled for him. He walked, head down, carrying a stool onto the darkened stage. Sat, spotlighted, guitar across his knees. The hall went stone silent at once. He sang one of Cleve's ballads, head still bowed, as if performing for an audience only he could see. As the last notes faded, the curtain behind him rose, the lights came up, and the band launched full blast into twenty-four-cylinder rock and roll. The uproar again. From the dark, the crowd's clatter was cacophony. Maybe this, she thought, was what Dante had meant in his welcome to hell. It rose in her ears and gathered itself into one great roar. Odd to see the band in full formation, Leslie barely dressed in black bugle beads, Cleve at piano grinning big at Gard. Fascinating. Cleve never even smiled at Gard. This must be a world in which she was a foreigner lately arrived. The mob quieted, a little, and Evermore blew right out of the building any assumption that no rock band ever required any genuine grasp of true musicology.

*   *   *

She is reminded of the discipline necessary to achieve opera. And the audience here is as absolute as any she has seen for *Aida*. She sits when others sit, stands when they stand, folds herself into the mass of bodies all around her. She draws her elbows in, moves closer to the empty chair on her left, the chair for which she has bought its own ticket, and she tries not to worry about breathing. The beat reverberates from instruments to equalizers to speakers to cement floor beneath her, through her boots, to her heart, to her solar plexus. If she leans her head back, she can feel the sound pulsing like an intruder vein in her throat. And yet the amps are not so loud as to deafen, the instruments clear but civilized, as if she is listening in her car, her house, or her dreams.

A neat trick, and she brushes away the faint longing that comes with the realization she will never be able to ask him how they do it. He is called the Hellion Tenor in the press. Now she understands it is the perfect title for him.

Leslie moves out, a flashing, feline thing, uncovering her dimples and sings counterpoint into her microphone. He tilts his head at her, she leans into him, looking for all the world as if she is going to swoon, as soon as the number is over. In the air are sex and drugs and rock and roll, and Gard, Deesh sees, holds the reins to it all.

She does not know this man.

*   *   *

But millions did–knew him well, intimately, intensely. Millions, she thought. What a horror. Cult figures, she knew, draw uncountable human flies just like honey. But it was what he lived for.

Unself-conscious, his eyes were closed, weaving in and out of the band, dancing but not dancing, obviously ridiculously happy. Sweat began to seethe, as it will on a big man working under hot lights. He shed his jacket, rolled his shirt sleeves to his elbows, all without dropping so much as a single note. A mist seemed to envelop him, though there was none. And his voice.

God, his voice.

A living thing, in a cage at last big enough to hold it. Her body responded, telling her to listen, listen dance and listen, take it all inside yourself and feel the music wrap around your ribs. Let it open up your own cage and send you out. Come on, come on, there'll be no turning back.

She locked her arms across her chest to keep from dancing. Her bones seemed ready to fly apart, and only his voice was holding them together.

So this is how it went. Everything on the verge, and her blood churned with it, a verge that never passed to its other side. How long could this possibly continue? His back against Kas's back, playing for hellfire, separating, closing in at the mike, their heads nearly touching, singing hellfire, too.

She looked around. People her own age crowded the hall, and people who were far too young to claim they had loved his music way back when. They all were his, every one, and all with him, arms out, mouths singing words with him, feet keeping time, thousands of heels slamming over and over into the concrete floor.

Divinity had to be terrifying.

*   *   *

Kas and Gard divide the stage, one to the left, one to the right. She watches him edge nearer and nearer the place

74

where she is. Down the guitar strap across his shoulder are the letters GARD spelled out in glitter. He comes close enough for her to verify the color of his eyes, but his connection is to the rising embankment of sound, the one coming from him and the one coming to him from every soul here.

*　　　　　　　　*　　　　　　　　*

He never saw her.

He wanted her, once upon a time, to wait in the wings for him, where he could see her, know she was there if he only turned his head. She could not comply. It took him years to fit together all the broken pieces as to why she could not; then he stopped asking. He had thought she refused because she loathed the thought of appearing a hanger-on, a "gropie" as she sarcastically called it. He was right, of course. It was just his information was incomplete.

*　　　　　　　　*　　　　　　　　*

As hers has been.

She watches his face, sees the anger, rage even, still in him, escaping through the throng of guitar chords and of keyboards gone berserk. They all of them are so in love with him, this Gard she's never met, but having seen him from a distance she knows now she will not always be able to save herself from him. And what of this adoration, this blind worship, this tearful shouting love that crawls up the apron of the stage and snakes around him, the band, the instruments, 'til it is a wonder they can still play?

*　　　　　　　　*　　　　　　　　*

She must never, she knew now with the conviction of the eyewitness, be a part of this. It would be exactly the same as standing before a flaming building, an inferno ready to consume her. How easy it would be, she thought, gaining an exit door and withdrawing into the shocking silence of the night, to allow herself simply to stand there, and to burn.

The Devil's Disciple

For a long time, I didn't know for shit. What I had and what I didn't have. I met her in Paris, but I don't remember how. Don't remember a lot from those days. But I know she was stalking her Ph.D., studying languages all over Europe. I don't think she knew who I was. Maybe she did. She's never said, and it's not the kind of question you can ask. Not of her. After she put me off for God knows how long, we spent about a week in a Paris hotel room. Cripes, she'd thought about it long enough. I was probably more nervous than she was, and believe me, that was a first. It's a lot easier when you just get wasted, pick a chick from the followers, do it, and forget it the next day. Was she at a gig? I don't remember. Damn me. Guess I was lucky I didn't scare her off. On the other hand, she don't scare. I knew it right away. Took one look in her eyes, and I knew. She knew me, too. The Wild Man of Rock was confused as hell. All the time. Wondering if I should have been an accountant like I'd started out, or gone to Julliard that time it was offered. Or maybe I should have just stayed in Texas. Nah, I never wondered *that*. I don't know where she grew up. Imagine. After all this time. Asked her once, she got that look like somebody's just knifed her, and said it wasn't a story she wanted to tell. She told me some, way later, and I'm the only one who knows. I'm the *only* one who knows. Sounds like an album title. I've been around so long I started on vinyl, LP's, 45's, all like that. Thirty years. Geezer Rocker, that's me. Jeez.

There are no pictures in her house. Not one. No photographs, no paintings, no prints, nothing. You don't notice it right off, cause her house is a little much to take the first time you're in it. Like an antique fun house; you never know when another room is going to be ready to jump you when

76

you round a corner. But it's funny, in a way, because she was a painting major when she started college. She did tell me that, but not why she left it. Not for a long time. We both began one thing, left it far behind for another. Course, it's not hard to figure why I shunted accounting–who wouldn't if they got the chance? Never even finished college. I'm a dropout, and she's the Queen of Academe. Go figure. I got pictures all over my place. Me and the band. Me and Deesh. Deesh. She thinks it's stupid, having photos of her around, but she doesn't criticize. Her walls blank, my walls full. Story of our life; nothing in common. What we have in common is knowing that, I guess, and not caring.

I've read most of her books. Only interesting history texts I've ever seen. Just like in her life, in her books she says what she thinks and tough beans if the dead presidents and dictators, and the live ones, don't like it. She writes a new one every couple of years, puts out updated editions of old ones. If college required reading had a best-seller list, she'd be number one. I like to watch her work. She wrinkles up her forehead, mutters to herself usually in languages I don't know, writes all over her documents and books, and then–she's done it. I couldn't in a trillion years. She's says no big deal, she can't sing a note so we're even. She's right about that. Her talking is great. It's beautiful. Her singing is another subject. She doesn't do it, says she knows she's got no cords, so what's the point? That's Deesh. If something's got no point, she's not interested. Being apart six months a year is a bitch, but she doesn't agree. People, even me, wear her out. She can stay in that house for days without seeing or speaking to another living soul. She *likes* it. I know. And I know why. After what she's been through, why shouldn't she feel uncomfortable out in the real world? When she travels, almost never these days, she books a flight that brings her back the same day. Once she spent eleven hours on a plane to London, four hours in the British Museum, and then another eleven on the ride home. Don't you want to see some of the city? I asked her. She said: no. She'd seen it before and doubted the useful parts of it had changed any.

Useful parts? Yes, she said, like the ravens at the Tower of London. She reminded me a goodly number of people had been executed at the Tower, and I took the hint. I can shut up when I need to.

She hates explaining herself.

I know how it is. I hate trying to explain me to anyone, including me. It's a good thing we don't worry about making sure the other *understands* everything. We just do. Beats me how. Sometimes I ask her stuff about what she thinks about something. And she'll tell me whatever I want to know. And I tell her the same. She doesn't seem to need to ask, though. When she's with someone, or a group, you can see her intensity. When she listens, it's like there is no one else in the world she gives a damn about but you. How she does this when the whole band shows for dinner, I don't know. But nothing gets past her. I think that's why she has to be alone so much. She's not faking it when she listens like that. She gives you the total of her attention. Very empathetic, too. Most people don't know that because she does like to sharpen her wit when she talks. But mostly she keeps her edge talking to me. I know when she's being funny and when she's not. I know.

I write her letters when I'm on tour. She won't read them or write back. Won't talk on the phone. It's like, go do your thing, guitar boy, and when you come back, I'll be here. But, you know—whatever she does is right.

When she's in the same room, she can do anything, like push her sleeves up over her elbows, or click her nails against her teeth, and I want to tell her she's fascinating. But I don't. She'd roll her eyes, and tell me I'm too easily entertained or something like that. I don't want to hear it. She doesn't get it, that she really is one of those people who has an economy of movement, has a gracefulness and a precision that makes you want to admire even the smallest things. I always want to touch her. All the time.

I'd do whatever she wanted. If she asked to me to cash it in on the singing, the touring, the whole scene, I would. I wouldn't like it, but I'd do it. I think she'd pretty much do the same for me. Hell, she's already done more than the same for me. Saved my life. I wish sometimes I could save hers. Just to show her I don't take what she did for granted. But I think she knows.

No pictures in her house. Nothing to give her away. Besides me and Lily, I don't think she even lets people in, except for the band. She and the band have a sort of mutual admiration thing going, have since the beginning. They're my family, them and Deesh, and they know it. They pretend they just put up with me, but they don't pretend a thing with Deesh. She's not a person you can take one false step with, even joking.

I want her to marry me. She won't. Says marriage kills romantic passion, the hunger that's always there, and she's taking no chances. I tell her to believe me, that nothing would change, I swear, and then she says so what's the point in doing it, and I get mad for a couple of hours and ride my bike like I'm on the fast track to hell, and then it's over 'til the next time I ask. Every few months, just to make sure she hasn't changed her mind. To tell the truth, as long as she's here, with me, then she can have it any way she wants it. Married. Not Married. As long as she stays.

Those photographs that aren't there? Reflects her take on herself–if someone is aiming a camera, metaphorically speaking, she'll see to it that there's no usable film. Parts of her life she's destroyed–even the negatives. I don't believe she forgets any of it, then or now, but there's a lot she doesn't want in her head. Ever. No reminders. Therefore, no film in the cameras.

So far, it's been about twenty years. I don't know what's more amazing: that she would stay for so long, or that I would. That I would want to stay, no matter what. Well, not so amazing on my part. I mean, there is only one of her. Prowling around anymore–what for?

She doesn't know it, but if she were gone my life would be over. Done. Finito. I'd go on living, but it would only be an act. So what would be the point? I can't tell her that. She'd feel I was putting pressure, too much responsibility on her. I know I'll never leave her. I don't know if she would leave me. Wish I knew.

I do know her better than anyone else does. I know her better than I know *every*one else. But I learn all the time. From her. About her. And some days I don't know her at all. Wish I did.

"You will," the Voice soothes. "Just a little more time, and you will."

"Yeah? You can do that?"

"Oh, yes. Miracles of that sort are quite easy, and ridiculously simple."

"Why me? Why are you helping me?"

"Because," the Voice barely conceals its great power. "Just because."

And like a child, Gard sees that's a reason good enough.

Swimming to Oblivion

"I'm starving."

"You're always starving." She patted his arm absently.

"For food, please."

She looked up, pulled her glasses off. "Oh. Well. By all means."

"Is there anything here?"

"You know there is. The freezer is crammed to the gills. Lily was here right before you came home. She cooked for three days."

He was surprised. "You must have loved it. Had you a course of action?" He hoped she was impressed with his elocution.

"I did. I went to the movies."

"For three days?"

"Mm hm."

"You didn't see all the ones with kicking, punching, and blood spattering, did you?"

"No. I saved those for you."

"You're a peach."

She yawned. "Aren't I, though?"

She stood, stretched, dropped the book. He picked it up, looked curiously at the cover. It seemed a little lurid for her usual reading.

"What's this?"

She took the book from him. "Trashy romance novel."

"You're kidding." She had surprised him again.

"You, of all people, should know that as far as reading goes, nothing is beneath me."

He grinned at her. "I still don't know what you're doing with that." He sounded as if she had brought anthrax home in a jar. "What can be new? We *are* a trashy romance novel."

She considered, or pretended to. Then, "Your point is well taken," and she casually pitched it into the fire where it blackened and crackled quickly.

"God, Deesh. I never thought I'd see the day *you* burned a book!"

"There are a good many days I expect you will never think you'll see."

He shook his head. "What if I had wanted to read it?"

"Oh, you'd probably have thrown it at the wall after a chapter. But, if you are so broken-hearted, I know where we can buy another one."

"Oh, that's okay," he said, hastily. He looked at her. She began to laugh. He joined her.

"Now," she said, hooking her arm through his, "shall we go to the kitchen and see if I know where anything is?"

*   *   *

Later, they sat together, her head on his chest, drifting in and out. He looked down at her. "Comfy?"

"Not as much as I'd like. You're not soft enough."

"Shall you adapt or should I reach for a cushion?"

"Adapt."

He nodded and they returned to their separate, silent contemplations.

*   *   *

Sometime into the night, she sat up from the sofa and looked at him. "Let's frolic."

He groaned, assumed an air of irritation. "Do we have to?"

"Yes," she said, "particularly if you have any designs on my body in the next eight hours."

"That's blackmail."

"Oh, more like leverage, I think."

"Deesh. You know I do not frolic. The disproportionate always make a mess of it."

She laid her fingers against his forehead. The room was darkening as the fire gave up the ghost. Odd shadows met each other across the masses of books shelved around the fireplace. "Oh, so we're back to that. Fine. I'll frolic and you can be lifeguard."

"It must be after midnight. Is this your night to be nuts?"

"One moment while I check the scorecard." She paused as if thinking it over. "Yep. My night."

He sighed. "We'll have to go to my house."

She waited.

"You know, we wouldn't have to roust ourselves if you'd get a house on the other end of town."

"And live next door to you? I think not. Besides, that neighborhood is too rich and too crowded for me."

"I don't have many neighbors."

"You have neighbors, period. I'll bring the Hayden. Best accompaniment for frolicking."

"Oh, goodie."

Across town they went, she driving alone in her own car. She would not ride behind him (except that once) on any one of his damned motorcycles. He thought it wise not to leave a Triumph bike unattended, even in her neighborhood. There was no one around, but the Thunderbird's chromed tank badge was likely to draw any number of bike robbers looking for lots of torque at low revs.

*   *   *

The lights blazed across the back of his house, every room lit for the purpose. The beach was dark, but they could discern themselves and where they were.

"Simon says you can't go farther out than where I can see you," he said, setting up a boom box on a ledge of his beachfront boulder.

"How am I supposed to know where that is?"

"If I begin to appear grumpy, you'll know you've gone too far."

"And heaven knows, we certainly do not want you to get grumpy."

"The voice of experience, I presume?"

She hopped from one foot to the other. The air had dropped from chilly to cold. The hideous sweat shirt she saved for these occasions flapped about her.

"Is there another kind?" She blew him a quick kiss and leapt across the sand into the ocean.

The night and the dark water were equally black. He sat down, his back resting against the rock. *Chaos* issued forth at ear-shrieking level. He knew she wouldn't hear it two feet into the surf, but this particular piece of music was essential to frolicking.

Eventually, she was back to the beach, kicking at sand, sitting in the shallower water, throwing back into the darkness any item washed in with the tide.

Sometimes she liked to be twelve. And why not? She never *was* twelve. He had been and was still learning to forget it.

Eventually, she ran out of the water over to him, gasping air. Her hair hung in drowned sheaves over her face. He pushed some behind her ear. Her eyes were so bloodshot with salt water that she had taken on the air of a vampire, and the sweatshirt was a soggy wreck.

"God, you're beautiful," he said simply.

She wrung out her hair and laughed. "I bet you say that to all the girls."

"Just the ones who promise to put out."

"I hope it works better on them than it's working on me." She shivered.

He took off his jacket and wrapped her up. "Are we done frolicking?" he said.

"I should say." Her teeth chattered.

"Now what?"

"Bath. Hot water."

"Step this way." He collected the boom box, silenced

84

Hayden, put his free arm around her, and they slowly made their way back up into the house.

It would be the last of their evenings on the tide line for a very long time.

Wanted: Dead and Alive

"What do you remember?" Shrike asks, "as the best of your life? A time in which you could have asked for nothing more, because at that moment there was nothing left to ask?"

Gard wonders why he wants to know, supposes it is an ingredient for Shrike's ever-spinning Happy Machine. What's the harm in confessing? No images flash, interchange, crowd in Gard's mind. He knows the moment exactly and at once. He would live it over and again until Armageddon if he could.

"New Orleans," he answers, unaware of the expression on his own face, as if facing the memory is like gazing on God, Himself. "About twelve years ago. We were stuck playing lousy little clubs and junior colleges, trying to get back. I . . ."

He's not sure he wants to recall what had led them to ruin and a painfully slow resurrection. Shrike probably knows anyway. If you're made of light, aren't you supposed to know everything? Shrike has hinted at this any number of times.

"Do go on," Shrike says in so cultured, so encouraging a voice Gard is again reminded he is dealing with his own personal Immortal here. Why he's been chosen he stopped asking weeks ago. Whether supreme good luck or as reward for something good he's done and doesn't remember is no matter. He's here, the Voice is here, what else is necessary? Not a thing, he tells himself happily. Not a blessed thing.

"Uh, yeah. New Orleans. Big record company convention, *every*body there. We'd cut a new single; Cleve was leaking genius again, finally, and we were hoping for a two-album deal." He shakes his head. "But nobody was sure. Not us, not them. Turned out we'd got invited to the gig 'cause another band's drummer and lead vocalist had OD'd in the same week–you know how it is–and we were the replacement band. We figured they'd put up with us, then dump us. But Cleve's song was so good, I didn't care. I just wanted to sing it."

"And you did," Shrike says silkily.

"Oh, man." Gard lets out a breath. "I got lost in it, forgot where I was. When it was over, I was afraid to open my eyes 'cause the hall was so quiet. I figured, well, this is it. Cleve has finally bombed out and I'm the one gonna take the heat for it. I thought everybody'd gone home while I was singing."

"You never give yourself enough credit," the Voice remonstrates him gently. Gard senses that somewhere in this dazzle of white illumination, if Shrike has a head, he's shaking it.

"Didn't that day, that's for sure." Gard is shaking his own head in wonder. "But nobody'd left. Just out of nowhere, there was this wall of noise, like a storm surge, it rose up and kinda crashed down over the stage. And it just kept coming and coming; I opened my eyes, and Leslie was looking at me like 'Can you believe this?' The whole place, I mean, *the whole place*, just lost it. There were these *huge* names in rock, blues, CW, jazz, *standing on the tables.* They were screaming and clapping with their hands over their heads. People so far above me in the business I couldn't believe it was for *me*. All of it. For me."

"Yes." The light wavers slightly.

"And, er, the band, of course," Gard adds perhaps a fraction too quickly.

"Oh, yes," Shrike says dismissively. "The band. But it was YOU who'd done it. Wasn't it?"

"Yeah," Gard answers softly. "Yeah. And suddenly we were hot again. I was hot."

"Memories do become tattered with use, though, don't they?" The Voice asks with the faintest of regrets.

Gard sighs. "Yeah. But I've still got 'em."

"Wouldn't you like to remember the event as if you were actually living it again?" Shrike's voice is so soft Gard nearly misses it.

"You can *do* that?"

"Easily. And," the Voice adds, "in color."

"Goddamn!" Gard drenches himself in anticipation, then flushes. "Oh. Sorry. No offense."

"None taken. Apologies unnecessary. We know you—all of you—express joy without regard to the niceties of language. I rather like it," Shrike adds. "So spontaneous."

Gard grins. "You don't judge, do you?"

He could have sworn the light shrugged. "Not my job."

"Wish you'd been there that night."

"I was."

"No shit? You were in the audience?" Gard is astounded.

"Yes, indeed," Shrikes says warmly. "I was. In fact, that was the evening I first began to take a real interest in you."

"I didn't know." Gard's voice skitters around awe. "Why didn't I?"

"Because you weren't really ready for me then."

"I am now?"

"What do you think?"

"Well, I can see you. See color. Hear you. Recognize you. I guess I'm past ready."

The Voice was pleased. "Then there," it says, "you are. Now, let's talk about other things you can have."

Turn, Turn, Turn

(Gard and the Evermore Band On the Road)

May, June, July	Tour I
August, September, October	Home
November, December, January	Tour II
[Interruption December 20-29]	Home
February, March, April	Home

Map Lesson

"Why are you in such a study?" she asked, from her desk.

Down the length of the room, his boots were visible, crossed atop the back of the sofa. He raised his head.

"How'd you know?"

"Because I've been working for two hours and you have yet to suggest I find something better to do. Preferably with you."

His voice grew hopeful. "So, you wanna? Find something better to do? With me?"

"Gard."

"Hey, no problem. I am a patient man."

"Sometimes," she smiled. "So do you want to tell me what's going on down there? Need a new album title?"

"Yeah. Got one?"

"Aging Rocker Ravages Wretched Writer."

"Miss Calder, you alliterator, you. And you are so wretched."

"Aren't I, though?"

"It's my week to be wretched."

"Oh? Well, then. Wretch away."

It was quiet a few moments. Then he asked, in what he assumed was a casual tone, "What's Jahanna?"

"Your biggest record in 1986?"

"No, not Johanna, *Ja*hanna."

"Write it for me."

She heard his feet drop to the floor, his steps crossing down the room, rounding the desk to stand behind her. She felt his breath on the back of her neck as he reached for a pencil. He wrote.

She studied the word a moment, then raised her eyebrow. The English translation is 'Genneha.' 'Jahanna' is

Arabic, if memory serves."

"A place in *Arabia*?" He seemed confused.

"No," she said, studying him with ill-concealed curiosity. "Could be, metaphorically. But I don't think so. It's an ancient Arabic word meaning '*incineration*.'"

He stared hard at her, his eyes unreadable. Time passed.

"Gotta go," he said suddenly. He turned away from her and left the room.

What? Whatwhatwhat? But honoring their understood agreement of time and space–the fault of its existence being hers–she did not follow him. She did not ask. She waited, without reward. He never said another word about it.

Deesh Reads

"I wanted simultaneously to understand Hannah's crime and to condemn it. But it was too terrible for that. When I tried to understand, I had the feeling I was failing to condemn it as it must be condemned. When I condemned it as it must be condemned, there was no room for understanding. But even as I wanted to understand Hannah, failing to understand her meant betraying her all over again. I could not resolve this. I wanted to pose myself both tasks— understanding and condemnation. But it was impossible to do both."

She looked at him over the book, as she often did when she was struck by something she'd just read, or by something she thought might strike him.

"Good God, what is it?" The alarm in her voice was evident. Deesh, as he knew, simply did not permit herself alarm. What in hell was she staring at?

He glanced behind him before the truth settled in at him. On him. She was looking straight into his face.

"What? Me?" His confusion was genuine.

"Yes, you. You look as if you'd just witnessed a train wreck."

"Do I?"

"Yes. You do. What is it?"

There was nothing for it but to tell her what had washed over him. "Uh. The understanding and the condemning. That you can't do both. I'd never thought of it. But I see. It is one or the other—you can't have both.

"Why," she asked, leaning forward, "would you want both?"

"I don't know." He rubbed his forehead, gazed at the floor, as if the answer might be lying there, loose dust from the corpse of wisdom. "Just, suddenly, it seemed that if you really knew–something–you would condemn, and I could only take that if you understood while you were doing it. Condemning."

"Something?" The alarm had faded, but there was none of her usual amusement to replace it. "Something about you?"

"I don't know," he said miserably.

"Look, dummy," she said softly. "I had my chance to damn you and leave you, and I didn't. No nobility on my part. Just didn't. That was a long time ago. Why would I retry you on charges dismissed for fifteen years?"

He said nothing.

"Oh, I see. You've got something new you think has you re-tracking your road to hell."

He raised his eyes. Admission rained from them, though admission of what he could not have said.

"Gard." She put the book down, sat next to him, took his hand in gesture old between them. "Whatever it is, tell me or don't tell me, you're safe with me." She smiled, and his heart relaxed. "I don't see a thing, and if it's something from the tour, I don't care. Unless you want me to."

He shook his head. "No, it's not from tour. It's not here. I don't know where. I don't know what. Oh, hell, I'm probably losing my mind from those times I didn't and deserved to."

She laced her fingers through his hair and tugged slightly. "Chicago is over. Off the map. Dead and doesn't count. You know the rules."

"Yeah." The rules. *Don't look back. Don't look forwards. Look only now at who you are and what you do. Never look back; it might kill you.* But that wasn't it. He had no idea where visions of such danger came from, and he had no way to tell her he didn't. So he nodded beneath the rein of his hair in her hand and said,

"Right. Just having a spell of the vapors, I reckon."

She laughed obligingly, and he wished like a child on a star that she would forget everything he had said, while knowing full well that she never forgot anything.

Crayola Gardens

The countryside was startling. He could see colors, all of them. Crowded with wild flowers, blue, red-orange, yellow, pink, stretching up from green. Cultivated blooms in a maze all around. Now he knew what he had been missing all his life. Color as vivid as life; very clear air, with the occasional cloud against an unnaturally blue sky. Gard had no knowledge that hydrangeas do not grow wild in the same soil as Impatiens, roses and cyclamens are not friends, peonies smearing across freesia, tulips spreading like weeds– these things do not happen in real life. Nonetheless, he thought this must be what it was to live in another country, alone with spectacular, shocking beauty.

"Not really," said the Voice. "No animals to eat the flowers or trample them. Fields unrequiring of harvesting. Temperature unnoticeable and unchanging. Faint flowery smells, scents of breeze and air undefiled. Your country, if you want it."

Music, he thought, *tunes to frame the picture, chords to flutter the flowers. A little acoustic.*

"That, I cannot provide. My regrets."

I can provide. Give me an instrument. I can provide.

"Lovely idea, but impossible."

"No?"

"No."

"Why not?"

"Part of the contract when I acquired the real estate."

Gard's vision blurred.

Too much. It was too much. More than his senses could process. Color. What music looked like if you could see it. Too much. Time to go. Thanks a lot, *adios.*

But he did not awaken.

He struggled, but against what? He appeared to be

perfectly free, perfectly able to leave whenever he wished.

"Hey."

"Having a little trouble?" Shrike seemed unconcerned.

"Little. What's wrong here? Wait a minute, man. What are you . . .?"

Moonlight puddled through the French doors. His house was quiet. The ocean echoed through the glass; no need to fear. Something, though. He caught at the thought–something wasn't right . . . The struggling notion died in midair. Brushing away damp and twisted sheets, he fumbled out of bed. Much too late to call Deesh. Her sleep would be sound, and though he had awakened her for more troubles than this, he certainly would not for less. The marbles clacking in his consciousness were nothing more than three a. m. skitters in the night. Must be.

By morning, he would have forgotten any disruption to his sleep.

Chicago

He was too large a man to fit economically on the window ledge of a graceful old hotel too expensive to kill yourself in. His hair was much longer then, and it flew in strings around his face, into his eyes. Crouched there, wild-eyed, wild-haired, he was the very picture of the homeless drunk, the derelict damned, lodged on a ledge of the twentieth floor. The windows on either side of him were open, one screenless because he had clawed through, and when Cleve, trying to reach him, had attempted to cut away the remaining ragged edges, Gard had turned his head and spoken his only words of the evening.

"Touch that window again," he said in the voice of an animal, "and I'll take you down with me."

Then Cleve called her. Reluctantly. He knew the rules.

But she merely said,

"Do you think you can keep him from the fall until I get there?"

He was sure he could, he lied. He caught Leslie's dangerous stare, and lied more enthusiastically.

Later, no one asked her how she'd managed a plane and taxi that put her at the window just three hours after she'd hung up the telephone. They all knew, even with the time change, it was impossible. But there it was.

She came through the door without speaking, deliberately and without hurry. Crossed the wrecked room acknowledging no one. He was still out there. Rocking his upper body to and fro, as if holding a baby in need of comfort. She turned back to the room, to the now shattered remains of what had been elegant, took in empty Jack Daniels bottles askew everywhere, smeared and emptied plastic bags, phials of God knew what, the peripheral paraphernalia of destruction. She asked without preamble, "How much?"

"Lots," Leslie said, trembling, "and of everything. EVERYthing."

Everyone seemed bereft of word or action, scattered around the walls watching Leslie do the talking.

"We found him about six," said Cleve from his corner. "Couldn't get here til midnight. Goddamn New York airports." The words fell out of his mouth. "He's been here three days, maybe four."

"What happened at "Gard at the Garden?" she asked.

"Nothing." Cleve seemed confounded. "We killed 'em. Biggest smash we've ever been. We've been famous, man, but we've *never* been famous like we are now."

She was at the window. She leaned out, twisted around the frame.

"Gard."

He moved his head, slow motion, to the sound of her voice. Rivulets of sweat laid trails across his face, neck, chest. His shirt, what was left of it, was wet, sticking.

They locked eyes, and everything within her went still. In his eyes was nothing. Nothing.

Animate he might have been, but she saw clearly and at once that Gard, the one she knew, was departed.

With one look she understood exactly why he had crashed himself through the ragged hole at which she now stood. She could imagine all too well what it was like to continue existing when, within, there was no one home alive. He gazed at her, but she doubted his vision was translating anything useful or accurate. Across from them the city's lights burned in a profusion of blurred outlines. It was cold. Neither of them felt it. She held her torso out the window, but made no further move. A deep breath rose with her shoulders, and fell; she said nothing. Twenty minutes, thirty minutes, possibly sixty minutes passed without alteration in the scene. No one in the room did anything. The planet was not in the mood for turning itself around from its own unchangeable course.

She holds her gaze unblinking. Finally, she says once more,

"Gard."

He stops rocking. The wind returns, moderately, but enough to flap the tatters of his shirt, an unpleasant neon white in the moonlight.

She lays her hand flat on the ledge. Concrete grit and unknown detritus move and scrape her palm. For a moment there is a slow recognition on his vacant face. Before it leaves him, she says quietly,

"No point in worrying about hell for killing yourself, because hell surely cannot be any worse than this."

A glimmer of something wavers across his eyes.

"I know it, you know it, and there it is."

He shifts himself almost imperceptibly in her direction. He hears her as though she were far away, shouting but barely audible.

"I know you're already half way to the pavement."

Neither looks down.

"You've been waiting."

He stares in the same slack-jawed manner, but he hears more clearly. She must be coming closer.

"You want someone to give you permission? I will not."

She leans another inch or two out the window. Keeping her balance is requiring effort.

"But I'll give you anything else you want. If you can think of anything." Her voice is calm, but keeping it even is also taking effort. "Can you think, Gard?"

Her back is beginning to give out. The gravely ledge is cutting into her hand. She brushes bodily inconveniences from her thoughts.

"It may be that you can think a little. I know you can't speak. Don't worry about it."

Her tone suggests one old friend reassuring another about the inconsequence of a lost sweater.

"John. Can you come in?" Her voice thickens, some Texas slides in. "I think you might could come in. Just awhile."

She makes no move to touch him. She lowers her eyes, re-sites them out into the night. Her shoulders move again. Slowly up. Slowly down.

Inside, Leslie is crying silently. She takes no notice of herself. Kaseem moves next to her and coughs.

"Come on, baby," Deesh says to the night clouds. "Please."

Time is passing, but how much time? Nobody knows.

"I know it's not gonna be 'everything's all right.' I know."

The moon ticks. Gradually falling. There is no sight of day, but she believes it can't be long. She hasn't much time to hold her position.

"But maybe you could come in. Just for awhile. Sleep a little. You could probably sleep some now. That would be good–just leaving it all for a *while*."

He closes his eyes, opens them, as if testing the hypothesis. A single word floats across his brain.

Sleep.

She motions behind her, arm back through the window, as if she's waving away mosquitos. Cleve gets up, heads for the door. Holds it open until Kas, Vlad, and Leslie file out, he following.

*   *   *

When he slowly awakens, he can't remember anything of the last four days. They have vanished from him and will never be recovered. The heavy hotel drapes are closed against what must be day. The rag of his shirt clings like adhesive. His mouth tastes like the inside of a foundry. His eyes hurt. He doesn't feel nearly as bad as he should. Has he slept so long all the shit in his system has oozed out of him? Doesn't know. Can't remember. This isn't his room, he suspects. It is undamaged, clean, with barely any evidence of occupancy. No one but himself? No matter how rich the room, or long the sleep, an old familiar beast is snorting somewhere near. *I can't go home alone.*

He looks down at an unmoving form blanketed next to him. Oh, great. What has he got in bed with him, and what did they do? Whoever it is rustles in the sheets. God, he wishes it were Deesh.

He can't register. Wishes like his no longer come true.

The form next to him sighs in sleep. He slides back down into the covers, knowing the voice he most wants to hear he may not hear again, ever. When she finds out about this, her patience will be gone, and with it, him. God, he thinks. But his abbreviated prayers won't work anymore. A cold emptiness settles in his belly, and suddenly he has to get out of this room. Can he decamp without waking this stranger who wandered into his nightmares? *Please don't let her wake up. Please don't let her say anything.* Too late. Muffled behind the bedclothes is a voice rusty with fatigue. He holds his breath. It can't be. But it is.

"Gard?"

*   *   *

"I know it doesn't fit properly, but it was the largest one they had."

She handed him a shirt from one of the overpriced shops in the lobby. With his hair tied back, the week's excesses left in the shower, he looked pale and trembling.

"Let's go now," she said.

He glanced around the immaculate room. "Where's your stuff?" he croaked.

She reached up, laid her hand on his shoulder straining under the white broadcloth. "Right here. Now, shall we go home?"

They did.

He did not leave again for years.

You Pays Your Money and You Takes Your Choice

He sits in some tiny out-of-the-way room he's discovered. Wonders if even Deesh knows it's tucked up here in a vacated corner of the abandoned fourth floor. Drops his head into his hands. He wants to vomit himself out of himself. Pictures himself a flat, steaming mess on the floor. *Yes, that's the Gard we all know and love.* And it's killing him. *No, man, you're already dead and you're just too stupid to know it.*

His thoughts ricochet within the framework he has constructed; continuous motion, over and over, and he can't turn it off. His mind will not shut up, making him sick, perhaps he really will toss, his head has to shut up now, it bygod does have to, but it won't and he can't make it and he'll never be able to turn it off, this endless pattern going nowhere will not leave him, it will be all he has left, there is no running from it, it follows him, and he is screaming without sound to stop and stop and it does not stop and he has a flash he must be going mad and cannot stop himself.

"Gard?"

She does not appear to have been searching frantically for him. Why should she be up here? At this hour she's meant to be downstairs, closed up in her library.

He can't raise his head. She steps in, sits on the floor facing him. She waits.

When at last he brings his eyes to light they are echoes in an empty world.

"How can you do it? How can you let me stay here? How can you stay with me? What in hell good does it do?"

She looks around, follows the strip of afternoon sun making its way through the nearly useless window.

"What is it that you mean to say?" she asks evenly, no apparent concern registering in her voice. She gathers herself up, tucking her knees under her chin. The sun drops below the window before he tells her.

"I see," she says, when he has run out of words. His skin is paste, white and doughy.

He coughs.

"You wish me to tell you how much a failure you are as a man, how despicable you are as a human being."

He doesn't know whether to look at her or the floor. His hair drips in sticky strands, falling lank around his face.

"No, that's not it."

"Yes, that is it. Your lately germinating conscience is full of the sound and fury, isn't it? Will not let you rest? But if I referee your fight, just tell you what a malefactor you are, what a debauched libertine you've become, then the fight will be finished, won't it? You can assign yourself peaceably to hell."

That there is not a single note of harshness in her voice makes it worse, somehow.

"You won't have to continue living with yourself; you'll tell yourself you're a profligate, and there it is, that is all. Be what you are, or be what you were and there's no strain in it for you. But you would have me take you apart, examine all the evidence, pass sentence. Then your sprouting scruples will slink off in humiliated silence. You want someone to give you a valediction for what a miscreant you think you are. Then find someone. You are not going to get it from me."

The evening begins to blacken before a further word is said. At length she stretches her legs across the floor, flexes her shoulders as if to jostle stiffening muscles. They have been up here a long time.

He sighs. "Yeah."

The two feet of floor between them seems vast in this cell-like space.

"Yeah," he repeats tiredly. He nods to himself, slowly. For the first time since Chicago, he raises his eyes to hers and holds them. "How do you come to figure out so much?"

"You know how."

He winces. He's an idiot to forget. Her life before he knew her. He nods again, and his misery does seem faintly abated.

"That's all?" he asks, the dark patches beneath his eyes growing larger in the darkened room.

"That," she says with a ghostly trace of tenderness, "is all."

He will be hours more alone in the shadowed room, casting for a spark, any flame at all, to relight his nearly extinguished honor.

Fifteen years ago
Fourteen years ago
Thirteen years ago

Hangover

His face had shifted. The left side had sunk in and sunk down, forcing his demeanor into misalignment and imbalance. His natural color had evaporated. In its place was a cemetery pallor, and the boxing scars, the bar-fight scars, the motorcycle scars, the hard-party scars had disappeared into a yeasty swelling, as if his face were a plate of risen biscuits. His hair hung longer, and seemed unwashed and lank even when clean. He appeared overweight when he wasn't, and his eyes were flat–no windows to anyone's soul, least of all his.

The calluses on his finger pads softened, smoothed until his hands lost their edge. The Gibson, the Stratocaster, the back-up Strat lay somewhere within his house, though he couldn't have told you where. When he tried to run his vocal cords through their regular paces, he failed. A normal scale exercise produced nothing but a series of squeaks, a sort of crippled croaking. Fighting damage and irreparable strain, he knew the end was come. His voice was gone.

They trailed from one ENT specialist to another. They lost count. Each time she sat silently in the examining room listening for the hope Gard thought too dangerous to wish for.

No diagnosis differed from another. There was nothing observably wrong, they were told. No polyps, no tumors, no inflammation. Perhaps the slightest sign of sensitivity, to be expected coming on the heels of that last tour. No illness, nothing to remove or rehabilitate.

Thirty doctors later, the latest in a long line, Deesh finally heard something, although any inherent hope seemed doubtful.

104

"You've paralyzed a vocal cord," the physician said, briskly.

Gard looked at Deesh.

"What's to be done?" she asked.

Dr. Allende could not keep the shrug from his voice. "Nothing."

"Nothing?" Deesh repeated carefully.

"It will either fix itself or–"

"It won't," Gard interrupted.

Allende studied him. "Yes, those are your choices."

"Choices? Like I have a damned thing to say about it."

"Maybe," Allende said tentatively, "you do."

He looked at Deesh. She knew what he meant, even if the poor slob with the frozen throat didn't. He might as well tell him something, so he might think there was something tangible he could do for himself.

"Don't sing," he went on. Gard's expression of bitter resignation deepened.

"And?" Deesh pressed.

"Don't speak."

"And?" she insisted.

Allende sighed. "And it may be that eventually the paralysis will reverse itself." Gard seemed blank, as if English no longer penetrated.

There was nothing to do but go home.

*　　　　　　　　*　　　　　　　　*

For three years they lived together in their separate houses. He rode the roads for hours at a time, thinking nothing. She had Lily go to his house and cook for him ("Nice modern kitchen," she reported in a tone suggesting Deesh's was one of the culinary unfortunates). He read for miles from her library. She read to him. He watched sports on television. He began to run and lift weights. He was silent as he waited for his voice to come back to him.

Three years later he stood again on a stage; the fragmented Evermore re-formed. Chicago receded into a distance. At last he could say to Cleve, "let's rock and roll, man" and know that he could, in full clarity. Deesh completed a textbook on political corruption, *The American States: 1895-1915.*

The nightmare was over.

His strange dreaming, too faint and far between to remember, began then.

Foreplay

She answered the phone without looking at it. "Mm hm?"

"What're you doing?"

"Eating Fig Newtons and reading Robert B. Parker."

"Civil War?"

"Detective novels."

"What? This your day off?"

"Mm."

"Will you," he asked, lowering his voice to its sexual timbre, "read it to me?"

She sighed. "Honestly, one would think you were illiterate."

"Wouldn't one."

"Mm."

"It's your voice. If your voice is in my head, I'll remember everything."

"Well," she said doubtfully.

"What do you like about the story?"

"The two continuing characters remind me of us."

"Maybe this Parker knows us."

"Knows you, maybe. You're the famous one."

"And nobody but the band and your publisher knows you."

"You left out Lily."

"I mustn't do that."

"No, you mustn't."

"If I take you somewhere for a dinner a little more upscale than your present choice, can I spend the night?"

"Possibly."

"Might we even sleep downstairs?"

"Don't push your luck."

"Might be dancing with dinner."

"I'm listening."

"So wear the black thing."

"You are pushing your luck."

"Okay," he grumbled over the line, "I'm pushing my luck."

A moment passed.

"I'll wear the black thing," she said, and hung up.

History Vs. Romance

He sustained the distinction as the President who clung to the belief that less is more, particularly in governing. Never were his convictions more apparent than during the economic summit for which he failed to crack the seal on, much less read, his briefing book. He explained forthrightly, "Well, ya see, last night The Sound of Music *was on TV." Perhaps he will be best remembered as an unfailing supporter of the arts.*

"You're really good," he chuckled, not raising his eyes from the page. You shouldn't speak ill of the dead, though."

"I shall," she answered briskly, "speak ill of whomever I like."

"And whomever you don't like, too." From the depths of the sofa, he was laughing. "Bet the kids in History 101 are going to love this. Nobody's better than you."

"So you've said," she answered dryly. She stood at the edge of the sofa table, having materialized from some other part of the house.

"I mean as a *writer*?" his impatience hovering.

"Oh. Then you've changed your mind about the other?"

"I have not," he said, mimicking her sternly, grabbing her wrist and drawing her over to him, "changed my mind about one bloody thing."

She settled deep into one end of the sofa. "Uh oh. Too much time in England this last tour."

"Jesus! Will you be serious for five minutes?"

She looked over at the clock–mocking them both–on the mantle. "Yes."

"Why won't you let me tell you?" he said sadly.

She shrugged. "I don't know. Really. I don't." A

momentary sadness passed over her own face.

"I think," he said, stretching, sliding his feet under her knees, "you would write killer fiction."

She regarded him a moment. He wondered what the hell she was thinking. "Fiction is your department, Fluffy. I would never encroach."

"What're you talking about?" He was puzzled or suspicious or both.

"You know," she said, leaning back into the cushions. "Love arrived, love lost, broken hearts, mended hearts, what happened, what happened?, somehow it will all be solved by the eighteenth bar and one change of key."

"You think that's fiction?"

"Mostly," she said.

"Still?"

"Oh, Gard. Don't take the whole of the world so personally. I'm not speaking in particulars."

"Yes, you are."

She sighed. "Today is today. All in all, that *is* all."

He sat up, shifting position to block her exit from the corner where she sat muffled in the upholstery. Putting his head close to hers, he said in a voice without puzzlement, suspicion, or doubt,

"We are no fiction, babe. Today is today, all right. But today is all I've ever wanted, and tomorrow's gonna be just like today. Because," he said as certain as if he were on stage facing ten thousand people, "I said so."

She touched his face.

His voice was low and intense. "I say so."

For a moment so fleeting it might not have happened, he saw her mask of factual habit slide askew; her eyes grew darker and larger until they seemed to fill her face. In one slip of a second, she exchanged merciless self-control for the hedonistic indulgence of abdication.

His voice was in her head.

She shivered.

Fights with Cleve #4819

"I want to do a cover he hates." He lounged in between the doors to the library.

"On the tracks you're recording now?" She looked up from her desk, laid down a magnifying glass aimed over some mysterious document. He would not try to guess.

"Yeah."

"?" her face said.

"'Cry Me a River.'"

"I cried a river over you?"

"The very one," he said lightly, as if it didn't matter.

She rolled her pencil around in her fingers. "That is so old it would be new to anyone under ninety."

"My point."

"And Cleve will not consider it because?"

She fixed her whole attention on him. He trembled almost imperceptibly, as he often did under her scrutiny. Was it in fear or amazement that she could lock in on him down to his very breadth of bones?

"Because," Gard sighed, "it's been done. Done to death, he says."

"Isn't it your turn to be producer this time?"

"Yeah," he spoke cautiously, nearly punctuating himself with a question mark.

"How nice of you to let him think he can win."

"Well, maybe he should. Maybe it is a bad idea. Maybe I don't have the kind of voice suitable for that old stuff."

"Yes, you do. But it has been done. How would you sing it differently?"

"Just–I don't know. I can't talk about it. I just want to sing it. It'll come out however it comes out."

She considered. "Show me."

"Right now?"

"Why," she flipped her pencil at him, "not?"

He shrugged. Picked up the pencil, held it as a microphone. Stepping in, leaning slightly against a support column, circling his arm around it in a gesture of defeat, surrender, and barely contained anger, he narrowed his eyes and slippered himself into a few notes. By the second verse, he closed his eyes and let it go.

The hair rose on the backs of her arms. Her usual concentrated expression froze into fierceness. Had he seen, he might have mistaken her look as disapproval.

He finished. After awhile, opened his eyes. Took a deep breath, raised his eyebrows at her.

In a low voice, she said, "Oh, yeah."

He smiled. "You never say 'yeah.'"

"Sometimes I do. Now, for example."

"Ah." He unwound from the column, twiddled the pencil unaware.

"How did you do it?" She rubbed her arms.

"Went somewhere else. You know."

"Yes," she smiled for the first time. "Where?"

"Never tell."

"I never do."

"Went to a place where you used me for sex, told me you did, and walked off. I was old toilet paper. Then you called and started it all again."

She chuckled. "Your worst nightmare."

He scratched his head. "Maybe not the part about using me for sex."

"Feeling usable?"

"*Yeah,*" he said.

*   *   *

Later, she asked, "How long for you to talk Cleve into it?"

He rubbed at his face. "No way to tell. Two years? Three or four? Maybe four albums from now."

She wrapped herself in his discarded shirt, pulled her knees up to rest her chin. "Too long."

"Too long?"

"Yes. You and Cleve do not have time to fight forever; we're none of us going to live that long."

"In that case," he said, mirroring her compacted position, "I'll tell him you said so."

She wrapped his shirt tighter, reached for the scrambled sheets and blankets.

"Cold?" He rubbed her shoulders.

"Autumn is coming early this year."

"And this house is drafty as hell up here in the guest bedrooms."

"Yes, yes. How about more insulation for my next birthday?"

"I am not bringing you insulation for your birthday." He drew the bed covers around them. "Maybe Groundhog's Day."

"I am happy to hear it." For a brief moment she was shaking.

"Hey, babe, you really are cold."

She shook her head. (*Don't worry me with it. Don't get up for another blanket. Just don't.*)

"And what's with this we're not living forever thinking? That's not like you."

"Not much." She considered. He ran his hand through her hair. "It was a thought taking words too soon, I guess. I don't know. Just a strange feeling I've bumped up against lately."

She did not like the look on his face. Leaned her head into his palm, spoke against his calluses,

"Pay no attention. Probably reading too much. You know, losing touch with reality, that sort of thing."

He took his cue and did not pursue farther.

She went on, "Why not tell Cleve to play nicely and you promise he can launch a hostile takeover of the sandbox next time?"

He laughed out loud.

She smiled. He nodded. They sat resting their chins for a time, looking at each other.

Call for the Lady with the Alligator Purse

One night without dreams, he hoped. At least one night without dreams he remembered. Back in the good old days he could have blamed the nocturnal weirdness on whatever controlled substance he had ingested before retiring. But the good old days were melted into a psychedelic past, for better, for worse, not to be re-invented. So, what now? What troubled him that he could not define? Why did he fear dreams of Shrike and want them, too? It was a muddle and it would be pissing him off if he weren't so tired thinking about it. Deesh should think. She was much better at it. No way, though, could he tell her what was in his head in the darkest hours of morning, when the sun was hours away from the window. First, what could he say? He had no language for it. There weren't any English words that applied directly, exactly. Dreams were like that, though, weren't they? Second, if he could explain, how could he make it clear he had no clue to why he tried to avoid sleeping, but was happy when he did. The pictures. The peace. The light. How could he tell it all and why and where? Stupid to try. He feared probably because he was so far out of his league. Yeah. Little lessons in humility, most likely. He was still too arrogant, too self-centered, too convinced of his own invincibility. Just accept the truth, he told himself, and you'll stop being afraid. Deesh would agree with that, wouldn't she? Be good to drink himself into a blackout. No. Not good. But useful. Maybe he could sleep through the night without all these universal mysteries being revealed to him. No. He knows it is no option, and it irks him that he knows it. Cripes, what the hell was he supposed to do?

The answer materialized: nothing. Do nothing, say nothing, think nothing. Just let it be, and he would understand it all in time.

It was a rare evening he was alone in his house. She had things to do, he said he had things to do, she said, see you tomorrow. Yeah, he said. Good idea. So now he could just goddamn well stop watching the clock and get his carcass in bed. Sleep was part of voice preservation the doctors had told him in the black years. Fine. Go. Racktime.

The dream arrived almost before he was asleep. Birds flew thick as blizzards. No color anywhere, no reforming realities, no astonishments. Just white birds. Who knew what kind? He didn't. Interesting that the feathers were so many, the sky was feathers, and the ground and the air in between, yet he felt no touch of them. He supposed they were beautiful, but there was something wrong. What? He was afraid, and afraid as he had never been in all his life. The other places weren't like this. They were soothing, hypnotic, taking him out of himself, giving him a respite from himself. Here, everything except touch was much too real. The whir and flapping of wings grew louder, the whiteness surrounded him. Right, he thought. It's a Hitchcock movie, and I'm the guy at the filling station who dies dumping a cigarette in a gas puddle.

They are not a movie.

He heard the words clearly. The speaker sounded firm, female, human. Good. Maybe someone could help him out.

The voice came from behind a wall of soundless birds. Silence came abruptly, like the volume on the wing machine had turned off. He looked around. Where was she?

It is no matter where I am.

Yeah? he thought.

Yes.

He waited, unsure. Kept himself very still.

Do you know what you are doing?

There was no accusation there; rather, a genuine question wrapped in a cloak of assurance that he most assuredly did *not* know what he was doing.

116

Do It To Me One More Time

"Is it too early to come in?"

She's taken a place on the parquetry, become an island rising from an ocean made of paper. He hears muttering. She looks up, as if torn from the only home she's ever known.

"Yes. But come in, anyway."

"Need help?"

She shakes her head, seems to have trouble focusing on him.

"No. I'm adjusting chapter sequence so I can deliver myself of the whole mess. As soon as you're off again, I'll be outlining the next one."

"About that . . ."

"Hmm?" She removes her reading glasses, looks at him expectantly. Now he has her attention.

"I . . . don't know if twelve weeks is enough time. Here, I mean."

She is surprised. "Since when?"

"Since–I don't know. It feels okay," he touches his throat, "but I'm not sure I should be singing again so soon." He sits on the floor, back against the chair opposite her.

She stacks paper piles crosswise, moves closer to him. They are knees to knees, chins resting on kneecaps as their arms wrap about themselves. They do not touch.

"I do not believe you," she says evenly.

"Why not?" He feigns innocence.

"Why do you think?" The question is gentle, with a tinge of he-ought-to-know-better-than-ask-such-a-question.

He sighs heavily. "Okay, you shouldn't believe me. But I don't know what to tell you."

"You don't want to do the tour," she says quietly.

"No. I mean, yes. But I don't want to leave here, and don't ask me why."

"I wouldn't think of it. 'Here' means this town, my house, your house, me, or a singing-less existence?"

"Yes." He lifts his hands, confused. "I guess I can't ask you to go with me?"

"You can ask, but why would you? I have another book to launch and six months in which to do it, and I don't like Europe unless I'm alone. Or we're alone. Furthermore, the countries are all too small. No place to hide."

This is old news.

He wants to touch her. Something about the conversation suggests it would be better for him to not. He supposes he has to keep his hands off her *some*times when they are together.

But laying his hand on her kneecap. Resting it there, next to her face. That he would greatly like to do.

"Besides," she goes on. "Europeans have gathered in massive crowds to hear the new song, the hit already, and I cannot listen to it if even a single other person is there."

"This is some kind of compliment?"

"It is."

"You could stay in the hotels."

"Agoraphobia begins at home."

He smiles. He can't waste even one small joke in this here and this now. He needs it to remember later, when he's alone in his room in a country he's not certain of.

"What is it?" She rubs her forehead. "We've had this tour stuff settled for years. You can't wait to go. I can't wait to stay home. When those choices begin getting old, it's usually right on time for you to come back. Where," she adds dryly, "I believe the management awaits you with open arms and no sexual morality whatever."

"Yeah. I'm being stupid."

"You are not being stupid. You are being something, but for once in twenty years I cannot discern it."

"We could fight about it," he says, hopefully.

"To what purpose? Our argumentative skills seem

pretty well honed without practice."

She makes him laugh. Even now, she makes him laugh. And why is he troubled? He has no answer, but if she would come with him, he would breathe more easily.

"What?" she says after some minutes.

"Uh, poetry. Thinking about some poem you read me."

His voice drifts, fades. She watches him carefully; he sees her eyes, and yanks his own chain–back to her, back to now.

"Let's go to breakfast," he says abruptly.

"Let's."

"Where?"

"Why tinker with tradition?"

He shrugs. "Good point. Pearl's Pie Palace it is."

*   *   *

They crowd themselves into one side of the booth. The place is nearly empty. Still too early for most.

"Who's in the next book?" he asks, drinking another orange juice. Their thighs are paired closely under the table.

"Neville Chamberlain, Oscar Wilde, Adam Smith, Charles Dickens, Sarah Bernhardt, Grand Duke Alexander," she says, wiping syrup from her fingers.

"Want any help?" He stares at her hands.

"Not here. You know what would happen." She replaces her napkin in her lap.

"I've got a pretty good idea," he grins carnally.

"I have syrup at home if you feel the need for licking it off somebody other than yourself." Under the table, she nudges one of her ankles between his.

Good. This is good. This is normal. This is life as it should be. Life as it is. What was wrong with him an hour ago? Nothing. Just the pre-tour crazies he has dodged and collided with as long as he remembers.

He will sleep in Belgium. And Greece. And wherever else they're going. He doesn't care, really. He's been to them all so many times. He will sleep every morning and every afternoon it will be a new day, severed cleanly from the old. *I have,* he recalls, *lost all my mirth.* To hell with that. If the mirth is gone, then it's time to get it back.

"So how come," he says, forking sausages from her plate, "Neville Chamberlain is hanging out with the Romanovs?" His pronunciation is correct, a point with which he once almost impressed Vlad the Implacable.

"Think about it," she said.

He drinks another orange juice.

"Oh," he says.

"Thought you'd get it." She tongues more syrup from the corners of her mouth. He would do the job for her, but they have their Regulations. No sharing anything in public. Let the public watch somebody else grow slightly short of breath, someone else feel the beginning of a heat behind his eyes.

"Are you going to have to suffer public research?"

"Not much. Just the Alexander exhibit–it will be up-state for a few weeks. I need to read the letters, see the watercolors before the thing packs up and disappears back into Petersburg."

"Where?"

"S F Museum of Fine Art."

"They gonna give you scholar status?"

"Yes. I could not possibly examine the materials in the middle of the tourists gushing through the doors. The curator would think that a greater horror than I would." She chews a corner of toast, contemplating.

"Deesh."

"Hm?"

"We have to go. Right now."

His urgency is even, low-keyed, but nonetheless dangerous.

"All right."

He drops too much money on the table. Unfolds himself out of the booth, waits for her, insists she walk ahead of him down the narrow path of linoleum. At the door, he opens it, waits for her to pass through. They cross the parking lot. He opens the passenger door of his truck, waits for her to get in. Walks around, lets himself in. Keys the ignition. Fires the engine. The sun still has not reached far above the horizon. He lays his forehead against the steering wheel.

"Gard," she says. Waits. Then, "Are you ill?"

He raises his head. "Yes."

"Your house?"

"Yes. All right?"

"Of course."

Her voice gives up no emotion, but she keeps her eyes on him. His complexion is not the corpse-like color he so often awakens with these days. Still, she will put him to bed. Call Lily to come and cook for him. She will prop her feet up on his bedclothes and read to him. Call the doctor regardless of the fuss he'll make about that. She turns her library upside down in her head, shakes books off shelves. Restoration Comedy. She's not got him into those plays before. She is considering titles when he turns the truck into his drive. The morning is graying, itself the color of corpses. She doubts the sun will show itself today. It looks to rain. Good. Perhaps he can sleep far from dangerous dreams. She will remain in his room until this passes. And what 'this' is it?

They go straight to the back of the house. His bedroom is there. He drags the cover off the bed.

"You have fever?" she asks.

"Yes."

He rolls the counterpane across his arm, reaches under the bed and extracts his weights bar.

"What do you think you're doing?" Curiosity, not reprimand.

He takes the weights bar the few steps down to his part of the beach. Lowers it onto the bedcover, climbs back to the house. He grabs her wrist and pulls her to the glass doors across the far wall.

"Wait. Wait a minute. I am not wrapping up in a blanket and sit to watch you tie weights to your legs so you can drown yourself."

"Not my plan," he says tersely. The sky sags with impending rain. A slight wind hovers.

He jerks at her arm. She stumbles after.

"Okay, I'm coming. You can let go."

He ignores her.

Drags her across the yard onto the edge of the beach. Sea brush grows in a clump at a pair of boulders down near the water.

"So what's the comforter for?" she gasps.

"We wouldn't want you to get any sand up your ass." His voice is harsh under the sound of the outgoing tide.

Such vulgarity about her person is unexpected, not his style.

"I thought you were feverish."

"I am."

They reach the sand, the boulders, the brush. He keeps her wrist tight in his hand.

"So what is this? Back to your endurance training for Monsieur Rock Star? Still a bit early, isn't it?"

He ignores her. Still keeps her in his grasp. Easily.

"Not a picnic, I'm guessing," she says, amusement creeping into her voice.

"Not in the way you think." From his back pocket, he withdraws a knife, flips the blade open with his thumb.

She raises an eyebrow.

Watches without flinching as he brings the tip of the knife closer and closer to the exact spot between her lungs. She raises the other eyebrow. Her expression is as sarcastic as he has ever seen it: *Okay, big man. Now what?*

The wind rises a little. The water at the shoreline is still clear.

She puts her free hand on her hip. Twists her lip. *You want to play in the traffic? Think you can leave the streets alive?*

He knows the nature of her sardonicism, can almost hear the words. Telepathy between them has never been much of a miracle.

He narrows his eyes, slides the blade under her shirt at the collar bone, and cuts it to the hem in one stroke. As it hangs from her shoulders, he puts the knife between his teeth, and tears the rest of the shirt off her back.

"This is original," she sneers.

He takes the knife from his mouth.

"How do you know," she continues, "I didn't have a sentimental attachment to that shirt?"

"Did you?"

"No."

He barks a short laugh without smiling.

"However," she says, looking down at herself, "I am rather fond of these underthings."

"Pity." He cuts her brassiere away right between her breasts. He wiggles the blade under the waistband of her slacks, tears. The linen makes a rusty shriek as it disappears into shreds.

She has yet to move.

Squatting, he cuts the rest of the garment away. Still squeezing her wrist. In the wind, chill bumps rise on her arms and thighs. He glances briefly at her panties, leaves them. Leans down for the bedroll, fixes it flat with one hand. Forces her on to it. The margins of the material begin to blow up at the corners. He sticks the open knife into a back pocket of his jeans. Lifts forty pounds off the weights bar, lays one of the freed discs flat on a corner where the blanket curls around its own goose down. As without effort, he repeats the process three times. He catches her about the waist, presses her down. Straddles her with his knees, keeping his own weight above her.

"So what now? I freeze to death on a dreadfully expensive array of silk and chicken feathers while you contemplate the sails on the horizon?"

"Don't talk anymore," he says evenly. Reaches for the remains of her brassiere, ties her wrists as tightly as he dares. Her lips twitch. She bites her lower lip to lock down her laughter. "Put your hands up there, over your head."

She complies.

He loops what's left of the lace tied about her over the tip of a thin outcropping in the boulder. Reaches behind himself, brings out the knife. Lays the blade against her right hipbone, slides it between her skin and remaining underwear. Slices upward. Her chill bumps spread. He cuts the material at her left hip. Tears the whole scrap into two strips. Stares into her eyes. For once, she cannot read his expression.

He is deft but leisurely as he threads the first scrap through a weight, ties one ankle to it. Ties the other to an opposite weight. The distance between weights forces her feet apart, keeps them there by the discs' inertia. The ocean is gray now, gray as the sky and clouds under it.

Surf's up.

"You're cold," he says.

"Yes," she answers.

"Good," he says. "You won't be in a minute."

"You think."

"I know."

He pulls his shirt over his head, lays it over her upper body.

"I don't think that's going to help much," she observes.

"You won't notice when the begging and screaming start."

"Why should you beg and scream? I appear to be at your mercy."

"Not me who's gonna scream." He plants the knife in the sand. She restrains herself from phallic repartee.

"Oh, and I suppose you're going to make me beg and scream. You know I do neither. Even for you."

"Today you will, and you'll do it for you." She looks at him, shaking her head at such a boast. "I can make you."

"You and what man's infantry?" she says, witheringly.

He lowers his head, kisses her. Serious kissing. She watches him while he bites at her lips, brushes his shirt off her. He slides down to her neck, beginning a trail of mouth-made bruises to her breasts. She closes her eyes.

124

"Beg me," he says.

"To stop?" She is breathing irregularly.

"You know better." His voice is cool, but its register is dropping. "Beg me."

"No."

He is kissing again, without gentility. Her mouth is already beginning to swell. "Plead," he says.

"No."

He lays another trail down her neck, begins one across her breasts. He feels all the muscles beneath her skin pull taut. An odd sound escapes her. She pushes her feet against the weights. Mouth against her ribs, he laughs. A low, scratchy chuckle not familiar to either of them.

"Cry."

"No."

He is correct. She is no longer cold. Her hair is beginning to mat at her forehead. Irregular breathing grows shallower. She cannot see, but can feel the strain in his Levis against her. He won't, her brain mumbles, be able to tease her much longer. Now what is he doing to her?

"Beg?"

"No."

He does it again. She feels some kind of sound vibrating up her throat. She recognizes that she and rational thought will soon part company. Feels his mouth on her lower belly. Her pelvic bone, the inside of one thigh, then the other. Sucking the resistance right out of her at too personal a place for her to keep quiet.

"Uhhn."

"Beg."

"Unnmm."

"In English."

In the little breath she can summon, she spits out, "No. Not ever."

He hasn't shaved. His face rasps up her thighs, over where he has already been, back up to her face where he begins again. Licking a circle at her jaw line. She bites her lip, but no longer to dam up laughter. Laughter left her

125

sometime back. Nerves just under the skin are jumping unevenly in places she wouldn't have expected. Her lungs are barely dragging in enough air. Her heart is skipping oddly.

"You will beg me."

She doesn't answer. The sentence never leaves her brain; the words are not forming in the correct shapes. He wets her lips, draws them between his teeth until they both taste blood.

"Feel faint?" His voice is sandpaper.

"Hmmhm." The sound she makes is faint, all right, and her regular alto has gone out of it.

"Beg."

She shakes her head, eyes remaining unopened.

Another path of bruises from his mouth, down her neck, across the tops of her breasts. She feels his hand between her legs.

"Beg."

"Hm mh."

He takes this for a "no," and, barely touching, drags his thumb up. Down. Kisses new discolorations across her nipples, down and under her breasts. Presses his thumb. Her hips jerk violently. He brushes the pads of his fingers over her belly and her feet clench. A stain of flush begins spreading from her jaw to navel. If he is breathing, she can't hear him anymore. Once, years ago, before she had known him, she had fallen into shock. Now the experience is coming back to her. Numbness around her chin, down to her shoulders, a sub-epidermal shaking, chills that are not cold. The feeling in her palms disappears. Her fingers flare and won't bend.

His mouth between her legs, he says, "Beg" and drags his tongue after the word. Numbness in her knees, around her waist. One did not go into shock from doing this sort of thing, or allowing it to be done, did one?

*   *   *

She was sure not, but her conscious attachment to her body continued shutting down. Except whatever half-inch of flesh he took with his mouth. Flitting across her brain was the broken thought, *Is this what he does to women just by singing to them?* Then no wonder his last two CDs had sold twenty million copies.

The voltage was leaping, and wherever he touched, it was if that place and his mouth were a lone existence. All that was left of her motor skills was reaction. When her body began to go rigid, he stopped.

"Well?" he said softly in her ear.

She opened her eyes; supplication in them was obvious.

"Gotta hear it," he said, moving back down her body. He would push her far enough for the rigidity to begin, and stop. Over and over, waiting as she came closer and closer, then abruptly cease. She watched his head moving, rising back to her face, and words came at last.

"You bastard," she croaked.

"Tsk tsk," he answered, and began unbuttoning his jeans, pushing them down. Now she would use her foot to toss them aside. Except, it came to her, her foot could not obey her commands.

Every nerve she possessed began shrieking.

He stood up and took his jeans all the way off. She thought not for the first time that a man might be measured by the size of his voice, if you were looking for a correlation.

He knew down to the last word what went through her mind, even with as much static as it was generating.

How long had they been out there? The gray dismal morning seemed to have passed into late afternoon. The tide was returning.

He laid back down, fitted himself against her, skin to skin, limb to limb, and edged his way in a little. Held it there, withdrew. Did it again, a third time, a fourth. Ran his thumb over her cheek bone, smiling tenderly. His eyelashes came close enough she could feel them flutter slowly on her face. He kissed the base of her throat.

Her voice came out in a cracked scream. "All RIGHT!"

"All right, what?" he said into her ear.

"PLEASE."

"No," he said in the same calm tone she had used on him sometime earlier.

"PLEASE, Goddamnit!"

"No."

"Please, I beg, please."

"Please what?"

"Have mercy."

"Please what?"

"Oh, God–PLEASE do it to me!" She didn't see the relief in his eyes. There was a limit to his endurance.

He shoved himself into her. She drew a clear breath and screamed,

"Oh God, oh God ohGod."

Maybe it was "Oh Gard, oh Gard, ohGard," but he couldn't hear the words exactly. There seemed to be a landmine going off beneath him, and all he could do was rise with it and drive it back down.

"Please, please, please." The words were a recitation, and was she moaning, or crying, or laughing, or all three?

He reached over her head, slipped the scrap of underwear over the rock, fumbled it off. She dropped her arms as a loop around his neck and pulled him down, held on, buried her face in the shallow near his collarbone as either the sea water or his own sweat ran over both of them. He heaved and a roar exploded out of his throat.

Wherever they'd gone in the past, there were in a new place now.

*   *   *

She opened her eyes to darkness and dry air. Sheets around her. Faint glow from a light in the bathroom. He stood in the doorway, a black outline, pushing his damp hair back with both hands.

He knew she was awake. Crossed the room to sit on the edge of the bed. Stroked the tangled mess that was her hair. He smelled of soap and clear water.

"Will you," she whispered, "be the death of me?"

"I'm working on it," he whispered back. She nodded. "You've arisen from your sexual stupor?"

"You're a stupor."

"You need food? More sleep?"

"A bath, cold water," she said, hoarsely. "Now."

He had to carry her to the tub, an outrageous fixture of black marble sunk into the floor. It might have doubled for a small pond. He lowered her into the water, turned on a lamp in the corner. "Mind if I join you?"

Her head resting on a rounded edge, she opened one eye and said, "It's your playground."

He washed her hair. Soap bubbles ran into the water, floated on the surface, burst. He massaged her scalp.

"If I weren't so tired," she muttered, "this could be dangerous."

"Deesh."

"Hm?"

"You okay?"

"And then some."

"Sure?"

"Quite. Why?"

"I'm afraid I left you in something of a mess."

She slid down, let her hair breathe underwater. Came up, laid herself floating on his lap.

"I am never a mess."

He held her carefully.

"Never. But . . ."

She sat up, examined one arm, held it where the light shone faintly on it. A maze of pale purple against her wintry skin. "Good thing I don't get out much."

Silence.

"My, my. What *won't* the neighbors say?" She was laughing at him. His serious expression remained.

"Don't be a dummy. None of them hurt. Even a little." She flipped bubbled water at him. "You must know you could not hurt me even if I wanted you to."

"Did you have a good time?" he said, clearly wanting to know.

"Hated it," she said, languidly.

He ran more water into the tub.

"And you?" she said, her amusement palpable.

He soaped a sponge down her back. "Yeah," he said, beginning a smile into the back of her neck, "me, too."

Bar Tab

They are in the days in between. Last homecoming and next home leaving. The days between his readjustment to waking up after three months in the tornado alley of touring and her falling alone again into whatever are her dreams when he's gone. She is sitting on the stairs to the third floor, watching him dig out wiring he's convinced will burn the house down. Besides, wrestling with the many hidden possibilities of the house relaxes him, gives him a chance to find, to fix, and not to sing. He's talking to the wall.

"Come on, give it up." He's groping around inside the hole he's made, searching for suspect wiring. "Gotcha." He gently withdraws a bundle of ancient electrical conduits, looks it over, shakes his head. "Nope. Won't do. I keep telling you," he turns to the stairs, "you've got to replace it all. Copper wiring. Right now."

"You won't be home long enough to do it all." She leans an elbow on one knee and looks up at him.

"We could get a real electrician in here? Oh, all right, never mind. Damn it." He lets go the wiring. "But I can do some, and some I am going to do." He gives a look daring her to deny him.

"My hero." She smiles and he gets out his serious tools.

"Stay and talk to me awhile." He's pretending to be casual.

"You mean as in conversation?"

"Yeah."

"Can you converse while performing surgery?"

He drops down next to her, leans into her knee. "But, yes, madame. We do ze wireeng so many times, it is, how you say, ze snap?"

"Your French is improving."

She moves her elbow. He rubs his chin on the vacated knee. "It's my German I need to work on."

"Want me to help?"

"Naw. I learn on the job."

He moves to his tools, begins replacement therapy. "Whatever you do, don't change anything in the breaker box, or I'll be Fried Chicken the Electrician."

"Breaker box?" she inquires. "I don't," she lies and he knows it, "even know where it is."

"I am getting some of the *Deutsche*, but there's always some surprise somewhere."

There's a point to this, she knows, and waits.

"I met a guy in a bar on the *Schedestrasse* on the last gig. I think two days before we came home, and I was tired and wired at the same time, you know?"

"Just don't be tired and wired at the present moment, Chicken Man. And yes, I do know. That stage of mercilessly sober disorientation."

He nods. "Exactly. Anyway, I'd gone down to this place after the sound check and I had a few hours to see the sights."

"Yeah, those German taverns are all listed in Baedeker."

"Ha. And then ha. I like to hang with the locals, and the only places you can find any with educational value are in the bars. Anyway, I keep thinking about it, because I think I was supposed to know him, this guy, and I didn't. Not like people who pretend you're supposed to know them, but the real confusion. I know he knew me. Knew *me*. Sort of creepy, but I can't define how."

"Scary?" She leans back against the banister, plants her feet on the wall opposite.

"Yes. But not to me. More in general."

"Scary how?"

"I don't know. I never met anyone, ever, who was so–powerful. And he wasn't much over bantam weight. He looked like a freakin' Ralph Lauren *model*. But his mind–or maybe I mean to say his will–seemed unmovable once he set to something."

"How do you mean?" She waits as he does something electrical she doesn't understand.

"How *do* I mean?" He stares into the hole he's carefully widening. "No fear. The only person I've ever seen with absolutely no fear. At all."

"No wonder you can't stop thinking about it. I've never known *anybody* like that."

"Except for you."

"Save the jokes for your audiences."

"No, really. The way his eyes were, the way he moved himself, the way he held himself still. Like he was driving a tank but had nothing enclosing him." He pauses. "Actually, he kinda looked like Cleve did thirty years ago. Waist length curly hair, blond. And scary like Cleve. No, much scarier.

She waits.

"There I was with my oh-so-bracing club soda, and he's somehow sitting next to me. Orders straight bourbon–said he thinks German beer tastes like thick piss."

She laughs. "He would be correct on that point."

He pauses in his labors, says benevolently, "Yeah–said the woman who eats Fig Newtons for dinner."

She smiles serenely. "Straight bourbon?"

"Yeah." He is thoughtful. "A whole quart. Just like me. Or another me from another time." A flicker of sadness passes over him.

"Still miss the old Jack?" she asks neutrally.

"Not always."

There is silence between them.

Years ago on the beach, they both remember. In the days after the international hysteria, thousands and thousands chanting "Gard. Gard. Gard." in sold-out stadiums. The days after he'd lost his American audiences, his record contracts, his place on the charts. The days after Chicago. The days after his voice had finally come back, but not far enough.

The day on the beach behind his house. She lay

prone, scribbling on a parchment copy of a seventeenth-century document's obscure answers to annoying questions she had to resolve before finishing her next chapter. She made notes all around the margins in pencil. Smiling to herself. Gard didn't know it was only a copy and she didn't plan on telling him. It would be interesting to see how long he could contain himself before breaking into his usual horror at her desecrations. Back in Texas, you wrote in a book, you got expelled. Lost your library card. Suffered public humiliations. Hanged at high noon.

"No one ever taught you how to read a book properly," she had once told him.

"Before you I only read books about football and motorcycles, anyway."

"Which accounts for you being the world-famous star you are now."

"Don't call me that. I hate that."

"Sorry," she had said, not at all sorry. "I forgot your tender sensibilities concerning self-denial."

Now she lay, scribbling away at the arcane French, waiting for him to object to the ruin of the parchment.

He sat against a dune he'd made himself. Staring out to sea. Behind sunglasses, his eyes were unfocused. All his concentration centered on looking a very model of the modern *laissez-faire*.

An hour passed. Translating passages into a notebook, she was frowning as she went.

He stared out to sea.

Then: "You know," he said, apropos of possibly nothing, "a beer would be good about now."

She raised her head. He was aiming his shaded eyes in her direction. Without changing her position, she said levelly, "then go and get one."

That's all? That's it? No protest? No warning? No concern? He watched her return to her work and held his breath. Let it out. A moment passed.

"Oh, never mind," he muttered, taking the Strat off its blanket and diddling a chord.

She did not look. And she was far enough away that he could not hear it when she, too, let out her breath.

They remember what they would like to forget.

She stops the mental videos. Time to come in from out of the past.

"Okay. So this guy orders a bottle of Jack, and chats you up. And made you feel weird because you're supposed to know him and you don't and you think he knows you but he looks like no barfly you've ever met."

"Right," he says, smiling again.

She shifts her legs against the stairwell, breathes comfortably. He'll get around to it when he gets around to it.

The smile fades. "Right," he repeats, softly. "And we had the strangest conversation I think I've ever had with anybody. I mean, we talk about football awhile, I figure the closest he got to the field was being a cheerleader; he's got all this halo of hair and skin like a girl's–I mean he's really *pretty.* And he's got no accent, so I can't tell where he's from, except that he's talking to the barkeep in what sounds like perfect German to me, and I can't find a clue to him from his English, also perfect. I tell him I'm working on getting better at the German, but it's slow, you know? I'm thinking, how does he do it? Like, is his cousin named Berlitz or something? Maybe I should just ask him who the hell he is.

"And he takes a long drag on the bottle, just like I used to, and sets it down and says to me, 'You won't find out a thing that way.'

"I think, oh, great. He's an alcoholic mind reader, and what the hell am I doing with him? And he says I don't have to know, not yet, and I'm starting to feel a club soda drunk coming on. So I start thinking stupid stuff, like all the words to the Micky Mouse Club, and how Annette just never did it for me, right from the start when I thought her name was Funi-jello, all sorts of tripe. To see if he'll tell me 'C–see ya real soon!!' And the guy goes on drinking his Jack, like if this is a test he ain't takin' it. I down another club, and there're people all over the place, and it's getting later and later, and I just can't leave. Don't ask me why. I've gotta find out what his story is. Like did we go to grade school together? He remembers and I don't? If he does, how much does he remember that I hope I don't? I swill two more club sodas. After awhile, the crowd changes, and this–I swear– this *nazi* comes in with his girlfriend, they take a table. He's talking to his girlfriend in German, and I got an idea of what he's saying; I'm getting teed off. He sees me giving him the "you are an asshole" look, and he switches to English. Just to make sure I don't miss anything, I guess. And he is mean. He is nasty. He's gonna make this girl cry, but not too soon, cause then his fun'll be over. He's saying stuff I'm gettin' in the mood to kill him for, and the girl looks like she could crawl through the cracks in the floor, if that's what it would take to get out of there. But she can't, 'cause he might–make her pay. He's just like–" Gard stops. Looks at the wire cutters in his hand. Studies them as if they are an archeological miracle. "Well," he says. "He's just like –"

She nods. "Sounds just like." She knows he is not speaking of the living. The ghost of Gard's daddy rises fast between them, fades faster.

"So, finally I get up and walk over and ask the bastard didn't his momma ever tell him not to talk like that in polite company, and he gets out of his chair, and asks me how my momma liked it, living in the whorehouse, so I gotta tell him I'm gonna have to mess him up if he keeps on bein' so socially unacceptable and all. He's laughing at me. Says, 'you're Gard, aren't you?' Well, yeah, I say, I am, but what's that got to do with anything? So he picks up his beer bottle and knocks the neck against the table. Beer foams out all over the girlfriend, and he laughs some more, waves this broken bottle in my face and tells me it ain't got to do with nothing but that I think I'm God's gift to women."

Gard rolls his eyes, as if to say *Yeah, right.*

"He goes on, he's getting louder, the jagged end of the bottle's getting closer and closer to my face. Says I am the ugliest son-of-a-bitch he's ever met, and I can just leave him and his woman the fuck alone."

He stops, tests the grip on the cutters.

"You never could stand a man bullying a woman. You know." She raises her eyes as if calling up memories. "You never could."

He shakes his head. "Bully is too kind a word. I've worked my way up to 'nazi asshole shit-for-brains,' and tell him if he don't put the bottle down he's gonna have some serious regret about it.

"'Yeah?' he says. 'Let's see what the great god of rock is really like.'

I can see he's not familiar with my full biography, so I tell him I used to be a boxer, and I can still remember how it goes. He tells me to do something unspeakable with some unmentionable part of my body. Everybody's either left by now, or is hanging out to watch the inevitable conclusion: tomorrow's headlines, 'American Rocker's Throat Sliced in Tavern.' Some of them don't look too upset about it. Not that they wished me ill, I'm sure."

She raises her eyebrows.

"No, really," he goes on. "It's just that sometimes any fight is better than none, especially if the fight looks to promise blood and broken bones."

"You would know," she says without remonstrance.

"Wouldn't I. So, I get ready to break his bottle arm, and he gets ready to dispatch me to bloody shreds, and suddenly, there's my old buddy, standing right there. I'm surprised. He wasn't in my peripheral vision, and I was pretty sure he'd left some while back. Looked like the type to get bored real quick with nickel-and-dime bar brawls. Plus he wouldn't be of much use in one, anyway."

She nods.

He sinks down on his haunches, abandons the pretense he's really rewiring and that travel tales are just to pass the time. Shifts the wire cutters from hand to hand.

"So here's him and here's me, and I'm a lot for one guy to deal with, a point not overlooked by the asshole. Makes remarks about two against one, and I'm wondering that this little guy has drunk almost a quart of Jack and he seems as stone sober as I am. The jerk-off says he ain't worried. But he was."

He looks around the hallway as if he's come back to a German saloon.

"I could tell. I'm thinking, well, one of us has to back outta this, and it can't be me, being that I started it. I'm telling the mind reader that I appreciate the help, I really do, but we gotta play by the rules, and the first rule's the one about an even field. While I'm explaining this to him, the nazi takes advantage of the lull in the proceedings, and jumps me. The girl is screaming and crying, still dripping beer off her hair, and people are yelling in German, and I see the broken glass coming right at my eyeball. Both eyeballs. You remember why I was a lousy boxer?"

"Yes," she says. "Reflexes too slow."

"Yeah. My arms are coming up to block him, but they're coming up in slow mo, and my new friend pushes me aside. Like I was a chair on casters. I mean, Deesh, he was one-fifty at the outside, and I'm not so easy to push."

"No, you're not." she says.

"Yeah. Then, the asshole tells the guy he'd just as soon cut his nads off and do mine later, and changes his aim with the goddamned bottle. Then he's on the floor. Just like that. I was *watching* it from two feet away and I never saw the move. Never saw the mind reader even shift position. But there's the ass-wipe staring up like whaaa? and then the little guy leans down and takes the guy by his tee shirt and drops him outside the bar right into the street. And stands there in the doorway telling him he's never gonna come in this bar again, and if he tries there's stuff going to happen to him he doesn't even want to think about, much less experience. The nazi's trying to get up, but he can't, don't ask me why, and the guy says to him, in German, something that sounded like

'Thou art banished now and forever. Take thine evil to that place which awaits you. There you may increase in evil day by day, until the time when thine own damnation shall be complete.'"

He looks at her face, shrugs helplessly. "Really. I

swear."

"I didn't know your German was accomplished enough to handle sixteenth-century vernacular," she says, puzzled.

"It's not," he says, shaking his head. "But that's what I heard. I asked the bartender, who'd apparently shrunk to invisibility during the festivities, what the guy said, and he says pretty much the same thing, wonders if the guy's just come from the monastery or something. I say maybe he's into Goethe, and the barman looks at me like how the hell do I know Goethe, and I would've told him about you then, but it was a place completely inappropriate to mention your name."

"None is the place appropriate for mentioning my name."

"Only in the generic sense, I promise. Your name outside the house is This Girl I Know."

"Ah," she says. "So how *did* you get what he was saying? The mind reader, I mean?"

"Beats me," Gard says. "Maybe I read his mind and it was translating for me. Just a joke, Deesh. But I don't know. I just know for a fact I understood every syllable, and I can tell you, so did the dickhead on the street. He looks up like he can kill everybody, especially this guy that's just tossed him, and he'll come back in his own sweet time to do just that. But old Cleve-Ralph Lauren there didn't seem impressed. Just stood there in the doorway like he had a flaming sword or something, and stared back until the poor stupid fuck finally got on his feet and left."

"What happened to his date?"

"She didn't seem to get any of it, except she was all wet and needed to go home and get a new boyfriend. So she went."

"Hmm."

"Just what I said." He grins at her. She smiles with half her mouth, motions him to continue.

"It all happened so fast, like in twenty, thirty seconds. Just takes a long time to tell."

"Not too long. And you're not finished, are you? There's more."

"Oh, yeah. The weirdest part is yet to come. Believe me I thought it couldn't get any weirder by that point, but you know when I'm wrong, I'm the wrongest man in the universe."

"Hmm."

"I'll take that for a reassuring contradiction."

"I love it when you talk in multiple syllables."

"Okay, okay. So there I am having this little *tête à tête* with the bartender, and the guy turns around from the door, and gives me this real long look. Real long. And I'm feeling like an idiot, like he heard me talking about him. So I stick out my hand to shake his and tell him 'thanks, man.' He tips his head towards what's left of the battle table, and we go over there. And he shakes my hand."

He draws a breath into lengthening silence.

"Gard? You still here?"

"Huh? Oh. Yeah, yeah." He blinks, as if emerging from a darkened room into morning sunlight.

"Okay. This is the weird part. Handshake probably lasted two seconds. In that two seconds I saw stuff, saw it like I was at the movies, and the movies were lasting way too long. Things I saw about me. And maybe you."

"Maybe me? Your movie go blurry there?"

"I don't know. I saw somebody with dark hair wearing that black thing you wear when we go out dancing. I just couldn't see your face. Like every time I could get a clear shot of it, something passed between us, blocking my view."

She does not seem skeptical. "What did you see, then? Can you tell me?"

He know when she uses the word "can" she means it exactly, as in "are you able?"

He thinks it over.

"I don't think so. I can see little pieces of it now, like you can sort of remember a dream. But you know how a dream can make perfect sense while you're having it, and then later when you try and describe it to someone, you just

140

don't have any words that fit right?"

"Yes. I know." She looks at him intently, as if to hold him to his visions, to keep any more pieces from cracking away.

"I can't." His voice is anxious. "I can't figure it out, except that I saw myself and a woman I'm sure was you, and something else. Something between us so I couldn't see you, you couldn't see me. Something too awful to talk about, even if I could."

He passes his hand through his scalp. His hair has become damp.

"Then it all just fades. I'm taking out my wallet without thinking about it. Pay the check, pay the damages, and get back to the hotel any way I can. And this guy, he pushes my wallet back at me and thinks,

'You'll have to fight your way in. Then fight your way out. Between the beginning and the end you'll think you can't do it. Remember that you can.'

"Of course, I've got no idea what he's talking about, and I'm wondering what happened to the curlicue language. And I *heard* him say it, except his mouth never moved. He just looks at me like 'don't be such a dumbshit, boy' and says,

"This one's mine. You pay later."

"I take it he wasn't inviting you for another round on another day."

"No. I think he was threatening me."

"Why? About what?"

He makes a gesture of quick frustration. "That's what I don't know. I'm not even sure that was it. But I got the same feeling I used to have when I was about to get in the ring and they'd be telling me I was gonna wipe the canvas with the other guy, and I wondered what they were telling me for, 'cause there was just no way it was gonna happen."

"Did you see him again?"

"No. But I can't shake the feeling I should have recognized him. The whole thing was–creepy. I'm not sure what was real and what was the club soda talking."

141

She swings herself off the stairs and moves to the floor beside him.

"Whatever it was, there's one thing in it that I seriously doubt could be real."

"Yeah?"

"Yeah. There's nothing going to get between you and me."

"You think? What happened to living the day you're in and trying not to cash out on the tomorrow which might not get here?"

"Nothing happened. And nothing's going to happen. Maybe I'll die. Maybe you will. Maybe my house will burn to cinders or suddenly suffer neighbors. Maybe you'll lose your voice again. Maybe the sun will be late coming up next Tuesday. But nothing is going to come between us, especially nothing that could block our view of each other. You can leave me for another woman, I'll still see you as you are. I could change into the Queen of Bedlam, looking for sanity in all the wrong places. But we would still know each other. You will always see me as I am and I will always see you as you are. Even if we wanted the comfort of illusions, we can't get them. Not now."

She holds herself very still and does not touch him.

"No," he says, some relief seeping into his voice. "Not now. It's been too long." He feels his unease loosening its grip.

But he's got to wonder what it means. He knows no harm was intended, but when the man in the bar had shaken Gard's hand with his own much smaller one, it had felt for all the world like every singular bone in Gard's had liquified.

Fights With Cleve #10560

Uncharacteristically, he slammed himself through the front door. She heard wood crash against wood, and returned to her notes. If he wanted to slam into the library, she would know soon enough. Had the house been a thin, contemporary one, the walls would have rattled.

He was in the doorway, a blackening presence. Smelling fumes of rage, she waited. Without preamble, he said in a voice she rarely heard,

"He makes me so goddamned fucking mad." He came into the room.

"You and Cleve fighting at recess again?" She appeared to be only mildly interested.

"Son of a bitch, some day I'm going to strangle that ratfucker." She raised one eyebrow.

"GodDAMN it!" he bellowed.

She sighed and moved her feet from desk to floor.

"What in the name of hell is wrong with him?"

She shrugged. "You know."

"Yeah, yeah, I know. He didn't get famous enough, and I got too famous. When's he gonna get over it?"

"Never, I imagine."

His roar dropped a few decibels. "Well, I don't get it. Without him, I'm nothing, Evermore's nothing, everything is just too fucking NOTHING!"

She leveled her gaze at him and said quietly, "You are not nothing under any circumstance, and neither is the band." She spoke calmly, as if she were reading a grocery list. The rage in the room lessened almost imperceptibly. She tapped a pencil lightly against the arm of her chair. "But Cleve is fundamental to your present success. He knows that, probably more than you do."

He sat on the edge of her desk, gave her a questioning look.

She said, "He cannot or will not accept that your public positions were inevitable."

He shook his head. "Nothing is inevitable."

"Some things are. Most people, for example, prefer the emotional response over the intellectual."

She twiddled the pencil. Thought for a moment, then looked at him with 'Do you really want to hear this?' clear on her face. He waited.

"Look," she said. "Cleve is the creator. He's God. You are the interpreter of his works. You're Superman. He's always going to be God, but or because he can't sing."

"Yeah," he said.

"Something to do with a biker chick in a bar and an injury, if I recall," she said.

He smiled for the first time. "She broke his nose in three places. He was lucky to get out alive."

"I should say." She watched him slide a little farther in on her desk. Papers rustled. "Think of it this way," she returned to the subject. "People see you, people hear *you*. They react viscerally. And they like to. It's part of the moment no one wants to spoil with cognitive analysis. And," she noted, "it is the human condition to prefer the emotional over the abstract. It's faster, easier, and feels good." She sighed again. "For Cleve to be world famous, everyone who sees and hears you would have to go home, study the lyrics, consider the music with an educated ear, consult all the liner notes, analyze all the material, and arrive at a reasonably unemotional conclusion. Believe me," she smiled, "if all your audiences, including the ones who never see you, did that, you wouldn't even cast a shadow standing in his."

"Oh, thanks."

"This isn't about you, it's about human behavior in general. Cleve will always be angry at the injustice of fame. The concept of Superman has made what?–a trillion dollars? He's a hero, and he is entertaining. God is not entertaining. People can feel moved by a Superman movie. Most of them sleep through the Sunday sermon. It's easier to love the cool guy who flies and saves the world than to remember the invisible guy who made the world."

"How'd you get so smart?" he asked, only half jokingly.

"It's a byproduct of spending the greater part of my life weighing and drawing conclusions about the irrationality of famous men. And women. Write about the denizens of world history for a living, and you soon learn that people never change, nor politics. Just clothes and custom." She stopped, moved the pencil to her other hand, and twiddled further. "Also," she added, "if I am smart, it's because I live with a genius."

"Oh, come now," he said, slightly embarrassed. "I don't know if I'd go that far."

She leaned back in her chair, returned her feet to the desk. "Who said anything about you?"

"Ha. Ha." He reached over and fondled her toes through her socks. "So writers are gods and don't get no worship. Why doesn't it bother *you*?"

"I never wanted to be famous." She wiggled her toes in his palm.

"But you are famous, kind of, aren't you?"

"In certain obscure circles, I suppose so, but there is nothing connected with the physical me. My face is unknown, and as for names, great god Gard, who in hell is E. Calder? Could be any one of dozens of people."

"Speaking of the physical you . . ."

"Not on your life," she interrupted. She sat up, shuffled her notes, and went back to penciling them. "I'm still in the studio recording."

He looked disappointed, but could not argue with the analogy. "Okay." He stood up, restless with himself. "Aren't you even tempted? A little?"

She chewed on the pencil. "As far as you are concerned, my life is nothing but temptation."

He saw sweetness in her face as she said it, and felt glad to be where he was. Anger forgotten, he bowed, and went on his way in what he thought was peace.

Père-Lachaise

He had come because it had been recommended as a quiet place to walk unmolested by his devotees. The beauty of the place struck him, as did its age. It was a clear day, and he decided there and then to spend rest of the afternoon pursuing rare solitude among those who now already had it—forever. Wandering slowly, he pondered the names caught in stone, surprising him in their familiarity. After an hour, he found himself far from the entrance gate, a bit lost, and unworried. Most of the occupants here were uncomfortably close together, the land at a higher premium with every passing year. He stopped in interest then at a well-kept square, the only one surrounded by an iron fence rising at least twelve feet, ending in sharpened spikes. Two rectangular stones lay close together on what must have been, he thought, a good quarter acre. Who were they, to have so much space to lounge around in? Mr. and Mrs. God?

On a bench just outside the fence, wearing a broad straw hat and sunglasses, a girl was writing furiously in a mess of notebooks and loose papers. Ha. A chance to mingle with the natives. No way was she a tourist. He eased himself into her hearing.

"You writing a book?"

She looked up at him from under the brim of her hat.

What an idiot. He'd forgotten the essential first question.

"Uh, do you speak English?" She nodded. He sighed in relief. "So, you writing a book?"

"No." Her voice shook him. It was pleasant, low, and absolutely the most self-assured he'd ever met.

"Do you write books?" Talk to me, baby. Talk to me.

"No. Mostly articles for obscure magazines read only by academics."

"Like what?" It struck him he might actually want to know.

She looked at him sharply. "Are you interested in cultural history?"

"I *am* cultural history," he blurted, then wished profoundly to kick himself in his own ass.

She raised her eyebrows over the dark glasses. "Are you now? Come here to visit your colleagues?" She indicated the scope of the visible horizon. "Lovely day for it."

He knew he was being insulted, but not quite sure how.

"Are you writing about them?" He nodded in the direction within the fence.

"Yes."

"Why?" Why should he care? What was wrong with this picture?

"Because," she said.

"That why you're here?" He tried again. "Soaking up atmosphere?"

She sighed heavily, clearly wishing him elsewhere. "You might say that. I wanted to know if I could pick up anything from a couple dead for eight hundred years."

Was she serious? He couldn't tell, and it maddened him.

"A couple of what?"

"Heloise and Abelard."

"They got all this space 'cause they've been dead the longest?"

She actually grinned. Finally, a reaction.

"Probably one of the reasons."

"So what makes them famous?"

She considered him a moment, then said quietly, "They loved each other."

Now he knew she was ragging on him. "That's all?"

"Yes." She pulled her hat lower on her forehead, as if drawing down a window shade. "That's all."

He actually blushed. It had been a long time since he

147

had been outranked in conversation. From every pore she exuded disdain. He was sure of it. Understandably, his temper took command.

"Who the hell do you think you are? Who the hell do you think I am?"

She looked up again. Slowly took off her sunglasses. Her disinterest was palpable. "On the first count, I'm not certain. On the second, who you are or are not is your affair."

She slid the sunglasses back up her nose. He thought the lenses were prescription. They must be, because she sure as hell was blind as a household of bats.

"Maybe I *am* here to 'visit my colleagues,'" he snapped. Let her figure out who—maybe Chopin, or Wilde, maybe Sarah Bernhardt, or how about Heloise and Abelardass. Whoever.

"You're in the wrong section, then." The words sounded like good-bye, good-bye, good-bye. "If you are looking for Morrison, just follow the graffiti arrows. They're everywhere."

Now he knew her game. She *did* know him, and was pretending otherwise to entice him. The salvo had been tried—and had failed—before.

"What makes you think I've got any interest in Morrison?" he growled.

She shrugged. "You're American and you're wearing black."

"So?"

"No one but American Morrison Mourners wear black here. Most of them, however," she seemed amused, "weren't born when the Doors had their day."

She tilted her chin in the direction she assumed he wanted to go. "Easy to find. The grief-stricken will be lighting candles and sobbing over what's left of his headstone. *Chacun á son goût*," she finished absently, returning to her papers.

Were-ent, she said. Not wernt. What a bitch. So why was he still here, angling to hold her attention? If she thought he was here for Morrison, then she did know him, and was faking her boredom. Wasn't she?

He sat down on the bench. She moved away.

"You live in Paris?" Now there was a line that always worked. He considered again a self-inflicted boot in the behind.

"No," she said, closing and stacking the papers and notebooks between them. He got a feeling the posture was less conversational and more a raising of the drawbridge. "I don't live anywhere."

What the fuck did that mean? He would not, he told himself, be distracted. He pressed on. "Traveling, heh? Me, too. When I'm working." He checked her closely. Her expression was unchanged. "So, what're you doing, traveling?"

"Studying languages."

"Yeah?" He was surprised.

"Yeah," she emphasized the word while vacating the bench. A slight wind blew up, flapping the brim of her hat.

"Gonna be in Paris long?"

"A few months," she said, looking back at her skirt to ensure the wind hadn't blown it high, as well. "Perhaps longer."

"Not me," he continued as if she had asked. "Another week here, then we're leaving for Belgium."

"We?" she said, shifting her notebooks more firmly into her arms.

Damn. She thought he was picking her up. Didn't she?

"Uh, some friends and me. But," he added—and why he never knew—"sometimes I come back here between perf— uh, between traveling. You know. For weekends. Or something."

Shut up, he raged at himself. Shut. The. Fuck. Up.

She bit her lip. To keep from laughing at him? But her face. Her face. Look at her skin. God, it's gorgeous.

She looked at him quizzically.

"You interested in dermatology?"

It took him a moment to be startled. "What?"

149

She smiled at him. Miracle. "You must be an actor. Everything you think is plain on your face." She turned to go. She went.

He watched her back dwindle into the trees.

Shit, he thought. Goddamn it. SHIT.

He did not rush after women. It was totally unnecessary. She could just walk on back to her cave and hang with the other bats. She must be disappointed he hadn't fallen for her shtick. Too friggin' bad for her. She'd never know what she'd missed, *who* she'd missed. Stupid bitch. Just as well he'd lost interest. Cold as ice, that one. Frigidaire. Probably never made it in her life. Fine, he thought. FINE. She could just go flap right back into hell. As for himself, he might as well pay some respects to Morrison. Why not? He kicked up dust starting down the path, which widened into gravel. The crunch under his boots quite satisfied. Felt like her bones.

In the cool breeze he felt himself beginning to sweat. He glanced behind, just to make sure she was gone. She was. Good. Excellent. Most excellent. She could rot before he'd ever think of her again. A narrow escape. He was lucky this time, and he should count his blessings, because . . . He risked his voice shouting at the top of it, "Wait!" Reversing his course, "Wait a minute," he yelled in a dead run after a girl, or maybe a ghost, he had just this moment come to find in a graveyard.

Black Horse, Black Knight

She is expressionless, a sign of vague indecision. The morning sun an intruder, all the drapes are drawn; the room is dim. Wherever she looks, there is no light. The telephone is cold in her hand.

"I want you to go with me to a publishers' dinner."

"Yeah? Like on a date?"

"Like."

"Oh, dear me, what shall I wear?" His voice noodles to a higher register; maybe he can get her to laugh. He hopes she isn't clutching the phone like the last tree on the mountainside.

"Anything, but your evening clothes would be nice."

"As in tux-eee-do?"

"As in."

"Your wish is my desire, Tootsie."

"Thank you."

He can't tell from her voice how this will be for her, and knows well enough not to ask directly.

"Think nothing of it. Any varmints there I'll be needin' to pertect you from?" Texas oozes in his voice.

"Just about everybody in publishing," she answers, "is a varmint."

"Oh, hell," he says

"You can protect me some other time."

"So where," he asks, contriving a flippant tone, "are we going?"

She tells him. He hears the drag in her voice. "Ballard's getting some sort of prize."

"Yeah? I thought you were his prize." He pauses, taking in that she's breathing shallowly on her end of the line. "You want to go and come back in the same night?" He hopes he sounds casual.

"The only way would be to fly." Her voice is matter-of-fact and distant.

"I know," he says. "All those people tinned up too close together."

She sighs heavily. "I just don't think I can do it."

He wants to come over, to touch her, to pretend with her there's no problem here, then thinks the better of it. She might interpret it as sympathy, or worse, pity. He knows better than to give voice to either. There were, he had discovered over the years, other ways.

"Who says you have to fly commercial?"

He has surprised her.

"What are you saying?"

"I'm saying that there are always planes to be chartered.

She seems to absorb the information slowly. As she nears the inevitable protest, he counters,

"Or, we could hire up a limo. We can spend the night necking in the back seat."

She smiles weakly. "Nice try."

"Deesh," he says in a tone that will suffer no argument, "Ballard asked you, so you think you've got to oblige him. So we fly or we drive. It's one or the other, and it's my treat, so choose."

"Ah," she says, conceding, perhaps because there is no energy to stick to her usual guns, "the power of money."

"Damn straight," he says with a camouflaged note of triumph. He likes it when he wins.

*   *   *

He calls her in the afternoon. "You're not hyperventilating, are you?"

"I am not," she says dryly, "that much of a wimp."

"Are you sure? Are we going to this thing just because Ballard is getting touted? Or tooted?"

"No. He and I have been having a hell-fired affair for years, and I thought you should meet him to compare notes."

"Ballard would be dead after one night with you, Sweetheart."

"Is that," she asks, feigning suspicion, "a compliment?"

"You bet your tidy sweet ass it is."

"Hm."

"I could pick you up on the big bike. Or the Ford?"

"Please refrain. Having a driver is conspicuous enough."

"What, no bike? No truck? No fun."

"Exactly."

"Okay, okay," he grumbles. "Anything else Madame wishes?"

"A sense of decorum, please. This is business."

"Decorum, huh? I'll have to check under the sink to see if there's any left down there with the rat poison." She can hear him gearing up to laugh. "Maybe a bike would be better. I can be decorous on a bike."

"Auto," she says, "mobile."

She knows he is grinning at her. "And," she adds, "please do not arrive in something vulgar. I do not mean your clothes, so do not even start."

"Me? I don't start anything I can't finish, or would be finished by. Sir Gard will rescue you at the appointed hour."

"*Oy vay,*" she says, and hangs up.

*   *   *

He lets himself in through the front door, ringing the bell as he crosses the threshold. Twirling his keys, he passes across the front hall, through the anteroom, the living room, and the library. He pauses at her bedroom doors and wonders if she knows he has come.

Stupid question, he knows, as she opens the doors, looks up, slides her arms around his waist, and, rising on her toes, says into his ear, "Whoa."

He brushes at his sleeve. "Hey, not every ugly guy you know looks this good in a tuxedo. Oh, do excuse me," he

153

affects an accent of east coast snobbery, *"evening clothes."*

"True," she said. "You're quite the sex god in white tie. Now, please let's go before I'm struck with a bad case of the fantods." She steps back from him.

He drops his keys.

"Really, Gard, we should go now."

"Not yet," he says roughly. "Not just yet."

His expression is indecipherable. "What's the matter?"

"Nothing," he growls. He stares. "I didn't–uh, I didn't know you had a dress like that." His eyes follows the sweep of the skirt as it drags, glittering, along the floor. "And your hair. You never do that."

"Oh," she says, airily, "as with you, I can on occasion clean up sufficiently for public emergence."

"God, Deesh," he breathes.

"God," she says, "had nothing to do with it. Three hours in the bathroom and ten thousand hair pins got all the sacrificial altars tonight."

He gapes.

"Gard," she laughs, "snap out of it. Do take me away before I lose any mood I've mustered up to do this."

He follows her out to the car, still gaping.

She says nothing during the drive up the coast, even about the chauffeur, which he would have bet would have gotten a rise out of her.

As she sits, a starched mannequin, even her eyes unmoving, the car, dark as blackened ashes, delivers them through the afternoon and into the night. He doesn't touch her, though he wants to. He can feel her gathering forces about her, readying for a long and much too-peopled evening.

"Park far away," she says, as they draw closer.

He looks at her, amused. "Done." He lowers the black-tinted window between them and the driver, motioning them over.

They walk quietly. Her fingers are dry in his hand. From a distance, the valets are bugs, shadows scrabbling in and out of the lights. Nearing the doors, he feels change in her, as if she is folding and putting herself away, leaving only a dressmaker's faceless model as animate surrogate.

Ballard would never have kept asking her–until she acquiesced–to these damned dinners, if he could rustle up even a hint of the cost to her. But he can't. No one can, except Gard. Leslie, Cleve, Vlad, and Kas understand the edges of it, but only he is party to the whole of how against her nature is this descent. Still, there are things unknown to him even now. Twenty years, and she has yet to make him privy to all the fragments she has somehow re-pieced into a self.

*   *   *

In the maw of the hotel, the publishing world, crowded and vaguely noisy, adhered to the spirit of the evening and went about congratulating itself. Not one face could he put with a name. "Maybe you should read me some books written after 1940," he whispered.

She came to, smiled slowly, shook her head.

"Oh, come on," he wheedled.

"It wouldn't help," she whispered back.

"They'd still look like a slew of department store dummies?"

"Ssh," she murmured, trying not to laugh. "Over there. Ballard. Let us convey our joy to him."

"For what?" he said, taking her arm, and heading in the indicated direction. "Publisher Who's Lived Through the Most Shit Writers Can Sling?"

She laughed, finally, out loud. "Not quite," she said, holding his arm lightly.

He wanted to stop and kiss her right there. If they were home–but they were not home, and he unwillingly pushed the thought aside.

They said hello to a swirling fog of people, and his anonymity here allowed him close observance of those who

155

populated a world so foreign to the wide one he knew. His own colleagues would, faced with this hall full of self-satisfied academic assholes, run out in a hurry, looking for any bar of greatest disrepute, or at least some primo dope to smoke. He shrugged to himself. Everybody's drawing room was somebody else's nest of maggots.

Ballard was pleased to see them, it seemed. Quick and dapper, but, Deesh had warned, too obviously going for "the Gatsby thing," (an assertion too faintly praising for a compliment, and too frail for an insult, to Gard's great amusement), Ballard fast bored him, and Gard wondered if Deesh found him equally dull as she remained hidden behind the mask of a public face. They mingled. It struck him as heroic, somehow, that she betrayed not a flicker of the exhaustion so much human contact was bringing her. When he felt her energy breaking into disjointed motes, he leaned down and said almost inaudibly,

"Please. Dance with me."
"Yes," she said.
"Will your, what is that, a train? Won't it be bother-some?"

"I see you haven't been to the palace lately," she said, lifting the seam loop, slipping it over her finger.
He was fascinated. "Hey. Do that again."
She bordered on a laugh. "It's not magic, Gard."
Women were just like peach pie, he thought. With ice cream. He saw she was reading him, and blushed. Shaking her head, she let her skirts drop, then re-looped. They danced. Like liquified sparking stars, her hem followed them around the floor, and for awhile they could be alone together in an overdressed glut of the self-important. The mob receded into ghosts, vaguely present but unacknowledged, and their voices died under the orchestral crush.

He was, he realized, content. Completely. He wanted to tell her that this miraculous thing had happened, but was afraid. Don't jinx it, don't test it, don't blow it. To want nothing more, even for an hour, was cool water running slowly through his soul, and he would take no chances.

In time, the speeches were spoken, Ballard was handed his plaque, and Gard had begun to think they might slip into the night and become ghosts themselves. They got as far as the foyer. Then he felt her shift beside him.

"Oh, goodie."

"What?" he asked.

"Bearing down upon us, quite determinedly, someone you are not going to like very much."

"Yeah?" He was interested. "Why not?"

"Never mind," she expelled a long breath, "just avoid, please."

He raised his eyebrows. "Please," she said.

He stepped away, rooted in a dim corner, close enough to see and hear. He crossed his arms across his chest, and took on an unreadable expression.

"MS. Calder!"

"Hello, Wilson," she said, making certain her back was between Gard and him. The couple with him, Gard thought, seemed mildly embarrassed. He took another look at Wilson and began to understand why.

"Well, well. Look at you. To what do we owe the honor?"

"Lovely to see you, as well." She smiled at the man and woman with him. "Hello."

They shook hands. The man was tall and thin, the woman not tall, and they had been together a long, happy time, Gard could tell. What the hell were they doing with someone like Wilson?

"Now–there you go with the famous Calder sarcasm." He was much smaller than the loudness of his voice would indicate; his skin stretched too tightly over his face, and hang too loosely everywhere else.

"Ah. What can I say, Wilson? You know me too well."

"I do. I do." He chortled, pleased with himself.

Gard smiled unpleasantly. What a fool this pudgy little creep was. His head, up to where it met his hair, was nastily pallid. Where did Deesh know such a cockroach from? Gard mused that if the forehead was the shuttered window to the mind, then Wilson's brains must be a kettle of snakes. Albino snakes. It was difficult for him not to chuckle in menace, but he sighed and refrained; losers were one thing, but so loathsome a loser was too easy a target. No wonder Deesh wanted him out of the guy's oxygen zone. The other man and woman seemed decent enough, and slightly uncomfortable in the company of this peckerhead.

"Published lately?" Wilson's voice affected lively curiosity.

"Yes. Eight months ago," she answered with no inflection whatever.

Wilson, however, was full of inflection. "Every year, just like clockwork. You know, I can't do it. Too big a chance for the writer to become repetitious and stale. I take my time; texts hastily published so often become fodder for the seconds-market graveyard." He pretended to shiver. "God, those sleazy wholesale nobodies buying right off the flats. Peddlers in whose-knows-what venues."

Gard's slight amusement withered. His radar went up and pulsed. Deesh, her back still to him, shook her head. He clinched his fists and stayed where he was.

"My last print run was forty thousand," Wilson was saying. "Can you believe it? Forty thousand. More than you're accustomed to, I would think?"

Deesh said something Gard couldn't hear. His alarm bells began shrieking.

"Yes, yes, I know. But really Miz Calder, is there

158

much of a market these days for your revisionist theories? Poor research always shows when the material gets thin. Don't you agree? You still in the university trade at all? Oh? I'm surprised. You know this kick all the trustees are on–to trash the experimental works and return to the DEWM. And rightly so, don't you think?"

"I'm very fond of dead European white men," Deesh answered. Gard was having trouble reading her voice. The couple's eyes widened, as if this were going farther than it should have, even for Wilson.

"Are you? I didn't think so. Surprised me again. Come on. Tell me." He imagined his voice as vaguely conspiratorial. "Whatever are you doing so far from home? Everybody knows you hate mixing with–shall we say, the more successful? I've wondered if there weren't some jealousy there. You should understand that we all can't be Edmund Wilson rolled into Voltaire. Nothing for you to be upset about." He shook his head mournfully. "Miz Calder, Miz Calder."

"It's *Doctor* Calder," Gard said, appearing from the shadows. He dropped his arms, loomed over the group. He spoke very quietly. "I'm guessing you were brought up in a barn, sir, but if you insult her once more–just once–I might accidentally hurt you when I'm throwing you through the lobby doors."

She tensed. When his voice held no expression whatever, anything might be next. She laid her hand on his sleeve, said conversationally, "Gard, Wilson Dane. Wilson, Gard."

They waited for Wilson to introduce the others, as he had not done for Deesh, and waited long enough the couple did it themselves. The man, Gard thought, seemed odd. He sort of nudged his wife, whose face gave way to slow-pulsed shock. The two of them looked at each other. Wilson Dane, without acknowledging Gard, said in a voice slightly laced with arsenic,

"Who is this thug, Calder?"

"Musical prodigy. Occasional collaborator. Friend

and gentleman."

"I suspect you overestimate him on at least two counts." He glanced at Gard's hair. "Certainly on personal grooming. Has no one told you–Gard is it?–that the sixties have been over for some time?" He smoothed the sides of his own sparse growth.

"I wouldn't say anything else, Wilson, were I you," Deesh said kindly. His friends were already attempting to edge him back into the general company. He brushed them away.

"Uh oh. Going to let your gorilla loose on me? I'm terrified."

Blood began to rise in the faces of the other two. They telegraphed to Deesh and Gard expressions of frantic apology. Gard grinned at them and shrugged.

"I'm so glad to have met you," he said to the pair, who couldn't make up their minds to be politely hostile to Wilson, or to find a subtle way to request something of Gard.

She knew their look.

They wanted to tell him how many times they had seen him in concert, how many of his albums they had, how long they had loved him, and when was he going to tour the States, it had been three years, after all?

"Perhaps we might meet again," she said.

"Oh, yes, yes, that would be great," said the man. Which one was the writer? Or the publisher? She could place neither one, but she thought them in need of some generosity; they were hanging on to their formal dignity by threads, but they were hanging on. Gard shook their hands; the woman had trouble letting go.

"What would be great?" said Wilson humorlessly. "Trying to converse with Calder's bodyguard? I feel the yawns already."

Gard moved slightly, putting himself in front of De-esh, who leaned into his back.

He seemed nonchalant, but she knew the tic pulsing in his cheek. Removed from Wilson's voice, dropped enough she couldn't hear it, she counted off how many more seconds she must let Gard enjoy his most primitive instincts. By a subtle shifting of his shoulder muscles she felt more than saw, she knew they were coming to that last moment before the needle swerved into the red zone.

"We have to leave now," she said calmly, stepping to Gard's side, laying her hand on his upper arm. Barely touching, but he knew it was there. "Good night," she addressed the man and the woman.

In her voice Gard read the warning to him. *Don't say a word. Do not hit him. Do not threaten him again. He hasn't the presence of mind to know what he's dealing with in you. Don't, Gard. Just don't.*

What kind of gallant was he turning out to be? When the fair maiden slew the dragon without benefit of even the white horse?

"Oh, please," Wilson said. "Did I hurt his feelings? I'm devastated. Well. If you must leave, can't say I blame you. Your taste in the inappropriate has extended even farther than your scholarship, I see." He waved without moving his hand. "Toodle ooh. That means 'good night,' he said in Gard's direction.

"Not right now it doesn't." Gard's voice issued every word from a fissure in granite. He moved a fraction closer to Wilson. "Apologize to Doctor Calder, Mr. Dane. Do it now."

Wilson Dane at last looked fully into Gard's face. Whatever retort he had been about to lob fainted dead away.

She wished they might just go, but it would be wrong to interfere now. Not on her own account; for Gard, whom she knew was not necessarily liking this. But by his agenda of Right and Wrong, necessarily doing it.

Wilson mumbled at her. She nodded at the other two, who slid reluctantly back into the crowds. Gard watched as she looped her skirts again and they left Wilson Dane standing abandoned in the foyer.

"And you wonder why I don't get out more," she tried to tease him. They walked three blocks, while his dejection seethed. "I know I embarrassed you," he said, regretting it but not allowed to say so.

"No. You didn't."

"I didn't?" Surprise overcame remorse.

"Not one speck."

"Why not?" he wanted to know. "Tell me why not."

"Tomorrow," she answered, and he knew she was losing the fight with fatigue.

"Okay," he said, taking his hand from hers and putting his arm around her waist. "I see your patience and fortitude fading fast."

"Hiding behind you is more fun than patience and fortitude."

"God, I hope so."

She rubbed her cheek against his arm as they walked. "I once rebuffed his advances, and he took it too much to heart."

"That swamp weed made advances?" He stopped. She shouldered him on, ignoring his face tightening into danger range again.

"He wanted me to work on a book with him on a subject about which he knew nothing."

"Keeping his mouth shut?"

She smiled. "No. More like an obscure eighteenth-century political movement, the agenda of which knocked over the first of two hundred years' worth of dominoes and the last one dropped was the Russian Revolution."

"Of course," he said sagely, his normal demeanor creeping back. "Lucky for you that is one of my areas of expertise. Allow me to *collaborate*." He drew the word out as if were a fun and filthy prospect.

She smiled again. "I thought you might appreciate my selection of nouns back there."

"Oh, yeah. Your nouns drive me wild." He was fully

restored to his better nature, and she felt the prickle of apprehension smooth and vanish.

Approaching the blackness of the car, Gard ran his hand through his hair. Idiocy always bemused him.

"TweedleDee must've been drunker than Cooter Brown," he said.

"He was," she answered.

"Why do trolls like that always say stuff they never mean and don't remember the next day?"

"He meant it," she said evenly.

He stopped. "Then you get in the car. I'm going back and kill him."

Oh, Gard, he's not worth killing. He doesn't, as you would say, *need* killing."

"He needs it."

"Gard."

They resumed walking. "All right," he said without agreement. "How do you know he meant it? Is he that big a cretin?"

"No," she answered calmly. "I know because when people drink, they–all of them–say *exactly* what they think. Every time."

There was silence. Their footsteps sounded louder than they actually were. Finally:

"Have I," she asked, "in drinking my fill, ever said things to you I would not ordinarily?"

He grinned salaciously. "Yep." He paused a beat. "I treasure the memories." Picking and sorting his words, he went on "But just because you wouldn't say them sober doesn't mean they weren't true. I like to think. And not in twenty years have you ever said a word to cut me, or revile me."

"Revile? Revile how?"

He didn't answer.

She suddenly knew the fear circling him.

"You have never," she reassured, "uttered one syllable to me you would have regretted. Even in your days of glorious debauchery."

Silence.

Now, she stopped, looked hard into his eyes. "Not even in Chicago."

He expelled breath. The tension of his expectation evaporated.

"Wilson," she turned the subject, "is a worried man. He would like us all to be worried. His wishes are ungranted." She shrugged one shoulder. "He does think my work is unworthy of Ballard's house, because he can't understand any brand of historian but himself. If you had taken it outside with him, he would have had something to talk about the rest of his days."

"Gee, I didn't mean to deprive him," Gard gruffed. They resumed walking. "So from your objective, writerly observations of life, a bucket of bourbon does not give you cause to tell anything but the whole truth so help you Jack." He shook his head. "Probably a good thing I never knew that. I thought getting down and dirty wasted was fun. And now you're telling me it's nothing but truth serum."

They arrived at the car. As he handed her into the back seat, she said, "You bet your tidy sweet ass it is."

He laughed, and got in beside her. "And what was wrong with those other two? They seemed nice enough, but they were looking at me with real weirdness. Don't they think I should have called that dickhead's bluff?"

"Nothing to do with it," she said, adjusting her skirts. "You are a sweet man. You really didn't see it, did you? Can't you recognize it beyond your usual haunts?"

"They knew me?" He was incredulous.

"Of course they did. I would venture to say that they would have killed Wilson before you could, except they would have lost the chance to stand next to you and worship."

"Deesh. You know I hate that."

"I know. Doesn't change anything." She leaned against his shoulder; he raised his arm higher around her. "Whatever you do to people when you sing, it seems to be permanent. They don't get over it. Or you."

"Your hair smells good," he said.

"Don't change the subject."

"I don't like the subject."

"You don't have to. But you do need to understand your impact. You have to be careful about it."

"I'm a geezer rocker. Who the hell cares anymore?"

"How much in royalties did you receive last year? How many concerts did you sell out in an hour on the last tour? How many women cried when you came on stage, just because you were standing there?"

"Deesh. Stop."

"I know it scares you."

"It does not scare me."

"Certainly it does. You are afraid of it, and at the same time, afraid to lose it."

"What makes you so sure?" The question was slow.

"Because," she wriggled deeper under his arm, "there was this one night, a long time ago, when you were too inebriated for any vertical activity, and you told me all about it."

He sighed. "*In vino veritas.*"

"Very good," she said, shifting to his lap.

"And in necking," she traced his jaw line with her fingers, "*veritas*, too."

He lifted her closer, and sang softly into her ear, "Then come on, baby. It's a cold dark night and I could use me some truth."

A Voice in the Afternoon

"Are you here?" he asked.

"Of course," came the answer.

"Haven't seen you in a while." Gard wasn't certain he should mention that. He didn't want to look too anxious.

"You've missed me, have you?"

Gard shrugged. Politely, he hoped.

"Ah. So you have, then." Shrike's voice was soothing. "I had begun to think you found my company tiresome."

"No," said Gard, doubtfully.

"Or dangerous."

"What could be dangerous about you?" Surprise filtered through his words.

"Nothing. Absolutely nothing. I hope I've never given you such an idea. With me, in fact, is the only time you are completely, inviolably safe."

The Voice felt like velvet rubbing slowly against his ears.

He was relieved, anxious to be relieved. "That's how I feel. This is the only place I'm safe."

"Even with her?" The Voice became liquid silk.

"Yeah," Gard sighed. "Even with her."

"She could leave you."

"Yes. Yes, she could."

"And that troubles you, does it?"

Gard hesitated. Something suggested to him it might be better not to give away his greatest secret, even to such sympathy. He brushed the faint warning aside.

"All the time. Every day. All the time for about the last eighteen years."

"I see. Before that, you thought you might leave her, if you wished."

He blanched to remember. "I didn't mean to think

that. But I guess I did."

"Your fears didn't emerge until you decided fidelity was necessary."

"I guess that's right."

"Well, see what it's gotten you. Fidelity is a tricky operation. Often backfires."

Gard did not understand, but somehow it made sense, when Shrike spoke.

"I don't know, maybe. Fucking around got to where it wasn't any fun anymore. Every time, I'd end up wishing it were Deesh. So I stopped. It's what I wanted. What I want."

"But she kept her own counsel about it, did she not? I believe she told you what you did traveling was what you did, as long as she didn't have to hear about it. Sensible attitude, but you were too afraid she didn't mean it."

Yes. He remembered. He hadn't thought she meant it. In his experience, no girl worth her weight in salt water would be so obliging, unless she wanted to dump you in the first place. She had known he was thinking that, and had said to him, "You don't understand why I don't pitch a fit. Haven't I any jealousy? What's wrong with me?" She had sat on the opposite end of the library from him, on the floor under the big Palladium window; they nearly had to shout for audibility. "If provoked, my jealousy would frighten us both to death, I think. But it's mine. Not yours. Just as your decision to do whatever you do on tour is yours. Not mine. I will not reassure you by letting you peek in at my less admirable emotions. And I would appreciate it if you would not try to assuage your uncertainties by telling me about anyone else in your bed. Or your head. Or your . . ."

She had stopped herself there. From the distance between them it was hard to know if her voice was trembling a little, or she was simply bored with the whole conversation, and thought it a waste of her time to go on with it. Or both. He had left then, gone to his own house. It was best, he thought, to back away and let her see he wasn't going to wash his guilt or confusion in her hair. They had never

*discussed it again. But for all the ensuing years, had she
called him in his hotel room after the show, if she hadn't had
her damned rules about that, she would have found him
there, every night, and alone. He was very mildly peeved that
she had never given him the chance to prove his reformation.
All she had to do was call, or let him call her.*

His memory tightened. It still rankled, faintly.

"And touring celibate for three months at a time is
dangerous," Shrike went on as if there had been no break in
Gard's attention. "It can diffuse your focus on your music.
So many gifted people believe they should want what a
fanatically conservative culture tells them they should want.
It's hard for them when their command-performance virtue
doesn't work out in their own best interests."

This, too, seemed reasonable. Gard marveled that the
Voice understood him so readily without his making any
effort to be understood. Here, he could say the things he
forbad himself to say elsewhere. Or the things forbidden to
him.

"You can change it."

Gard was confused.

"Of course," the Voice went on, "if you don't have
the courage, then . . ."

"Don't!" For the first time in their long collaboration,
Gard interrupted his mentor. "Don't say that. I can get over
this, I don't have to keep living with this fear. Why should I?
It's stupid."

"Ah. You do have the courage. Well, then."

"Then what?"

"Remove yourself to the time when you knew you
could get rid of her. When you had sufficient companionship
whenever necessary. When you knew you could have almost
anybody, because of your name. Which still holds true."

"I don't want to know I can get rid of her." Gard felt
the conversation sliding away from him, but he wasn't sure
how he should begin to pin things down.

"Not the knowledge, dear boy. Just the feeling.

That's all fear is anyway. Just a decomposing human emotion that never did any soul any good."

"Oh. I see. I think."

"Certainly you do. You've simply been living in terror so long that your natural intellect has lost its power to overcome any useless waste of time, such as time worrying over nothing, or nothing that is ever going to happen."

"Yeah," he said slowly. "Yeah. It is a waste of time."

"And you have no time to waste, have you?"

"God, no. I wasted too much in the beginning."

"Not another moment."

"Not another moment," Gard agreed.

"Then, there you are. Remember that you do not belong in a hypocritical right-wing society of fringe zealots who will tell you all too often how to think and feel, but who give you nothing when their plans aren't working."

"Yes, but, I don't really think the society I'm in is full of fringe zealots."

"You don't recognize it. And why should you? For the last twenty years it's all you've known. So long that anyone could forget the truth."

"The truth?" Gard found himself in difficulty trying to follow the serpentine thread of the conversation, but marked it up to the fact that he was a lesser being in the presence of a Greater Being.

"Oh, yes. The truth about *everything.*"

Gard let out a breath. "Seems like an awful lot to relearn."

"Have no worries, my child. I can make it easy for you. Have I not done so already? Given you eyes to see what you could never see before? An example, perhaps."

The air seemed to create a large circular screen swirling near them. Gard looked into a widening gyre and saw within a world where the mess of his past had never happened. He had never made happen. From the beginning, back to that miserable clapboard house in Travis County. How it might have been. His heart literally ached with longing. Suddenly, the longing vanished, replaced with assurance, and the notion of letting the dead bury the dead. His future appeared, rewriting the past.

The pictures bloomed in turquoise, in celadon and scarlet and lemon, in maroon and navy and pastels enough to make him dizzy with the pleasure; the world as it could be. What Gard saw now and remembered from earlier visions the Voice had given him flashed in wild spreading palettes in his memory. Yes, it was true. The Voice had given him the impossible.

"And I can keep on giving it."

Oops. He'd forgotten about that mind-reading thing. Shrike laughed, sonorous and beautiful. Gard was suddenly pleased he could amuse so powerful a source. Still, a question nagged. And was answered.

"Why you? Why have I chosen you to take under my wing? So to speak, if you take the literal with the metaphorical."

The Voice chuckled as if there were a great and wonderful joke known only to them. Gard felt great peace come over him.

"I choose only those," Shrike soothed, "worth choosing. Those few sufficiently intrepid to stand equal to me." Another soft laugh. "Almost equal, I should say. You don't mind, do you?"

"Mind? No, man, no. I mean, no–Sir? I mean I can't call you by name, can I?"

The voice made a self-deprecating clicking sound.

"Dreadful oversight. You should have brought it to my attention much earlier."

Gard was embarrassed.

"None of that," the voice said quietly. "No. More."

Breathing in, Gard felt his old troubles falling to pieces in front of him. Right. No more. No more no more no more.

"Excellent. Not many put my teachings to work as quickly as you. You understand then, why I wish to help you." It was not a question. "Because you do have the courage to break out, remake yourself into the man you were always meant to be. And no one," the Voice took on a tone suggesting this was the best part of all, "will question what they see. You can appear to be anything you can think of, or want, or remember, but your power will be contained within so that you can control it. When you learn all it can do, we will discuss increasing it."

"How much increasing it?" Gard believed he asked out of simple curiosity.

"No limit. In time, you may come very close to being my true equal."

It was too much for him to absorb at once. So he let the general idea wash over him, leaving him clean with the future, the infinitely possible.

After some moments of silence, he asked, "and everything else will remain the same? We're not making some kind of hell-fired deal here, are we?"

He hoped the Voice would take no offense. It did not.

"We leave that sort of bargaining to those in Hell. And remember, I ask nothing of you. Except to realize what you are and live by it. No harm can come to you, unless you bring it on yourself. And that we are leaving behind us, are we not?"

"Yeah. Yeah, we are." Gard turned the idea over and looked under it. Nothing hiding there.

"Were I one of the Others, those who wish to deliver only damage and despair, I would make an exchange, yes? Giving you what cannot be in nature?"

"Like," Gard saw the right of it all, "changing my eyes so I could perceive color when I'm not here."

"Precisely." The Voice sounded like a courtly old professor quite pleased with his favorite student. "You were born color-blind. If I could change your original blueprint, I would not. That wouldn't be right, would it? But here, you have no flaws. You need to know the sensation of perfection in order to bring yourself to it."

Suddenly, the Voice took physical form, previously unseen. In shock, Gard stared. He nearly stopped breathing. Before him rose a great white luminousness. He stared into it easily, and there saw the proof the Voice had indeed flown out of Heaven. Deesh was right. He had asked her, and she had answered him "because it was you who asked." And she was right. He felt himself wrapped in sheet lightning, beloved and exalted. He gazed upon the impossible. An outline of wings, rising to the great height of the illumination, the outline of a head, face inaccessible, body slender and strong, all clothed in more light.

Angel. Oh, my God. I'm seeing an angel.

"Archangel to be exact. Never mind which one. You have been given sight for which few are ever privileged. Take it as a bond of trust."

Gard began to fear, and to feel he must look away. This creature was too massive, too golden, too awe-provoking, and Gard felt from respect he should cover his eyes. There was a monstrous cracking sound, as if the world were splitting in two, and a raging rush of wind. He knew now what fear of God meant.

When he removed his hands from his face, he was in his own bed, alone in the darkest early morning. He had been gone for ten or twelve hours. When had he lain down? And for what reason? What had he been doing to send him to sleep alone in the afternoon? He stumbled out to the beach, plunged himself in the waves. Fully awake now, he threw himself out of the surf and lay on the sand. He wanted Deesh, but it was just well she slept elsewhere. He knew without a mirror check that he was drained, ill, wrecked, from the wonder he had witnessed.

Knight Errant

"So, are you going to tell me why it didn't bother you last night when I interfered with your self-sufficiency?"

"Hm." She licked a trace of blueberry pie off her spoon. "You mean something you don't already know?"

"I'm serious. Please." He dragged another plate toward him, plunked a fork into the apple *à la mode*.

She leaned back against the booth. Whatever his reason, there was a reason, and she did not need to know what. "Because you are a dangerous man." His face changed. "And I like it."

He replaced his fork in the pie. Stared at her.

"You are dangerous to everyone, but you're dangerous *for* me. I know it frustrates you I can't let you beat up people you think need beating up for some transgression against me, but I like you because I know you could, you would, and you would want to. I like it that you are a man not to be trifled with, but it seems to entertain you when I trifle with, tease, or downright irritate you. I supposed it is something I must need, because I find it sexy that you have so much physical power, and when we're together you are completely gentle. I suspect because you're terrified you might accidentally hurt me. Which you could never do. But I like that the possibility gives you pause. I am completely safe with you, because I'm safe *from* you, and I'm safe from anyone else *because* of you."

He signaled Pearl, indicated the dwindling supply of full plates on their table. She nodded, began to load a tray.

"You like me because you're safe?" Was he supposed to be flattered?

"I like you because no one else is ever completely safe around you. Makes me feel like I matter to you in a way that is only for me."

"Well. Thanks."

"Believe me. My inclination was to never tell you what I just have. The fact that I let you in on it is overwhelming evidence of how much I care for you."

Pearl brought more pie, unloaded the tray, took the empty dishes, and pretended she hadn't heard one word.

They ate silently for awhile. She squashed meringue between the tines of her fork, held it upside down in her mouth.

"I'm thinking about it," he said.

"Mm hm," she said around the fork.

Finally, he put his hand over her free one, smiled, and said with a fervency that did not escape her,

"Thank you."

She withdrew the fork, laid it in a plate of key lime. Gave him a look that, had he not known was pure affection, would have broken his heart. "My pleasure."

Wordlessly watching
He waits by the window
And wonders
At the empty place inside.
Heartlessly helping
Himself
To her bad dreams
He worries
Did he hear a
Good-bye?
Or even
Hello?

Stephen Stills

Night

Dancing in daylight in some café. She tiptoes and kisses him gently, slowly. More dancing. This is a test, but what kind? She looks up. His lips are parted slightly, an odd expression crawling across his face. There is no window, but he stares off sideways as if there were; his eyes are distant, as if trying to decide something.

She writes about him, but in which book? She cannot read her own title. One sentence is there:

"*Somewhere in the years, they stopped jamming and began rehearsing. They went from rumor to legend in one performance.*"

Yes, that was correct. When did it happen? Before her time; therefore, not relevant.

"Fret action," she says to him, dancing again. He doesn't seem to hear.

"FRET ACTION," she insists, but he remains staring at nothing, as if he has not changed position since she was here with him last.

"Fret action," she tries, again. No reply. She angers, wants to stop dancing, but she can't. She can't stop him, and so is caught in his hold. She tries to twist away, but she is frozen, dancing only from her ankles.

"Gard!" she calls. This has got to stop. "GARD!"

When she looks, he isn't there.

*   *   *

In the waking morning, she is for the first time in a long time, afraid. If she tells him, he will want to protect her, but from what? No, better to keep it quiet; his own bad dreams are taking toll enough on him.

Interlude

She knows he's unusually tired. He says things he would never say, otherwise. Such as:

"You think I'm getting too old for this?"

"I'm sure you mean touring, and not the pursuit of mad passion?" she says.

He nods.

Her expression sharpens. "Right. You love it."

"I'm forty-nine."

"Assuming actuarial tables are gaining on reality," she answers, "you're only half way to death."

"Midway through the journey of our life . . ."

"What? Have you been reading again?"

"Just to impress you."

"Uh huh. Groupies in Germany getting scarce this year?"

"Not at all. I find of late my tastes run to older women. Of about your age, say."

"You know perfectly well there are plenty of those in six countries, all clamoring for your body."

"But they don't live in Gothic wrecks, nor were they born to sarcastic repartee."

"I am not being sarcastic."

"Neither," he says putting his face myopically closer to hers, "am I."

She pulls back slightly, kisses his cheek. "No, you are not too old." She stops, as if thinking a moment, then says to him, "You will never be."

He wasn't going to tell her whatever was clawing him, and she resigned herself. Eventually he would put the words together. But it was curious, his growing reluctance to leave. Why? Were his dreams worse when the Atlantic roiled between his nights and hers?

Restoration

They are withdrawn into his rooms in the hotel. A good thing she can order fluent room service. He isn't positive even how to say *chambre de vingt et cinq*.

Having laid herself down as straight and unmoving as a marble yardstick, the sheets pulled up to her nose, she closes her eyes. It's too late now. They have made up their minds to do this, or she has made up her mind (after what he considers several tiresome months), knowing once done, no way undone. Her eyes open, enormous. Or it could be, once done *she* will be undone. Her eyes close. Too late to think about this anymore. She rarely takes a risk. But she may. In a minute. Shadows diffuse through the room.

Behind the bathroom door, he paces. A girl on the other side is hardly a new scene for him, but he can't shake the sense that what he is about to do could put an end to all the other scenes in all the other hotel suites strung all the way across the continent.

He has come to no conclusion about whether it will be good to lose his promiscuity to this girl, but what the hell. They don't live in each other's back pockets. Who's to say he can't be re-promiscuitized later?

Such thoughts he has never entertained before; they crowd him, they and the urgency of his desire. He shunts his clothes aside, having no idea what she's out there thinking. Wrapping the hotel's robe about himself, an unaccustomed politeness, he puts his hand around the door latch and clicks it open.

The windows close so tightly in their casements that no noise from the Paris night floats in. Late, he thinks, it must be very late, the show closed hours ago. Into the unnatural quiet he goes, dropping himself casually on the bed, next to her.

She moves her eyes to him, everything else quite still. They stare. She looks at him as if to say "The light is green. Go, already." He props himself on one elbow and with his other hand barely lifts the sheet. Beneath the linens she is dressed to leave at any moment. He resists the idea to laugh. Why is she hesitant as a fifteen-year-old fixing to lose it?

"You *have* done this before?" he asks lightly.

She is silent, choosing an answer. Finally, "Not with you."

"Does it make so much difference?" He trifles a little, hesitantly, with her hair. She straightens the covers from underneath until they're back up to her chin.

"I don't know."

He isn't certain what to make of her voice. Is she confused? Puzzled? Afraid?

"You can change your mind," he says, surprising himself.

"So can you," she whispers.

Sexual tension thick in his throat, he croaks out, "Oh, I don't think so."

She's heard desire in her day, but never anything close to what she is hearing now. She is thinking of what he's just said, and she would like him to say those five words again, in exactly the same manner. To heave off so ridiculous a notion, she gazes at the shepherdesses painted gamboling on the ceiling, shuffles around under the bedclothes, and withdraws her dress. She hands the garment to him, to do whatever he wants to do with it. He would enjoy tearing it to pieces, just to keep her at his mercy. Instead, he folds it, lays it carefully at the foot of the bed. More rustling; she hands him a piece of lingerie, then another, and another. But the time her hand emerges with her sandals, he can hear blood loudly crashing through his head. She raises her eyebrows. It's his move. He lifts the sheets again, just enough to look. His eyes round, and his next words astonish him. He's never uttered them to a naked woman, because they are exactly what are in his mind. Dragging the vowels long down the road, he raises his eyebrows in some surprise and exclaims,

"Oooh. Cool!"

Her response is an hilarity he has never heard from her, clear, certain, long-lived. It swirls about him until he, too, laughs, and there they are, forgetting they are both afraid even as he kicks the top sheet and her folded clothes off the bed and she raises her arms and locks them around his neck.

In another moment they are no longer laughing, they are unraveling bodily mysteries, staggered by something they might never have anticipated, much less believed.

*   *   *

They remained in Room 25 for four days. By the time his management company was ready to break down his door to get him back on schedule, he was furious with himself. He had fallen, and he was inconsolable, and desperate.

So this is what it's like, he told himself. *This is* wonder.

He hated it.

Metal on the Edge

It was late before he escaped the studio. The house was dark, as he expected it would be. Knock knock. Who's there? She. She who? Shee-it, I can't go home alone. He pushed open his front doors, closed them behind himself, made his way through the opaque air. There *was* a light, a knife-edged strip showing underneath his bedroom door. Burglars, he thought. Good. He was pitching for a fight. He opened the door.

She was trying to wear one of his bathrobes. The effect was rather like a normal-sized woman suddenly shrunk back to childhood without changing clothes.

"My," he said, making stupendous effort to keep his voice casual, "what big shoulders you have, Grandma."

"Hi."

He looked at her suspiciously, hopefully. "You're up to something."

"Mm."

"You deny it?"

"No. I am up to something."

"You gonna tell me?"

"Mm."

His dangerous smile appeared. "Okay, since subtlety isn't working tonight, let's try the direct approach."

She raised her eyebrows and waited.

"Why here?" he continued. "Why now? Why what?"

"Because you have utilities here my house is lacking." She shook her head, apparently sad for her under-equipped house.

"What might those be?" A familiar tight tugging in his entrails began pulling at him.

She tilted her head at the mahogany canopy over his bed. "From your bad old days," she observed.

"Oh. That."

"Mm."

"What? You want me to smash it up. Make sure no peeking is allowed?"

"No."

"Then?"

"Mm."

"Well. Then I should perhaps remove my clothes?" A little hopefulness had slipped out under the words. The warmth in his belly grew more pronounced.

"I don't care."

His face drooped a little.

"You don't, really?"

"I don't, really."

"Oh."

"Now go lie down, please."

His droopiness departed. "Madame's commands are my every wish."

"Of course they are. Now, the price to pay for this evening's festivities is: you can look up all you wish. We should have more opportunities for reflection. But you may not look directly at me. If you do I shall go home immediately. Alone." He knew she would, too.

He bowed. "I play well with others and I always follow directions."

"Class suck-up, eh?"

He laid down on his bed. If only to accommodate him, it was the size of a small parking lot.

"Your eyes open?"

"Yes, ma'am."

"In place."

"But of course."

She came to the bed, the borrowed robed dragging well behind. The sleeves hung nearly to her knees, the shoulders were falling off. She climbed up on the opposite side, and knelt in the pillows at the footboard. Let the robe fall.

He let out a sigh of relief. She was naked.

"All that antiquing up there makes for a kind of hazy view."

"This is a soft-focus movie."

She reached under a pillow and drew out a knife large enough to make his pocket version seem a toy. He started to raise his head.

"Rules," she said.

"Sorry. Nearly forgot."

"Now, in this movie, you are the sound director. If you want sound, you provide. Dialogue, up to you. I don't help."

"Music?" he questioned.

"As long as it's not yours."

"Never." He reached at the table next to the bed, felt his way for the "on" button. Music that was not his came out.

"Good choice."

She held the knife up, blade reflecting. "I'm the action sequence director. Since you like to play with knives, we'll play with a *real* one."

"Do I get to touch you?" She could tell he was already having trouble holding still.

"No. You do not. At all."

"Do you get to touch me?"

"If I want to."

"Do you want to?"

"No. And that is my final collaboration on sound. You're on your own."

He thought of an excellent retort, and reconsidered.

She snaked herself around on the bed. Held the knife with two hands, hilt to tip. Straight blade, elaborate handle not giving up many details in the dim light. She laid the flat of the blade across her mouth. Ran her tongue down the surface. Gard made an unintelligible sound.

She licked the other side. More sound effects. Laid it, upright and flat, against her throat and carefully, very deliberately, dragged the blade down to her pelvic bone. Gard did not move his eyes from her reflection. She laid it lengthwise up her leg, slowly pulling it up and to the inside of her thigh. He made a sound somewhere between a moan and a hiccup. Her eyes remained on the knife. Bent her leg up. Slow motioned the blade down her calf, up over her knee. Lowered her leg, changed the knife to the other leg. Moved it up herself, down, around. This went on for some time. The sound effects were of a man in ever-increasing pain. She ignored him. Dragged the knife up until carved handle lay between her breasts. She stretched, a luxurious movement. Ran her right foot up her left leg. Writhed around the bed, avoiding him, tracing herself with the flat of the blade.

Gard showed signs of physical discomfort. The undefinable sounds he was making accelerated. She turned on her side, stretched again. More time passed. And passed again. Gard, shaking, began begging her name. Without turning his head his eyes followed her every move. He began to call her other kinds of names, most of them impolite. Eventually she planted the blade right through the covers, sheets, mattress, as if they were ice cream. With only the hilt apparent, she closed her legs around it, sat up, put her mouth over the handle and tongued it until saliva dripped down the side.

A bellow issued from the Sound Director; he sat straight up in one movement. She had pulled the knife from the mattress, considering it, as though planning where next it might go.

He knocked it from her hand, sent it flying four or five yards across the room, where it fell with a blade-dulling clang.

"Goddamn it, Deesh!"

She smiled, made a motion as if to put his robe back on.

"God DAMN it," he roared, and he was upon her, covering her body with his own, burying his face in her neck. He tore at his clothes. She waited. In his haste, he forgot to watch. She kissed the top of his head, and took in the view. He might almost have been glowing in the dark.

Paris Again

"You don't remember that," she said.

"I remember everything you ever said," he reminded her.

"So you say." She looked amused.

"So I say."

She smiled sadly. "I'm not sure that is a good idea."

"Can't help it."

She sighed.

"Besides," he went on, "*I* think it's a good idea. Whenever I get to feeling weird, I remember something. Like that time we went to Notre Dame, 'cause it was so dark and quiet inside, remember?"

"Just like you," she said.

"Dark is one thing," he said. "Quiet is something else."

"You managed, as I recall."

"Yeah, 'cause we sat there about two hours and you told me about the place in that voice you have, the one you read with."

"How exciting," she said dryly.

"No. Sexy."

"Come on."

"I can't explain it. Calm and sexy, too. Go figure."

"Thank you, no. If you want to go figure, be my guest."

"And a couple of weeks later, when I came back from Belgium, you read me that book?"

She rolled her eyes. "What was I thinking?"

"You were thinking I might like it. And I did."

"Did you." It was not a question.

"I still think about it."

"Yes?" She ran her hand through her hair, a habit he

185

thought often indicated her brain was sparking.

"Yeah. Wanna hear some?"

"Gard, that was eighteen years ago. Are you telling me you committed it to memory?"

"It just happens. Really. This was my favorite part:

'Oh, have pity on me, girl! You think yourself unhappy. Alas! Alas! You do not know the meaning of misery.'" His voice was slow, sonorous. *"'Oh, to have a woman; to love her with all the strength of your soul; to feel that you would give your blood, your life, your reputation, your salvation, immortality and eternity, this life and the next, for the least of her smiles; to regret that you are not a king, a genius, an emperor, an archangel, a god to place at her feet a grander slave. Do you know what agony he feels through long nights, whose arteries boil, whose heart seems bursting, whose head seems splitting, whose teeth tear his hands–remorseless tormentors over love, jealousy, and despair. Mercy, girl! Have pity on me! Have mercy! If you come from Hell, I will go there with you.'"*

Her look warned him to be cautious. "Typical Hugo melodrama."

"What's your favorite part?" he asked, ignoring the dismissal.

"Don't have one," she muttered. And he believed her even as she lied. In a fork of cerebral lightning the words all came back and she was silent for half a minute. Accustomed to this, he watched her, wondering what she was thinking. Then she began from memory, almost unwillingly.

"'All at once you began to sing. What could I do, miserable man? I strove to escape. Impossible. I was nailed, I was rooted to the spot. It seemed as if the marble of the floor had risen to my knees. I was forced to stay on to the end. My feet were ice, my head burned. At last–perhaps you pitied me–you ceased to sing; you disappeared. I fled; but, alas! something in me had fallen which could never be raised up; something had overtaken me which I could not escape. I had learned who you were–how could I doubt your

186

magic powers? Thus began your misfortune and my own. Not knowing what to do or what would become of me.' Yes," she repeated in a dull tone he could not read, "typical Hugo melodrama."

"Maybe," he shrugged, hiding–he hoped–the ballooning ache in his heart. "Funny," he said slowly, "I really loved the Hunchback, but I felt sorry for the priest."

"Because he was so pathetically wicked?"

"No," he said, looking hard into her eyes. "Because even though he could say those things, it would never matter to her."

"Better that than the other way around," she shrugged.

And he should know, he thought. "Arteries boil," he repeated.

"'And my body is burning like a naked wire,'" she said, anxious to leave Hugo behind. "You remember that one? Not Cleve's, but not too bad."

"No," he agreed, "that other guy. 'I want to turn on the juice/I want to fall in the fire,'" he finished. "And I know you're changing the subject."

"'I want to drown in the ocean/in the bottomless sea/I want to give you what I'm hoping/You'll be giving to me.' Well? How about it?"

"Not fair," he said, moving toward her.

"Maybe not," she agreed, "but the other guy's lyrics can sometimes have the same effect as you singing Cleve's."

He took her hand and they wandered to a far corner of the house. He wondered if she knew at all that she was–by denying him the words as important as the body–delivering him into the same teeth of envy as the hopeless priest.

They Don't Live Together Because

"What are you doing?" he asks, interested.

"Drawing a sketch of the library."

He peers over her shoulder. "Hey, you're good."

"So you've said."

"I mean this drawing. You still remember stuff from your college painting days?"

"I do."

"But you never paint."

"I don't." She spoke indulgently as she moved the pencil over the pad.

"So what's it for? Other than being good, I mean."

"You'll see in a minute."

"What? Is it for me?"

"You may say so."

He watched as her own library appeared in gray pencil line. Bookcases, furniture, carpets, fireplace, windows. From the Palladium window, a slant of light crossing diagonally to the floor. She feathered in some dust motes.

"Finished."

He took the sketch pad and examined it. "You are an artist."

"I am a writer."

"Okay, okay. Would you give it to me?"

"For you to flatten out under some of your floor detritus, or to display in your house?"

"I want to hang in it my bedroom. Please."

She clicked her teeth on the pencil, as if she were thinking about it.

"Hmm?" he asked.

"Hmm."

She sat and he stood in silence for awhile.

"All right," she said at last.

He started to take the pad.

"Not so fast, Wonder Boy," she said.

"What?" he asked, clutching the paper to his chest as if it were his first born child, or his Stratocaster.

"Oh, come, come." She laughed. "I'm not going to change my mind. It's just that if you really want to take it, I need to add two or three things."

He bent his head to one side and studied the drawing. "I don't see what you left out."

"I know you don't see. Hand it over." He complied.

She scribbled the pencil around, holding the drawing where only she could see it. He squinted his eyes at her. She ignored him. After a few minutes, she put the pencil back between her teeth, and gave him her work without comment.

The room was the same, but there were things added, things making it look like one of those puzzle drawings "What Doesn't Belong?" Leaning against the marble of the lower mantle was a motorcycle, in proper proportion. Leaning against the Harley was one of Gard's tool boxes, half open, screwdrivers dribbling out. One of the sofas at that end of the room was covered with open magazines, some draped over the back and arms. They appeared to be reading material about sports, motorcycles, weight lifting, guitars, and reviews of rock bands. Gard's massive stereo system completely blocked two of the bookcases. A stack of weights and a weight bar were propped against her desk, looking as if they might smash right through it. Three large television screens were hung at intervals around the room, masking more bookcases. A guitar rested in her favorite reading chair. Another lay across another sofa. Earphones dangled from the lamp on the console, reflected in the mirror behind it. CD cases were everywhere. Against the double doors leading to her bedroom was a shaky pyramid of black leather: jackets, pants, boots, and several black silk shirts draped on the pair of statues she had sent back from Greece during her studies. In her desk chair was a great wobble of Gard's book collection, English translations of the some of the books she owned in their original languages. And no birds sang.

"Jeez! You ruined it! What for?"

She eyed him before his temper caught full flame from the kindling she had just drawn.

"Your life and my life. Not an easy coupling."

"Deesh."

Now he was the one sounding indulgent.

"Both of us have houses more than large enough to accommodate another person. Or six persons, for that matter."

She was about to say something, but he beat her to it.

"I know you don't want to live in my house, I know you can't leave this one, and I don't blame you. But you don't really think I would do this to your *library*, for chrissakes? Or any other part of the house?"

"No," she said, thoughtfully. "I know. But the drawing is not about the room." He raised his eyebrows, wrinkling his forehead. She continued. "It's about me."

He lowered his eyebrows, then his head. Everything about him seemed slumped. He had no weapon against the inevitable, and the truth.

"This is what my interior self, whatever that is, would look like if you moved in." She told him this softly, as if the lower her voice the more rapid his understanding. He had, however, understood from the first eleven words.

"Yeah," he said, finally.

"Yeah," she said in tones suggesting he walked with the Immortals.

"Yeah," he said again. "But you know I'll forget from time to time."

"I know."

He put his arm around her shoulders, she leaned a bit into his chest. "This starch smells good," she said.

"Want to smell without the clothes?"

"Oh, probably. Later."

"Probably?"

"Probably later. Absolutely yes I want a sniff under the starch." She turned her head until she her mouth was right against his shirt buttons. "I know I'm disappointing you. I wish I could do otherwise."

He kissed the top of her head. "I know." She had her arms around his waist. He could feel the bones of her back beneath his hands.

"One thing you got wrong. Wrong wrong wrong," he said.

"Hmm?"

"The motorcycles would have to go in the dining room."

He felt her shoulders shake under her chuckle, and he smiled a grievous smile over her head.

Gonna Hit the Highway on a Phantom Bike
(Approaching the Dickensian Christmas)

"What are you thinking, if I may ask?" She looks up from her annotating and finds him with an open book and closed eyes. Television on, sound off. His expression just enough off the usual range her curiosity is piqued. This end of the library is cozy when the fire burns, and she likes to look around from time to time.

He opens his eyes. "I am thinking," he says, "of the forthcoming holiday festivities." Sometimes it entertains him to copy her speech patterns.

"I thought you looked like a little boy licking his chops, drooling for Claus."

"Not Claus."

She waits. His answer, deflating any hopes of clues as to what he most might want this year, is quick and gleeful.

"I'm drooling because I can buy you anything I want, as much as I want, and you can't do a thing about it."

"Oh," she says, dryly. "Well. Absolutely barring purchasing houses in the Bahamas, I suppose one must take one's victories where one can." She draws up her right leg, tucking it into the chair cushion.

"Yes. One must." He lobs her a practiced evil grin, and returns to his daydreaming.

She sighed to herself. Please, she prayed to the Ghosts of Christmases Past, don't let him lose all reason. But it was a useless plea, and she knew it. Oh, what the hell. Here was another chance to practice one of her powers: to make him forget old Christmases mercifully dead, the ones prior to his escape on the rocket launcher Rock and Roll. Let him think he was crashing over one of her most immutable rules. Yes, indeed, one must take one's victories where one can. And not a soul, except her own, would know what they were.

Perhaps this year, in choosing loot for him, she might teach him a thing or two about wretched excess. She had managed to locate a rare English motorcycle, and she now had less than two months to regret doing it. She shrugged at herself. Come on, if he killed himself on it, then she might festoon it with black balloons and ride the damn thing to his funeral. He would appreciate that sort of perversity. She closed her eyes and planned.

He glanced over at her, saw her reverie, the intensity with which she was thinking. Always so serious. Probably comparing Thomas Hobbes to Descartes or some such historical hooey. Maybe he'd name his next bike Thomas Hobbes just to tease her. *"Life is nasty, brutish, and short,"* he vaguely recalled. Poor Hobbes. Bet he would've felt different if he'd only owned a Harley.

Path Diverged

In his dream, they are dancing in some café. She wears the black thing she always wears when they dance. She arches her feet and kisses him gently. The kiss is a test, he divines, but of what? He knows she is looking up at him; he is staring off sideways out a window that isn't there. He must be trying to decide something. What? It was eighteen years ago or more. When he saw that groupies on tour and Deesh at home was not going to work. The fun was going out of it, he felt guilty at home, and clichéd and sleazy on the road. It was not a question of fighting for fidelity, he realized; he wanted no one else. When did that happen? In Paris? Why had it taken him two years to know it? He is shaking his head at himself; she twirls into his chest, and says,

"Obsession is part of passion. Don't worry about it."

Guess I am obsessed with her, he thinks. Obsessed for twenty years. Can passion last so long?

"You're obsessed with me?" she asks as they turn around the room.

"Yes. I thought you knew."

She makes no answer. He has not turned his head toward her yet. Is he speaking to her? She to him? Who talks, who walks, who dances in the night? She feels tiny in his hands, as if he could break her ribs without effort. But he doesn't want to break her ribs. He wants to break her heart. NO. No, he doesn't. No. But it becomes clear he may break her heart as a consequence of something else. Something to decide. What is it? He squints, as if to see more clearly through the nothing at which he stares. He feels her hand on the back of his neck. They dance faster, and faster again. Her eyes are closed, she flies with him around the room, an expression of great seriousness on her face.

Yes, now he remembers. He has to decide now. He's running out of time, standing on the outside, looking at the inside, the inside of yearning satisfied. He should be in, looking out. His lips part slightly, and a grin crawls over his mouth. Yes, he says. The decision seems gradual, somehow, like the way the band made itself a reality. Stopped jamming and started rehearsing. Yes. Time to stop jamming, being jammed up. It is raining outside. There are no windows, but he hears the thunder, the crack of lightning, the sudden downpour of furious rain beating against the café's exterior walls.

Choose, Gard. Choose.

Their dance has slowed. She is tucked in under his arms; she weighs nothing. She seems to be becoming corporally insubstantial as they move. But she is there, dancing in the black dress, so what can there be to worry about?

Choose. Choose, Gard.

Yes, he says, sure any danger can't survive their passion, obsession, twenty years together. They are safe.

Choose.

And the deal is done.

Yes, he says.

Yes.

Editing

They slouched on one of the library sofas, legs straight, feet on the low table fronting the fireplace. She was taking a pencil to a curling sheet of galley proofs, occasionally readjusting half-glasses up or down her nose. Head back, he slept.

More and more he was sleeping at odd hours, and long hours at night. He had stopped making even a pretense of going to his own house. She would not object. The tour was soon upon them, and as it came a day closer, then another, he was likely gearing up. She tapped the pencil against her hand. It was time for him to go. They both knew it, as they had known it with revolving regularity for the last twenty years.

She scribbled on the galleys. As a kindness, Ballard had them sent, rather than computer disks. Modern editing she left to iconoclasts and apprentices to the devil's workshops. To be set in one's ways was the vanguard of excellent armor. She considered, made another note, something about de Tocqueville, then scribbled something else on the flyleaf of a book she drew up from the floor. She wished briefly he were awake. As much as he hated her using books for notepads, it would be a little fun to watch him try to say nothing.

The fireplace fired. Already it was cold, as if deep winter had come too soon. She would ask him to help her carry several loads of wood to the upstairs bedrooms.

He insisted. He always insisted. "I'll just take a last look around up there, make sure everything's okay."

Her reply never varied: "Any rats you find are yours to keep."

"Ducky."

They said these things twice a year, every year. A

ritual so practiced it was nature to them now.

Still, she was uneasy, and irritated at the feeling. There was something so very not right, she knew. But she had already asked him and he had answered that life was good, thanks. She suspected otherwise, but if questions between them went unanswered, there was no revisiting the inquiry. A closed border to any country had to be respected.

She got up, crossed to a window seat cowering between two towers of shelves, and took up one of the reading blankets. She walked back and laid it over him, lightly. If sleep he wanted (needed?), then sleep he must have. She sat at the hearth, drew her knees to her chin. Staring into the flames, she slowly rocked back and forth. He would go the first day of November, and return for ten days just before Christmas, and why the hell, she wondered, was she so nervous about it this time?

Helplessly hoping,
Her harlequin hovers
Nearby
Awaiting a word.
Gasping at glimpses
Of gentle true spirit,
He runs
Wishing he could fly
Only to trip
At the sound
Of good-bye.

Stephen Stills

Charon's Crossing

He watches her from the door of the back stairs descending to the kitchen. One knee bent, one foot flat against the wall, her voice is uncharacteristically yielding. She must be talking to Lily There is no sign of anything but that it is Sunday night, the tour begins in two days, and she is making sure his house will survive.

"Yes," he hears her say, "in a couple of weeks. Only if you have time. Uh huh–no, nothing special. Just the dust and the plants, and open the windows awhile. No, just every few weeks." She smiles lopsidedly into the phone. "Oh, I don't know. Survey the area for any vagrants camping out in the living room?" She paused, listening, and laughed. "Of course, you're right. No vagrants in *that* neighborhood." She had yet to notice him. He gazed at her from the stairway, felt her running in his veins. "Oh, until February, I should think. You know I can never be sure . . . uh uh. Yes, Lily, I promise. Really, now, don't you think . . ."

He began to clear the doorframe in time to see her not finish the sentence. Quite silently, and at once, she crumpled to the tiles, the telephone handset still in her fingers. He was across the room in three strides.

"Deesh? Deeshee? DEESH?"

He lifted the receiver, said with the automation that comes with shock, "Lily? Listen, she'll have to call you back. Okay? No, later."

She was limp. Her face wore the same conversational expression, as if she had not been interrupted. She might have drifted into sleep, for all the trauma he could see. He lifted her from the floor. Carried her into the living room. Sat, holding her to him. Put his lips to her temple to know she remained warm. Kept her tight against his chest, as if he could will his own life force into her body.

Remembered with slow recognition a telephone, and an ambulance.

Admissions

They had got her into a room, and a nurse followed. "There are too many people in here," she announced sharply. Vlad, crouched in a corner, raised his head from the styrofoam cup protecting his Zubrowka. Cleve said, "Then you should leave," and if ever he looked as dangerous as he really was, it was now. The nurse turned to another subject. Wielding her clipboard, she said unpleasantly, "Who is the nearest relative–we need some signatures."

Leslie laid a hand on Gard's shoulder. He looked up from the corner of the bed. The bed was too small. She wasn't used to so narrow a space. Hardly room for him to sit, hardly room for her move about in her dreams. He must rectify this at once.

"Relationship to patient?" The nurse said at him. "Sir? Are you the husband?"

"No," said Leslie.

The nurse bristled. "We need a relative. Is there family available?"

"We're here," said Cleve, coldly.

"Brothers, sisters, aunts, uncles, cousins? Any parents still living?"

Silence.

"Mr. Gard? Sir. Whom may we call?"

"Me."

"Then I must know your relationship to the patient."

"The patient's name is Doctor Calder. Remember it," he says, weary and threatening.

"Mr. Gard, you must understand, I must have information, some next of kin–what is your relationship to the–er–Miss Calder?"

"Brother," he said.

She wrote that.

"Husband," he went on in an inflectionless voice. "Aunt, uncle, brothers, sisters, cousins, parents still living."

The nurse tucked up her clipboard, rested her hand on the shelf of her hip. "Mr. Gard, I understand from the floor nurse you are some sort of celebrity"–the word sounded poisonous in her mouth–"but in this hospital you are to cooperate with the staff, whoever you are."

Gard looked around from his seat on the bed. "Put it all down, or pick one, I don't care. Kindly take your goddamned papers, get the hell out of here, and stay the hell out." His look suggested he might begin throwing furniture at her any moment.

"Do it," said Leslie, calmly. She took the woman by the arm and push-walked her through the door. "I'll bring you the forms in a few minutes. It's all right. Believe me. Please."

"I can call security and have you all thrown out of here," said the nurse, shoving the sheaf of forms at her.

"Yes, you can," said Leslie. "But you really don't want to do that. There could be consequences. For you. We won't all be here all the time, we will not cause inconvenience to your staff. But we will not leave her alone. Ever."

"Who do you people think you are?" the nurse asked, but the edge of threat had fallen off her voice. Her expression remained that of a high security prison guard.

"Who we are would mean nothing to you, ma'am, but it would mean something to the hospital administrator."

The nurse departed.

Leslie turned back into the room, said, "Gard."

He hung his head and shook it slowly. She put her hand back on his shoulder. "Gard. Baby. Just sign where the x's are, and we'll be done with the bureaucracy." She put a pen in front on him, pointed at the signature lines. He wrote his name where her fingers led him. "That's good, baby. Now I'll just run this out to the nurses' station. I'll work out the "relative" idiocy. I'll come back soon."

He did not appear to have heard her.

"I did this," he said.

"No, you didn't," Cleve said. "How could you?"

"I don't know," Gard answered, dully, "but I did this."

For the next twenty-four days, each a robber knocking on the door of Deesh's dwindling life, his inexplicable guilt, breeding and warming itself, hatched in his soul until it displaced anything Gard might ever else have felt.

Poison Apples Revisited

After the first week, the neurologist agreed to release her if Gard would see to it she were confined to an identical medical prison. He swore. Nurses would be required for home care. He guaranteed. He must sign sheaves of papers removing the hospital from possible indemnity should she "expire off premises." Gard signed. Anything to rescue her from this terrible place. If awake, she would find a hospital abhorrent; no privacy, no quiet, no dignity, no life worth living. He did not intend for her to ever know such a moment. It would all be very expensive, they told him, and as she was uninsured–and once again he raged, rampant and terrifying. "I have twenty, thirty times more money that you'll ever have, *Doctor*," he sneered. "I can buy this hospital, and I can buy you and the medical school you say you went to. Would you like to see my lawyer for a full accounting of my riches?" Well, no, actually, that wouldn't be necessary, if he signed a guarantor release. He was not married to her, you see, which complicated the issue–he walked out of the room before they finished. But she came home, unaware, but home nonetheless, and was laid out in her own bed in her own room, the room of rounded walls and cupola ceiling, every foot in old conservatory glass. With her dark hair and white skin, she might have been Snow White, the nurse observed. He nodded.

"In a glass coffin."

"Which makes you the prince," she said, helpfully.

"No," he answered. "I'm all damned seven of those godforsaken dwarfs. Dopey, Dummy, Sleazy, Bleedy, Stupie, Creepy, and Bastardy."

"She needs a nightgown," the nurse observed gently. She had already been warned of the ensuing fallout from trying to argue with Gard.

"She doesn't own one. They bother her."

"Surely you don't want her to remain in the hospital gown?" she treaded lightly.

"I'll get something," he muttered, dully. He disappeared into the next room, closing the door behind him. Nurses did not need to spy on Deesh's closets or her bathroom. He would make sure they didn't.

He went looking for her one dancing dress. He had seen it, held it, breathed into it for years, and he could see it as clear as if it were in front of him. Scooped neck, low back, buttons in front, tight bodice flaring to an eight-gored skirt, cap sleeves. Black. The fabric of the dress was as tangible to him as his own skin. They were good together, Deesh and that dress. Deesh and he. His hand on the bareness of her back, the twirling circle of her skirt when he spun her, his bulk and her compactness coming together, flying apart, melding and dividing, dancing to the gods of rock and roll, the music of their childhood, the music leveling their playing field, the music of their lives.

She was careless of clothes; they were neither important nor unimportant. But the black dancing dress hung alone, separated from others, contented to keep its distance. Just like Deesh, he thought. What else? She would not need shoes; in any case she hated them. Underwear? He imagined himself lying in bed, dressed for decency and show, moving only when moved. No. Just one more thing to remove and redress. Something plucked at his brain. What?

It came to him his decisions were like choosing a costume for a casket. He sat abruptly on the closet floor. He would joyfully have awakened, still stoned, in a Chicago hotel room, his life smashed, future lost. He would have done it joyfully and a thousand times if it could mean he would not be here now. Doing what he was doing. Thinking what he was thinking.

Wondering what else does one need as couturier to the living dead? Or the dead living. Conjured up in his mind was childhood television, a riff on the old western title:

Wanted: Dead and Alive.

How could Deesh be both? And how could it be there was nothing he could do?

*   *   *

There was no telling how long he sat slumped on the floor of her closet. It was a corridored, wandering thing he'd built when he constructed the far reaching bathroom on some long ago birthday. When? A year after she'd moved into what she liked to call This Castle of Otranto. What was that? She'd told him—some book. But what about it? He used to know that. He did. Why couldn't he remember?

He stretched out, lay on the floor beneath her clothes, drifting. It smelled good in here, like Deesh. He stretched again, and something clattered down at his foot. He'd knocked something over. Fucking crab apples. He rolled out, rolled up to a standing position, and looked. He moved down the row to look again. And again. It took awhile to register what he was seeing: a scattered stack of CDs. Cases scratched, liner note corners ragged, and every one of them his. All his music from when he began to the album they'd done three years ago—his last. He and Cleve had to get the one in progress out of the goddamned studio and into production.

His thoughts accordioned, in and out, before he realized his brain had gone elsewhere, unwilling to accept the reality in front of him. And the implication of the reality: she did listen to his music when he was gone. The battered CD cases told him how often. His face grew numb. She did listen to his music. She did.

He wanted, but failed, to cry.

Hotel California

The Voice was cloaked in sarcasm, glee, triumph, evil.

"Where are we?" Gard asked, shaken, afraid.

"Just where we've always been. Accommodations not to your liking, sir? You've certainly liked them well enough until now."

There was darkness, air difficult to breathe, confusion, nausea. "What's happening? How have things got so . . . so bad?" Gard could barely recognize his own voice. Or the other, which had grown deeper, louder, sharpened like claws.

"You think you can continue so far so many times and always control the threshold you won't step over? A little farther each time. Dangerous game. But you *like* danger, do you not? No more drugs, no more of your celebrated whoring around, no more booze. No more trashing the world as you crash through it with everyone applauding you because you're *Gard*. And you miss it–you lie to yourself, and most convincingly, I might add, but you look back with regret. Those days were unspeakable horrors. And they were heaven for you. I did nothing but offer you just a *soupçon* of the old pleasure disguised in flowers and fireworks and you were on it like a duck on a Junebug. Of course, now *you're* the bug. Welcome to Hell."

*   *   *

Gard awakened, still caught in his dream. Deesh was as she was, unmoving in her bed. He briefly wondered why such dreams had chosen to return when he had banished them as his oath to her. He struggled off the floor, knowing that no nightmare could be worse than daylight reality. But, he thought shivering, it was plenty bad enough.

Orpheus

He tries to keep as much of the institutional as possible out of her room, out of her house. There is an IV running into her arm, with an octopus arrangement of tubes feeding into it. There are monitors, and a machine to measure heartbeat, and breath, and all small responses revealing she lived. She lived though appearing dead, and Gard's heart was slowly pulling out of him.

How long? How long? Two weeks? Two years? Two decades? Come back to me, Deesh, he begged, even as he knew somehow he had done this. He, by himself. The neurologist ("Call me Theo") told him her body might work itself back into life, but only God knew when. Gard had snarled: "too damned bad God isn't telling, if there is a God, and I don't much give a gold-plated friggin' goddamn if there ain't."

*   *   *

Nonetheless, Theo's reputation was wide. Everyone said he was the best, that Deesh was lucky he took her case, that if he didn't know the cause no one could, and what neurologist made *house calls* for God's sake? Calm down, they said, did he know how impossible it was she was home and not in a nursing facility, surrounded by linoleum and human vegetables? So many concessions to him, they said, unprecedented, they said. Your anger won't help her, they said. Your despair won't help her, they said.

Eventually, he turned them all out except the Nurse, who was the price he paid for keeping Deesh where she belonged. The Nurse whose name he could never remember, who answered to whatever Gard called her, often simply "You!" She kept things in order, kept Deesh's life in her body, and stayed out of the way. When she did speak, often in complicated metaphors, Gard ignored her. He supposed the nurse must have started out an English major.

Gard gave her her choice of rooms on the second floor, where she slept when Gard insisted she do so. When not sleeping, she sat in a chair next to Deesh's bed, one of the big reading chairs Gard had dragged in from the library, and in the chair the nurse watched Deesh. She never read, nor spoke on the phone, nor watched television, nor listened to music. She watched Deesh, changing the chemicals running through the IV, marking incomprehensible notes on her chart for Theo, and watching. Anything else Gard would permit to no one but himself. He washed her, brushed out her hair, put pajamas on her at night, the black dancing dress on her in the day. He laundered the dress himself in Deesh's bathroom sink each evening, and laid it out to dry for the morning. He slept on the floor next to her bed, and during the day he laid himself down in the bed with her and spoke softly in her ear. He read to her. He sang so that only she could hear. He kissed her fingers and held them against his cheek. He broke apart all the furniture in two bedrooms on the third floor, screaming like an animal as he threw chairs, tables, bedstands against the walls. He spoke not at all except to her. "You!" he would call, and point at Deesh's IV bag, or at a crinkling bandage battening down the cannula in her arm. Point and make his point. Why talk to the nurse? What was there to talk about? Nothing was Gard's answer. Nothing was his answer for everything. His sleep was dreamless now, night after night, a gray mist of nothing, just as were his waking days. While Deesh was dead, he was nothing more than a laser pinpoint of terrifying energy, aimed directly at Deesh's life force.

Lily came, and took a room on the third floor; saying nothing, she cooked and kept the house that she had tended sporadically for seventeen years.

On the twenty-third day of Deesh's dying, "You!" sat watching. Gard dragged into the kitchen to look over the larder and confer with Lily about groceries for the nurse and anything for which Lily could wear Gard down into eating. He slumped in the butler's pantry, too tired to live.

*   *   *

He heard himself think, *Go for a walk.*

Shut up. Gard spoke kindly not at all these days. He made his way back to Deesh's bed.

Go for a walk. For a little while. Breathe the air. Move your legs. Remember her as she was so that she will be. She will be. Go for a walk.

He went.

The wind was up, a late Autumn twirl of air blowing through the trees.

He would have sworn on all things sacred to him that he was out walking in a nearby park, and not asleep next to Deesh, or what was left of her.

And there she was, she of the white birds, a voice in their midst, hovering over a stone bench, as if waiting for him. Her face was indiscernible. As in dreams, she spoke to him as if their conversation had been going on for sometime. He knew, though he didn't want to, exactly what she was talking about.

He would have to go alone, she said. Even the evening shadows surrounding her glittered. How could he? He didn't know how to begin, he said. There would be a way. She could say when–on the twenty-fourth day–but she could not say where, It was important to remember simply that the readiness was all.

"You know Shakespeare?" he asked, not thinking.

"We know many things," she said kindly.

"But you can't go where I'm going?"

"We can't go beyond. The place is not of our making. Therefore, we are not obliged to it."

"But," he said shaking his head as if to clear it. "I'm here in the middle of Heaven and Earth, and I didn't make any of it."

"No," she agreed. "You made nothing." He knew the

209

'you' was generic. "So you are free to go anywhere."

"You're not free? I don't believe it."

She spoke very gently. "You don't because you can't." Feathers fluttered, cast sparks, stilled. "You can't imagine an existence," she went on, "where freedom means nothing, because it *is* nothing. Those who wanted freedom? It was granted them. And you will have to trespass on that liberation alone."

"Because none of you," he asked, straining toward understanding, "go there? Ever?"

"It was done. Once. Once was the limit to the necessity, as it will be for you. Once you return, no matter the outcome, you can never go back."

He tried to absorb it all, so much of which was so foreign to him. "So I will find a way back out?"

"I don't know."

"No," he said with the slightest note of fear, "you must know–how can you *not* know?"

"Because," she answered, "you haven't yet made the decision."

"To go in?" he asked.

"To come out," she answered.

Wrenched

"I'm going out." The Nurse looked up in surprise. He never went out.

"Everything okay?" she said carefully. Didn't want to scare him into staying in.

"Yeah."

"Going to the park?"

"Hardware store." He held up the crescent he decided it was it was time to replace, for no good reason he could think of.

Not the answer she'd been hoping for. He had awakened earlier from a restless sleep, looking half-wild, and begun to tear apart the upstairs bathrooms, determined to have them enlarged and remodeled "for the time when she comes back. See, if I do it now, she can't complain about my money, she can't insist on paying for it herself. And when she wakes up," he had grinned with a creeping hint of craziness, "it'll be too late for her to be mad. Ha."

He could take however many years he needed to finish the job. Or maybe months. Or maybe days. Nobody knew a goddamned thing. Just wait, just wait, they said, and it was killing him. Banging the hell out of walls, pipes, wires, and antiquated porcelain, destroying to rebuild, there was a way to pass the crawling time. However long it crawled.

"Take your time," the Nurse said, smiling gently, nodding encouragingly.

"Yeah." Her obvious patience was beginning to piss him off.

He rode his bike fast enough for suicide. People glared at him when he exploded into the parking lot. He ignored them. He was in as dangerous mood as he had ever known. Let some asshole pick a fight with him right now. Come on, do it. He flexed his hands, clinched them. It was a late, lovely, browsy afternoon. He did not notice.

The store seemed empty; not surprising. It was small and disordered, as old as the ocean shore, and he knew where every last cache of screws, wood, pipe, tools, and wire, were. As he pushed through the framed glass door, smeared with the hand prints of a thousand previous customers, he noticed nothing. But he stood there on the concrete floor, suddenly confused as to which direction to go.

"Help you with something?"

He turned to the counter. The voice was one he had heard before. And he wanted, with no reasoning, to hear it again. There was a woman there, and he knew she had spoken, but her head was turned to a tower of rusting buckets stacked off to one side.

"Excuse me?"

Slowly her gaze came round to him. His breath stopped.

It was she, and this was no dream. She was here in the hardware store, the mythical creature Cleve had written a lifetime of songs about, sitting on a nasty looking plastic stool, looking right at him. He abruptly took in air. She swung one foot against the rungs of the stool.

How could he define her in terms possible to be understood? She was there, that was certain, but ethereal was too heavy, too clumsy a description. Coloring too clear, skin too smooth as if airbrushed, eyes a color of blue that didn't exist in nature.

"Your . . . hair," he said.

She nodded once, with an expression of infinite understanding.

"What color would you call it?" He was sufficiently astonished to remember not one of his automatic gentlemanly manners towards the women folk. "Kind of white, kind of gold–you were born with it, right?"

A sense of *déjà vu* unfolded inside him.

She laughed. He forgot everything. The universe shrank. Even his despair seemed crowded away.

She was the new counter clerk? She was wearing

212

overalls, though white ones–pretty impractical for sitting next to rust buckets. A long-sleeved white tee shirt, the sleeves pushed up to her elbows. Very tall, evident even when sitting, almost as tall as he. She continued as she was, foot tapping the stool, hands folded calmly in her lap.

"I'm." What? What was he? "I'm . . . sorry," he stuttered. "Please don't take offense. I–you . . . you are the most beautiful woman I've ever seen."

Leslie, who made men collapse in the streets merely by passing them by, was a shadow next to her. In comparison this woman was a god, a god so gorgeous as to make him weak.

"It's all right," she said.

"Is it?" He had no idea what "it" was. Nor did he care. What could he say?

"Thank you."

Where had that come from? Was he thinking his own thoughts or not?

"Yes," she said. "There is no one in your head except yourself."

His relief was fleeting. Oh, Lord, she read minds, too? Or was he speaking unawares? Confusion gave way to fear, fear to panic, panic to a sort of black nausea he'd never known. Until now. He knew why he was afraid.

"You have blonde hair. You have blue eyes. Those buckets are the color of blood. I can see every color. I can't see colors." He stopped to take in air. "You're from there. Aren't you? Aren't you from there." It was not a question. He had the absolute conviction he needn't have explained a thing.

She shook her head. "No. Anywhere but there. Don't be afraid."

Was he hallucinating? He'd certainly been good enough at that in his time.

She shook her head again. "No. But why do you worry? Have you not liked it "there" for some long time now?"

"I do. I did. Not lately. Not anymore."

"Why do you worry?"

Damn it, this conversation had happened before, but he couldn't remember where.

"Why are you wearing coveralls the color of buttered cream?" he heard himself say. What the hell did he care what color they were? Buttered cream? What was *wrong* with him? His panic receded a measure. Was it really she enveloping him in such unease?

She laughed. What sound? He couldn't pin it down. She must be a singer somewhere. Leslie's pipes were as good as the best around–but nothing like what he was now hearing. And wanted, very much, to hear again.

"Very kind of you to think so. Your approving judgment is not easily won."

Like she should care. Whoever she was, he knew instinctively that she was no hiree of a hardware store, and that admiration was ever of no consequence to her.

"There is no need to fear."

He knew exactly what she referred to.

"But–you haven't seen her. She's . . ." He couldn't finish.

I don't need to see her. I've seen you.

He shook his head as if to clear it. What was he saying? What the hell were they talking about? "Are you telling me I'll get over it? That time heals all wounds no matter how fatal?"

"What you say is true, but it is not what I mean for you to hear."

He stood there. She rubbed her right wrist. At last, in a final effort to prove himself in the here and now, he said, "I need copper elbow connectors. Six inch pipe. And a new"– he held up the damaged tool. "Stripped the threads right out of it trying to tighten a two-inch wing nut."

She seemed to know exactly what he wanted. "Connections."

"I know where they are. I'll just get them and . . ."

"Later," she said very quietly. "Get them later."

"All right," he heard himself saying, as if she had

214

suggested he open a window, or take a different aisle than he intended.

She stood up, and he was struck all over again. The harsh light from overhead fluorescents caught at her hair, turning various strands of blonde into platinum. It occurred to him her hair, caught up in a formal back twist, was rather at odds with her clothes. Even under unforgiving light, her skin warmed, as if illumination came from a hearth fire, and her eyes seemed to have no pupils. Eyes so beautiful, so arresting, what in hell color would you call that?

He knew her. He did. But when? And from where? It came to him. The guy in the bar. The runty kid who'd waded in without blinking, whose physical power was so much greater than what it seemed. It was impossible to make a rational association, but the look about her, the imperturbable certainty, it was the same. But he could hardly ask her, Hey, Honey, ever hang out at a bar in Germany where this other weird dude shows up? When there's a fight?

Whenever there's a fight between the Mortal and the Light, or the Mortal and the Darkness, the other side always shows up.

She didn't say that. But he heard it. What was she saying to him? He wanted to think it out, but he could not look at her and think.

He realized he was staring, probably with his mouth open, and that she was again amused. He cleared his throat, or tried to.

"Uh. Sorry. I just, I was, I mean you don't see that hair style much any more."

She smiled.

"It's–it's so . . ." he breathed, hardly having sufficient mind to take note of the fool he was sure he was making of himself.

He thought her head like the prow of a ship, her hair pulled back like that, lines so clean and clear she might be a sculpture of flesh. Could he describe her later? He doubted it. Leslie would, he knew, tell him (if he could get it right), "human beings don't look like that, Gard. She's probably a

215

member of the Plastic Surgery of the Month Club." And how could he say she would be wrong, so wrong–wrong? Wrong. But he knew that even if human beings could not look like this, here was one who did.

Her eyes, however, made him waver in his certainty. For whatever reason, the hair on his arms prickled and rose. Her eyes again. Would Leslie sneer "cosmetic contact lenses"? Somehow, even with Les' eagled powers of observation, he doubted it. But, then, this really could not be. He searched her face, her hands for any flaw. And found none. He shook his head. He could never reproduce this woman in words, and who would believe him if he did? What took him more aback was that he was absolutely positive, for no reason at all, that with her, what you could see would be exactly what you would get. She had not one false or filthy bone in her body, he would swear on it. And, more, though it was not true–this he could also swear on–he *had* known her, met her, seen her before. The words came out before he could caution himself.

"Do I know you?"

Yes.

Puzzled with this familiarity he could not recognize. "And you know me?" He would remember if he had had this woman, no mistaking that. The thought seemed profane to even think, but why? Then what? Was she a foreign record producer? Perhaps. Some second string European royalty? She had the bearing of someone used to moving without regard for danger or discomfort. His confusion dissipated even as he tried to hold on to it. He felt an aching for her, unfathomable and inexplicable. But no anxiety, no guilt, nothing but surety he'd always known her and just now found her. Even Deesh, it hurt him to know, could not mix in him such a crosswind of peace and longing, though longing for what he couldn't say.

"You would go for a walk with me?" she asked.

Of course he would. "Thank you," she said. Reaching behind the counter, she withdrew a small backpack, smoothing it with her hand. Alligator? He watched her fingers curl around the strap, and he had a quick convulsive need to know what was inside.

She smiled again, turned it upside down over the counter and shook it. Out from it fell–nothing.

Gard had known a goodly number of women in his day, and one thing he knew was as certain as cotton crops when the heat rose up: "nothing" was in no way *ever* what they carried, clutched, and clung to 'til death did them part from their handbags.

"It's a prop," she said.

"Please. Who are you?" Despite himself, he tingled with pinpoints of fear.

She gave him a look he couldn't begin to describe, and again the fear vanished. He hoped they could remain here together in this small, uncomfortable, dusty, and badly lighted place forever. At the thought, "forever" suddenly possessed meaning; he understood the idea at once and completely.

In a moment he lost it, so fast perhaps he was unaware of the flash. In its faint trail was inexplicable recognition.

"Don't be afraid," she said again.

For a moment his mind was blank, then, as if an eclipse had ended, the world blazed in familiar light so recently disappeared.

"I'd only have to fear you," he said slowly, "if I didn't somehow know who you are."

She nodded.

He nodded.

"But why like this? Aren't you supposed to be a bird or something? Or a tongue of flame?" *Or a flock of white feathers*, he thought.

She smiled again, and this time he was convulsed with a terrible, unquenchable need to never leave her, to be with her, to be *of* her. His confusion spread, twisting with wonder.

"Because," she answered, "you like women, and you love them. You must see me as I am in your heart."

This was beyond him, but he believed her.

Deesh came back to him.

Peace fled.

"Let's walk now," she said, preceding him out of the store, the wind blowing the emptied alligator bag against her back. She eyed his bike leaned against the building, a silver and black mesh monster shading itself in the afternoon. "Nice," she said.

"Thanks," he said, automatically. "It's a Har"

"–ley Panhead Road Rally," she finished for him. "1984. V-Twin OHV engine." He was astonished. "Let's ride," she said.

Nothing she could have said or done would have caught him more off guard.

"Uh, okay." He paused. "But I don't have a helmet for you."

"I don't need," she said under the wind, "the protection you give to her."

No, he thought.

He got on, awoke his bike. He felt her materialize behind him. "Just put your arms around me," he said automatically, "and hold on." He knew when he said it she had no need for that, either.

"Don't look back." she said. "Nothing but trouble ever came from taking your eyes off the road."

"Yes, ma'am," he said, good Texas boy that he was. She laughed again. He leaned into the sound.

He fired out of the parking lot, having no clue or care as to where they were going. He hoped his hair wasn't flying in her face, or his stink, either.

*　　　　　　*　　　　　　*

The park was deserted, as the hardware store had been. Had he noticed, he would have wondered where everyone was, on such a day as this. Rather, he was noticing how apart she seemed from everything, trees, grass, wind, winding paths of delphinium, Ligustrum, camellias, Liriope, peonies, and who knew what else. *In winter?* Apparently anything grew in this region; Deesh had pointed out to him on a number of occasions that even she couldn't kill the hydrangeas flourishing despite her efforts in her back garden. He smiled at the thought, as if she were here now, telling him the names of plants and blooms, castigating herself as butcher gardener, while he wondered what she was talking about. The flowers in her garden were perfect. He thought of Deesh describing their different colors, almost as if he could see them. Oh, Deesh. A heart could actually, he knew now, crack.

He for a moment turned away from the swirling nightmare his life had become when the woman said, "Let's sit here." She took one end of the stone bench and drew her knees up under her chin. Just like Deesh, he thought. Just like–

He covered his face. Too hard to breathe; he'd have to re-expose himself to her gaze. There were tears on his hands, he saw, horrified. His body began to tremble, then shake. From his throat rose a rumbling, growing to a hoarse, coughing sob, which multiplied and gathered into a guttural scream. He sounded horrible to himself, as if he were being tortured, or dying from grief, or finding out what it was like to be damned. A grinding sobbing as if his soul were trying to tear itself out of his body.

She touched him, and it stopped. Just like that. From his end of the bench he looked up, and he was amazed. Who are you, he wondered, who are you who are you? It was still hard to accept.

His next thought must have been insane. Nonetheless. "Can she come back? Can you get her back?" For the first time in days he did not feel like death waiting on itself.

No. She seemed sad, a little.

No. Well, he hadn't really thought so. There was no one could get her back. And how many years would he have to live, watching her body, waiting for her to die? How many years before he could reach for whatever end to existence he might have for himself?

219

She cannot come back.

"So what's the point in talking about it? I can't. Anymore."

He didn't wish to look away. Being dazzled was actually a rest of sorts. But he could no longer sustain. His head dropped back into his hands.

Gard. She made his name sound as bells.

He wasn't worth it. Vision or woman, she must know it. What had he done, what dreadful crime had he committed? Why was Deesh where she was?

Because you wanted more. You have everything, and you wanted more.

Yes. His dreams of the last years congealed, turned to rot in his guts. "Shouldn't I have known? Why didn't I know? But there was so much light–sometimes that's all I could see."

It's an old act. You know–false prophets, sheep's clothing, ravening wolves."

"Yeah," he said slowly. "My old man used to beat that one into me. So why didn't I see it?"

To begin with, he had no business screaming Truth as a threat to an eight-year-old. What did you think it meant?

He was abashed. "Uh. I thought it was like cartoons. Where the wolf jakes up a real bad disguise out of an old sheep skin–and, like, who believes it? Not the sheep."

But you see now, this is not a cartoon. This is real."

He nodded miserably.

What you must face will appear as what it is not. Do not be distracted. Whatever visions are forced upon you, remember: there is <u>no light</u> there. There can never be. Demons have no generative powers.

He thought of all the moments when vague dissatisfaction hardened into something else, where he was temporarily consumed by his own wanting. Then it would pass. But it came again. He wanted more. Even with Deesh. He wanted more with her. More of her. More of it all. More audiences. More music. Higher numbers on the charts. It was never enough, and now he saw what the other, the Voice, had led him into. Shrike. Opening the doors. Showing him more. Always more. And all for nothing. No generative powers. His throat closed, and his skin burned with guilt.

Oh, Deesh.

She cannot "get" back. But she can be brought back.

He jerked his head up. Was there help for it after all?

His hope died as it was conceived. He knew what he'd known from the beginning. What he'd pretended otherwise. Now he was no longer safe from what was true.

"By me."

You.

"Why can't you?" he asked stupidly. Do this for me, I don't want to.

Because the place is not yet deemed for destruction. My presence would be as a boulder falling on glass; it would be crushed from the weight. So, I cannot go there. But you can. Once. A one-time-only offer. You need to do nothing except take it or leave it.

Again his fear oozed, and a shame too vile to endure. He wished this woman, this *lady* to take her overalls and her alligator backpack, and her glittering hair, and be gone.

You don't know Deesh entirely. She would forgive you.

He kept his face in darkness. "How? You tell me how. How could she?"

There was movement. She was sitting next to him now and it felt as if she had an arm around him, holding the pieces together. When he looked up, she was still straddling the bench, her hands in her lap.

She never blamed you. Nor would she.

"How can she not?" His humiliation grew greater; how much more? He felt his face flush to his neck, and dropped his gaze.

The question for her is 'how can she?' How could she ever blame so much and at the same time let you mean so much? One only. Blame or not blame. She made her choice.

"And you're telling me I gotta make mine?"

221

As you do every day. As any spirit must. Choose large, choose small, choose self or not self, choose shame or absolution. Every day, all your life. It is what you do. That is life as you can know it. Choice has been given you. Given.

And thereto was the war. The minute-long, infinite war that consumed him, consumed all, blighting the whole of him, leaving no prisoners.

Choose.

One would think the process an easy one. Only those who have survived it know better. Those who have known and have been to the gates of so deep a valley of decision. It was the closest thing he had ever in his life understood as Hell. He had mistaken many times and places for what he knew now, and he cursed his ignorance. Chicago had been as nothing in light of the present moment.

"But I lived through it. Through Chicago. And I built everything back. One frigging brick at a time."

Then you know how it is done.

"I hate this. I hate it. What if I'm wrong? What if I do the wrong thing? How am I supposed to know how to do it right?"

She seemed to shrug. *Take it on faith that you will. Deesh takes you on faith. Even when the choice is as hard for her as it is for you now.*

Hard choices for Deesh? He thought that process had been over for her before he ever met her.

It's never over. Not in this life.

"Then you have to tell me where she is. How can I find her? Where is she? Where is she? Please."

She put both hands on his arm. It felt like escaping a dark night lost in the woods. She told him.

Later he wondered what violence or insanity he might have committed had not the touch of her fingers kept him gravitational. The air in his windpipe grew hot again, and difficult to breathe. He felt it burn his lungs, and he would have given anything, you name it, anything at all, not to know this. The true nature of shame, of guilt without a trace of qualification.

"It's my fault. I did it, I know I did. But I didn't know then. It's my fault, and I never thought for a second it would have anything to do with her."

She withdrew her hand from his arm, gazed upon him serenely.

You walked through an opened door.

"That's all it takes?"

Sometimes.

"But why Deesh? I opened the door, *I* should have crossed the threshold."

You will. If you choose to.

"But Deesh?"

She was pulled through to serve as the purpose of drawing you into that place before your soul made the trip by itself.

It's working, he thought bitterly.

Which is why I have come. Sshh. Just listen a moment. Hell does not belong on Earth. She does not belong in Hell.

"And I don't belong anywhere without her," he blurted.

Perhaps. But when the natural order is confounded by unnatural means, eventually it must be restored.

"So you've come to restore order?"

I am here to have this conversation with you.

Gard had known despair, self-inflicted, as well as forced upon him. But whatever his memories of past pits of blackness they were as breaths of air in the here and now. Desperation in his head, panic behind his eyes.

"You're telling me that I can get her out. That I can get us both out."

And only you.

"Why?"

That you will know when you are ready to know. Gard. Listen, and attend. You will find yourself there if you wish to be. You won't see her, but she is there. She will know you are there. You must believe it. It is a simple matter of faith. Do not try and look for her or at her. You will be let in to take her out, you are granted your chance, but it is for you to decide whether or not to trust what I say to you now. You are given this chance. Don't ask for more.

He started. Deesh had said those very words, hadn't she? Once, when life was life and death kept decently to itself? "Don't ask for more," he repeated.

Nothing can prevent you. Ask if you will. Or refrain. Nothing can prevent that, either. It is your choice, and once made, no power of any sort can unmake it.

Power. He had so much in just making up his mind?

So much more than you have ever understood. The power of the emptiness that is evil is nothing before it. Nothing. But if you let It, It will convince you otherwise. Under no circumstances should you enter into conversation with It.

That he had already done so, and so very many times, stabbed him.

You did not see It as It really is. What is in the past is superficial. Now It will be as deep and as divisive as anything you will ever experience. Now you are in the worse danger. If you speak with It, It will turn your heart to ice. You cannot best It with words; It will try to induce hatred in you, so that It might have a common ground. No matter what It does, what It says, what It shows you, do not raise yourself in rage. Do not give It the power It must have from you to win. You are lost if you do.

"But what do I do? If I can't talk or fight, what's left?"

It is in you. Whatever weapon you choose. Again, it is your choice, and to make the choice is in itself the power to rend Hell. Now you may use it, and see its force yourself. There is only one thing more.

There were a million things more, and he had to ask. What kind of road map was there? He suspected the local visitors' aid would not be much help. But before he could order up his questions, he heard,

Don't look back. When you have her behind you, when you are delivering her, and yourself, from that place, no matter what, do not look back. No matter what.

"Why not?"

You will know when she is released. Then you must believe it without proof from your eyes. What you can see is very little of what matters.

"Why are you helping me? I don't understand."

Whenever there is this fight, the other side always shows up.

Wait. He knew those words, didn't he? Had she said them before? Was this a recurrent dream, and not happening at all? He had to know, and his panic rose again.

This morning, early, weren't you holding her hand and praying that you would do anything for love, anything for her?

"You would call that praying?"

That is what anybody would call it, except you. You would do anything for love, so I am here to help you do it. Whatever you choose to do. You must believe what you choose, and remember what you choose. It is difficult. It has always been so. Your will is at your own command. And Gard. For God's sake, don't *look back.*

"Why not?" He knew he was repeating himself, but he needed a different answer.

She shrugged again, as if whatever he might look back upon was completely inconsequential.

Just a minor matter of faith.

He shut his eyes in an attempt to clear his brain, make sense or nonsense of what he was hearing. He had to think about it all, somehow, without this tornado of emotion striking him without warning or mercy.

The other side always shows up. Is that the best thing? Or is it a curse? Depends, he thought, on who started the fight. Good. He was beginning, he thought, to get it. He would have said so, wanting her to know he did feel gratitude for her time and trouble. When he opened his eyes, she was gone.

Only later, as he slowly made his way back to the house, watching the late afternoon street slide away beneath

225

his wheels, did he realize. He had not awakened from any dream, because he had not been asleep. He was awake, and he was alone.

Prelude to the Damned

He awoke unpleasantly. Sweat stuck to his scalp, his skin felt as if something crawled upon it. His eyes burned beneath their lids. Where was he? In the glass coffin, slumped in a chair, halfway between this world and another. She lay unmoving, IV fluid dripping, drifting down the tube into her arm.

He saw her in his absences, alive and well, lying in bed, watching a starry night, listening to him, to every album he'd made. Why hadn't he known? *Because,* a familiar woman's voice whispered, *it was her way to keep you out of Chicago. To try to keep your head inside your hat. To hold you to safety and sanity. She couldn't let you know how much she admired you, wanted you; had you had the information, what would you have done with it? Drag her back to Chicago with you? Leave her to go alone? Neither would do, would it? She used to look at the glass sky and hope, "don't let him fall. Don't let him fall, again." She didn't realize how much she was responsible for keeping you in this life you wanted. Glorious Gard, invisible Deesh. She could never let you know how much you mattered because you mattered too much to too many amassed strangers. Someone had to save you from yourself, and you didn't volunteer.*

"Deesh," he whispered. "No crime was thine."

Nor yours, the voice pressed against him. Weakness, perhaps, but weakness is all the opening needed for those who would invade you and rejoice in your torment.

"Deesh," he said, low and miserably, "I didn't know."

You know now. Remember that. You know now. Evil looks more powerful than it is: Darkness appears to have borders you must cross to reach it, but the truth is that it must cross your defenses to reach you. It cannot invade unless it is invited. Wanting more is its welcome.

The voice vanished. He saw the shimmering hair, the eyes too blue to be human, the perfect face, sad and serious. Gone and would not, he was sure, come back. He unbent himself from the chair, stretching his cramping joints. It must be three or four in the morning, he guessed. There was no clock in her room. Watching it would have been more than he could stand. Tick tock, she's in hock, tock tic, he's a prick, tick tock, her life's in lock, no key you see tick tock tick tock tick tock—Alexander Pope, it's Alexander Pope, how did he know that, how did he dream Alexander Pope Alexander Pope—

He put his hands over his ears as it to shut his mind up or out or down. He was coming too close to the edge from which he had once toppled in Chicago. He remembered. There was more that he wanted, more that had been denied him. His voice ruined, and so, he thought, was his rocket-shot upward. He wanted that blast into the skies of fame. The world could be damned for wrecking it for him. The years come on, the years go by, and the skies are his, the highest clouds over Europe, Australia, New Zealand. But not enough. There should be more, he wanted more, he wanted the worshiping mobs of madness in his own country. The rest of the world was second prize. Not good enough. Not enough good.

His mind pushing the metal, driving faster and faster, making less and less sense, never shutting up, driving him crazy, driving him out the window, driving him to a familiar narrow ledge from which he miraculously had not fallen, or leapt.

Deesh. Deesh the miracle. "Deesh," he called, as if she were not beyond his voice. Far away. He felt a viper rattle of fatal grief beginning. It could strangle him, or he could choke the life from it. Give up now or go and somehow get her back. Chicago or Comeback. Be lost, Deesh, or come back. His career had been his to rescue or abandon. He remembered how hard, how tortured the rescue had been, and how easy the surrender would have been. Now it was come round again: Choose.

Claim or capitulate. This time he had no three years to decide. This time it was officially now or officially never. This time he was terrified. Listening to her breath whispering, he re-drifted into dreams beside her.

Stand by the stairway
You'll see something certain
To tell you
Confusion has its cost.
Love isn't lying
It's loose in a lady
Who lingers
Saying she is lost,
Only to trip
At the sound
Of
Hello.

Stephen Stills

Hell If I Know

He found himself on a strange road, the air so still there was nothing. Not even his footsteps came back to him. No color rose from the ground–all was gray and sandstone. Either that or his old hobbled vision had been returned to him. Something was wrong here, he felt it more than understood it. There were trees that were not trees, sky that wasn't sky. Only a rocky path bordered with boulders in all disorder.

There was no fear. He waited for it to seize him, moved his glance right and left, trying to see it coming.

Nothing.

At once he felt a blow to his heart so mighty as to take his breath and send him to his knees. Dizzy and nauseated, he struggled back to his feet. Slowly. Shaking dizziness off, he put his hand to his chest to know that his heart was still beating. Panic isn't pretty, he reminded himself. He might puke, but it wouldn't be from fear. Panic is not pretty, he admonished himself harshly. The landscape remained colorless, endless. He walked. *Come on,* he thought. *You can do better than cardiac interruption. There is nothing you can do to run me off. I'm here,* he heard his mind menacing and certain, *and I'M COMING.*

He'd played in beer halls worse than this. Back when the best gig he could get was a third-rate bar, where fifty people was considered SRO. When he'd had to face his own downfall night after night. After Chicago. But he'd done it; gradually the audiences grew bigger, grew into crowds, and then into mobs. Years. This was no worse. Hell, this was a quart of Jack Daniels compared to a glacier-paced comeback. *That* had been frightening.

I'm coming, asshole.

What's next?

Nothing. He felt a smile twist on his face as his boots clocked over the hardpan and the stones.

It occurred to him that he'd been given some sort of warning, hadn't he? About engaging the satanic in conversation? But he couldn't remember, and shook off the thought.

I am coming, now, and there is nothing you can do to stop me.

But the absence of fear does not mean courage is going for free. He didn't question his direction. The parched trail of rock led forward. He had nowhere else to go, except back. Back he would not go. Nothing moved, and gradually he became conscious of something far more ravaging than fear.

As if he were being processed through a vacuum, he lost all human connection, real or imagined. He was the last man on Earth. Or the last man in Hell. And there was no God to deliver him. He had never felt so alone in his life–he might have been locked in the blackness of a bank vault. No one would help him if help were called for. No one would hear, whatever came from his throat. There was no one. No living thing to absorb any sparks of his own spirit, and no living thing to which to send them back.

The absence of anything or everything he would not

have known could be so terrible. Something squeezed his heart, and the emptiness increased, if that were possible. A void over which he would have said no man could prevail, even the worst, living or dead. Loneliness he had known. But the cavern he was fast becoming was so great as to contain the loneliness of every person every lonely moment in the history of time. He could not endure. His mind, his spirit, were slowly snuffing out. Every fiber in him screamed "Get me out of here!"

Still, he went on, his soundless footsteps carrying him nowhere. No end to the road or the silence or the great vaulted emptiness beginning to dismantle him. Could his brain survive a loneliness so vast that it seemed the very stuff of which the universe was made?

Yes. His awareness would endure, would survive memory, body, heart. Locked into a vise of nothingness, he began wishing he were dead, until it occurred to him that he probably already was.

So where am I?

He knew perfectly well where. He could think the thought without acknowledging it, a good trick, but not one that loosened any pressure in the vacuum behind his ribs. He continued walking.

A new horror came upon him. He saw his boots moving colorless gravel, dodging dust-colored rocks. And there was no dust. His boots were as clean and black as when he bought them. He couldn't remember when and why did it matter? But it did. It did. *It's no big deal, except–except, you can't remember and there is no one anywhere to assist your recall, or do your recalling for you.*

She never failed in recalling for him. His Boswell, she said. His Pepys. Whatever was gone from him she could retrieve. Bring it back. Blow dust from any required memory, air it out for him. And he did that for her. Didn't he? Wasn't he the ledger she could open when she needed an accounting of a month here, a moment there, a lifetime that could not guarantee peace regardless of safeguards long set in place? His mind told him nothing. Would permit him nothing but his unnaturally clean boot leather.

Didn't I, Deesh? Didn't I do it for you? Kept the bad old days shut away for you? The bad old days you almost never spoke of, the terrible times before I knew you? Didn't I let one or two of those days emerge when I knew you were silently torturing yourself to death? Didn't you do the same for me? "And so my father made me thus, or left me thus . . ." *You were right, Deesh. No one ever knew me except you. So long ago, crouched by the radio, playing a stack of scratched-up 45s, teaching myself how to sing. Taking it all in because there was nothing else in the world, nothing for me to take. They're gone, those days. Gone for both of us. So why do I feel as if they've never left me?*

No dust.

Trying to work his thoughts around a desolation too great to bear, but which must be borne, he absorbed the dread of what he had been trying to ignore.

No dust because dust meant decomposition. Decomposition meant regeneration. Which eventually comes to dust, and begins the continuum again.

No dust meant no rot.

No rot. No life.

He wanted, oh *please*, he wanted to weep. To give way to the grief of having lost forever something he never thought valuable. No tears welled. Just a hideous ache of relentless regret to keep company with an abandonment that anywhere else would have driven him mad in moments.

Here, there was no comfort of madness.

*   *   *

Time lost relevance. He glanced at his watch, but puzzlingly, could not read it. The road went on.

She had read Dante to him. Somewhere in Europe, Germany maybe, on some tour when he'd fallen ill. He could still remember some of it, and he wondered why he should think of it now. He didn't know anything anymore. But her voice, a voice that could not sing however it reached, her voice reading had been two out of three. If not sex, the sounds she read were recreational controlled substances, were rock and roll. Maybe sex, too. Whatever it was, it had kept him in bed, kept him from speaking, kept him from going crazy over the number of concerts he wasn't giving.

What could he remember? Hear it, he commanded himself. He tried to focus on nothing but the past. Hear it like the radio, the only escape, the old Philco where he had *heard* and so taught himself to sing.

Hear! The flaying landscape receded. Her voice came back in fits and starts and, like the radio, was hindered by spitting static. Faintly, far away, he could almost get it.

Nel mezzo del cammin di nostra vita
mi ritrovai per una selva oscura
che' la diritta via era smarrita

Nel mezzo del cammin di nostra vita. Yeah, like the radio mezzo del cammin where he'd spent his long ago childhood, Nel mezzo del cammin, learning to sing. He saw himself crouched on unclean linoleum, getting himself out of the way, his ear to the box cabinet, feeling the music. Feeling. The sounds suddenly tactile, rumbling or whirring though him. Nel mezzo. Not a handsome child, nor a beloved one, something had happened as he had transfixed himself, consuming the original sovereigns of rock and roll.

And one day, long gone from linoleum and the Philco, he'd opened up his throat, and staggered even himself.

The vision dissolved.

Nel mezzo, he repeated, Nel mezzo, the magic words, magic beans, magic carpet. Nel mezzo cammin del nostra vita. Dante's travelogue to impossible places. Deesh's voice in his head. She had read and read until he slept, and begun again when he awoke. "In the noontime of life/I shall be consigned to the netherworld." Nel mezzo cummin del nostra vita. Midway in our life's journey. Midway in life I shall go to the gates of the grave. Midway . . .

Deesh's voice enveloping him, keeping him safe, he remembered. Whatever monsters had been under the hotel room bed, they cowered where they were when Deesh was reading.

Midway in our life's journey, I went astray
from the straight road and woke to find myself
alone in a dark wood.

Walking farther on and farther. No deep, dense forest here. But he was alone. He was forty-nine years old. Had no idea where he was going. And though he could see clearly, there was no light.

The landscape must have gone on for miles unchanging. Like walking a treadmill, he might be weary, but the scenery remained the same.

Che nel pensier rinova la pavra
Tant' e' amara che poco e' piu' morte!
Which even in recall renews my fear
So bitter–death is hardly more severe.

Morte.

Deesh.

Morte.

Euydice.

Morte.

When the last of his strength against the vileness of the place wasted away, he came to the end of the road. Before him lay a distorted edifice, part palace, part cave, the same sickening non-color as everything else. A shape made of rock, a shape not recognizable as architecture, but with an entrance. And it waited.

In the midst of my days
I shall go to the gates of Hell.

No boatman? No three-headed beast-dog? No cacophony of lost souls lined up at a filthy river? Dante, he decided, had certainly been more imaginative than the Devil.

No fire. No ice. No nothing.

All nothing.

A door was slamming on his heart, over and over, disorienting him, shortchanging his breath. He wanted to sit down, to lie down, curl up within himself and wait for the radio to turn on and take him out of here.

He wanted, but he did not get.

Come in, he thought he heard. *Come in or go back. No indecision allowed here.* Faint and hideous amusement behind the words. Wake up. Wake up! Now! But the words no longer offered his escape clause. There was none.

The truth settled about him like drifting cobwebs. "I'm not stronger than Hell. I can't beat it." One more yard and his heart would tear, split. *Stay or go.* Another revolting chuckle. *Your choice.*

Had self been so dislocated his capacity to protest no longer registered? If he might come back to himself just for a moment, he would have screamed, have shouted, and have damned the power to choose.

"Damn free will" he wanted to break from his brain. "God *damn* free will and damn everyone forced into its chains. God damn me. I should be damned. I am condemned because I can't decide. Deesh.

Can't leave.

Then what he dreaded arrived: a maelstrom of fear and revulsion and terror that whatever he did would be wrong.

Can't stay.

Alone complete.

No life no death no sex for salvation, no drugs for disappearing from himself, no rock and roll to keep his soul alive. *Abandon Hope, All Ye Who Enter Here.*

Choose.

Escape. Or Deesh.

He passed through the doorway and went on, stepping on rough stone, a stairwell winding down in darkness.

*   *   *

He couldn't have said what he expected. His mind had closed into its primal level.

How bad? How bad can it be? He felt his way, circling down, until a darkness visible showed him the bottom step.

At the end of it, the Voice was palpable. Like poisonous gas, the air was nearly unbreathable; this was the smell of despair. Every fear, every doubt, every insecurity, every hate he'd ever known bloomed wide, like fireworks in a night sky. Gard thought he must die. Now. Death must be better than this. The Voice, all hospitable persuasion gone from it, laughed. The hair on the back of Gard's head stiffened.

"This is *death, you useless fool. The real thing. The classic brand, so common to the other garbage in your 'profession.'"* The Voice circled him, a devastating merry-go-round, leaving him dizzy and disoriented.

"This is real, and it ain't the Lost and Found, you fat-faced motherfuck. So you've come for her. Gallant Gard." Hideous chuckle. *"The damsel is retrieved from hell in mythology and fairy tales. This is* real.*"*

He could hear her voice. Or remember it. "This is real." she had said, and he'd nearly shattered at the words. She would not say a thing if she knew it to be untrue.

Now he grew cold. From his own fear, turning him fast to ice? Or from the other's hate, the like of which Gard could never have imagined? He pressed on, issuing silent orders to his boots: one; now the other; one; now the other; walking blind and sick with terror. His body seemed to be compressing, his thinking–gone. Nothing left but to feel, and such feeling as nearly forgotten from Chicago.

"Chicago," intoned the Voice, *"was amateur hour. You knew you were in hell then? You knew nothing."*

Gard felt tears begin, freezing on his face as they tried to flow. He must find a voice he could use. His paralytic silence was taking everything; sliding away through invisible crevices were any reasons for him to try and live. He sucked in as much breath as the lethal air would allow. The pain assured him Chicago *had* been so little; homemade hell in a handbasket.

He blew out.

"Where?" his voice creaking

"Where? Oh, you mean the bitch in twigs over

there?"

From the foot of the stairs Gard's eyes tracked—nothing. "Not," he gasped, "part of the deal."

"What deal?" The sound of the Voice made Gard's fall into fear move faster. *"The deal was about you—and voilà!, here you are."*

"Can't," he panted, "keep her."

"As long as she lives I can. When she dies, then she slips my grip, true. But," the voice ground with gravel, *"you know these cases. Coma, unknown origin? Coma, diagnosis inconclusive? Coma, prognosis just any idiot's best guess? Living death—and it can go on for* years. *Just think of it. Years!"*

No. He would not allow it. He was physically powerful, she, physically helpless. He could send her far and forever away from here in less than a minute.

The laugh, high and lewd, came again. *"Yes, you do that. She'll fly off to wherever; you'll be a murderer, and shortly thereafter you will rejoin us on a more everlasting basis. You will be accommodated a place in the building where you can be alone with your own consciousness. Forever."*

Gard heard the glee. He pulled in another breath like shattered glass, let it out.

"The deal was me. I didn't sell her soul."

"No. You sold your own to rock and roll—isn't that how the lyric goes? Yet you are *here—your choice. So, unless you leave, you are voluntarily well and truly damned. And by the way, you don't have all the time in the world. Or,"* the Voice hissed in his ear, *"in Perdition."* The hiss lengthened to another laugh. Gard would have covered his ears could he have raised his arms.

One foot, then the other.

Again.

How long? Ten seconds? Ten centuries? He stopped. Here was the place to stop.

She was here, somewhere. A greenish glow akin to the surface of evening swamp water appeared.

The Voice lounged in a corner. It had taken on concrete form, unspeakable and indescribable. Whatever Gard had left to pay for, it would be with what he saw now. And what he would have to remember. Saliva rushed under his tongue. Bile rising, vomit he wouldn't be able to withhold. The Voice came at him.

"That all you can do? Not surprising. Spewing? Your singing? One sounds the same as the other. Pathetic. Just what did you hope to accomplish showing up uninvited? There is no getting her back, Great Gard the Puke Machine. No hope, asslick. None."

No hope. That was so. None here. None left. None likely to arrive.

"You should stay, though. Stick around, watch me fuck your whore. If she ever wakes up, she'll bolt if you touch her hand. Her experiences here will displace your useless fumblings. Doubtful you'll want her then, anyway. You'll always be able to smell me on her. In her. Unless necrophilia makes you hot. Does it?"

Give me my voice, he thought.

The chuckling oozed on. *"Your voice is dead. Good riddance to that fecal horror."*

What could he use? What did he know? Deesh. He knew Deesh, knew *her* voice over all the years she had read to him, and read and read more 'til her voice would devolve into a scratchy whisper of itself.

What did he know?

Something—there was something—but what? Different stories ran together scrambling poetry and memory. *You've done this before.* He had not, so why did he feel as if this were the second show of the night? *Doesn't matter. Push it away. What can I remember?*

Bile rose higher, stripping his throat, burning the walls of his mouth. He forced it back. His throat felt flayed.

"You like TV, you stupid shithole? Let's watch some."

Before Gard a sort of holographic tunnel opened. He

239

saw what was in it. He closed his eyes. Uselessly. He could still see, and at close range.

His life flashing scene by scene, but only the bad ones, only the killing ones, only the ones so well equipped as to drive him where insanity would be relief. The things he never spoke of, never acknowledged, things Deesh could only guess at. Every horror he ever perpetrated or was perpetrated on him. Every second of depravity and filth, every libertine scene he'd ever made. In clarified, color-wide detail. Humiliation too overwhelming to bear. Impossible to turn from. How could he have done? How could they? The endless gyre of misery once inflicted widened, spreading until people he never knew were caught in it.

I didn't know. I didn't. How could I?

"Well, now you do. No excuse in ignorance, blubber boy. Let's change the channel."

Gard before Chicago. Gluttony on all counts. Food, whisky, recreational drugs, one night stands which he had forgotten before the next sun gave way to the next moon. He was gross, bloated, body an insult to function and form. No tangible relation to the hard discipline which had changed him so completely.

"You haven't changed one crapulous iota."

"I don't want to watch any more. Stop it."

"I don't want to watch any more. Stop it." The voice imitated him in a high screech. *"This is my little party. You watch what I want. You really must admit, it's pretty inventive–if disgusting–stuff you've got going there. Let's see Mommy and Daddy, what say?"*

NO!

"Oh, yes. Yes, indeed. It'll be fun. Nothing like these little sentimental journeys down memory lane, right? Especially yours, in all its glorious degradation."

The images changed, the sounds heightened, voices he'd spent a lifetime driving out of his head. Sadistic ridicule, horrors at the hands of those who should have most protected him, a child dead so long ago. A childhood he had shunted aside too early in exchange for a ticket to survive.

"Let's see what's happening on HBO. Ah—look. Quite the self-centered little bastard, weren't you? Twenty-four and ready for Rikers. Oh, no—I forgot. No jails for you, you're a Rock Star. You do what you want, take what you want, break what you don't want. My kind of folks, the Great Gard."

The screen swallowed itself and changed. He saw Chicago's aftermath. His band scattering, hustling to play backup for studio recording sessions, avoiding mention of the years they all made millions with Gard. Millions gone, smoke in the sky. Cleve disappearing for months, writing nothing, Vladimir treating himself to a ten-month drunk, Leslie, sleepless, peaceless, jobless, unable to figure out what had happened to them all.

I *happened to them all.*

"Right again, Gardo."

But that was a thousand years ago. We've come back, we're the same, we're better than we were before.

"You're even stupider than I thought, snotwad. You think dragging their asses all over Europe 'cause you can't get a local gig makes up for what you did? They loved you, and you pissed all over them. They stink of it yet."

Was it true? Had they never forgiven him or each other? It didn't seem true. Now they were having what they missed the first time—fun. Weren't they? And they did a stateside tour just three years ago; people had waited for them to return, they sold out all over, they got standing ovations before they played a note, life was far better than it had ever been. Wasn't it? Wasn't it?

"Doubt yourself, kiddiefucker. That's what you do best, isn't it? Doubt them. You know you'll never last. You know it, or you wouldn't have found my company with all its vague promises so irresistible. You can make your futile attempts to sustain your body, but what's that worth? It'll run to pus now or later. But you still want more—always more."

He had to stop listening to this. But how? What was there for him? He couldn't see Deesh. He couldn't hear her.

If he could make her hear that he would get her out no matter what then he would get her out no matter what.

She will know you are there.

The memory was loud in his head, coming fast from nowhere and leaving as it had come.

"Deesh," he spoke aloud. His throat was killing him; he seemed to be swallowing carbolic acid instead of bile and fear. *Do it anyway*, he told himself. *This is your chance. Take it now, even if she doesn't hear, I have to say it. She has to let me say it now.*

"Deesh," he began again.

*   *   *

He has to make her understand. And will she let him tell her, now, when it all might be too late? Will she finally allow him the words he has never had her permission to give? Words that, in their suppression, have taken on their own life of nagging shock, as would a shattered bone or a leap from a hotel room ledge? Into the blackness where somewhere she is, he speaks:

"Deesh. I can't. I can't remember. I can't remember a time when I didn't love you. Can't be a time when I won't love you. I've wanted to tell you and tell you and tell you 'til I wore out the words. But there's stuff you don't say, gotta be sacred so you don't say them. Well, I'm sayin' them, even if you don't want me to, I say them." His voice grew lower, tighter. "I love you. I've been in love with you for half my life. I will be in love with you for the rest of it. Deesh. I love you. God Himself couldn't love you the way I do. If I die in here and you survive, somehow you gotta remember I'm telling you. I'd rather be dead and damned than not love you. Deesh. Oh *God*, Deesh, I love you. I'm *in* love with you."

The Voice sounded as if it were vomiting. *"Peeeee Yewwww. You think that crap is going to help? It's melodrama written in shit, you hairball, and you know it. So what if she hears? So what if she remembers? Which I seriously doubt, by the way. It's just words, and we all know*

*how much words are worth. As much as you, maggot:
nothing."* His sickening laughter boiled up *again. "Nothing.
NO THING. You're nothing, and it would take more than
nothing to make any difference now."* More laughter. *"You
are such a stupid motherfucking coward. There is no magic
in words."*

Yes, there is, he thought.

*"Oh, yes, indeed. You've got your mouth open spew-
ing words night and day, and they meant so much you
jumped at the chance to grab something else; you weren't
even sure* what, *but you wanted it. Didn't you?"*

It doesn't matter, he thought. I told her. That matters.
Matters to me, matters to her. I know it does. You don't
know anything.

"Oh, but I do," the Voice snarled, a taloned thing
reaching for him. *"Rewrite history all you like, you know
every word that I'm saying is true. You were so easy, you
screeching fool. Never satisfied, always looking for more
and more and more. My kind of self-serving cocksucker."*

Yeah. Just like–someone. Someone from the days of
the dead, the old life just now reopened for him to see. All
the memories that he would have to spend who knew how
many years to forget again. When all answers, all correction,
all attacks were forced upon him by quotations his father
whined or shouted or beat into him using the same ragged
black book. What was the answer? *You're fallen!* was flung
at him over and over. *Just like . . .* One never satisfied. The
itching edges of his mind strained to recall. He didn't want to
know. Why did he need to remember now? For what
possible reason? Why revisit nightmares long gone by?
Never mind, he shushed his own brain, *just wait, don't
reason, don't argue, just wait for it, it won't take long.*

And he remembered.

He knew.

You mean just like you? He heard his own voice,
though it was soundless again.

"Careful, shit-for-brains."

You *wanted more, as I remember it. Man, you had*

everything, and it didn't do anything but piss you off.

The Voice snarled, *"You don't have time for supposition, not if you plan to escape before you can't."*

"Son of the Morning."

The catalogue of his pictured shames went black. He saw Deesh, then, eyes like a flat-faced doll. Insubstantial. Her hair hung over her face. *She's not really here. Just something looking like her. Let it be.*

Knowing no pretense he could invent would remove from reality that she was here, in this place, he dragged his mind back to his host. What else did he know? From times far removed from childhood torment?

Better to reign in Hell than serve in Heaven.

"*The cunt read you that Puritan faggot? Thought he was the great writer. Wanted more. Fixed him. Had to finish writing that piece of dogshit blind, bedridden,* putrid."

He's not here, though.

"*But YOU are. And SHE is. And ding-ding–oh, sorry, contestants, your time is up. Game's over. You're lost.*"

You were said to be most beautiful. And most loved.

"*Mythology.*"

But it wasn't enough, was it? It was you who wanted more, wanted everything. It was you.

There was no response, but immediately Gard felt his limbs pulling, yanking out of his body, straining against sinew and socket. In dismemberment, every nerve endlessly screaming as his arms and legs separated, his joints serrated. He gasped, his mind closed. Nothing but a body cramping in excruciating physical anguish. Was it actual, or illusion? No matter. The agony was real enough. He grew clammy. Sweat like ice stung him everywhere, colonies of hornets shredding him. *Stop. Just stop. Please. Please stop please stop stop stop. Stop or kill me.* Just as he was on the verge of being completely pulled to pieces, the torturous slow murder ceased.

"*Ready to pay attention, now? Good. Let us begin with something even you were too dumb for–this will amuse you. Think she'll go for sodomy? Well–whether she does or not, doesn't matter. You get to watch. Maybe she'll sleep a hundred years. You can be the Drooling Fatboy Prince. If you can slobber her awake, she'll still suspect us of this little fuckfest, and that you just sat there, taking notes."*

He closed one–coil?–around the silent Deesh, and her eyes came alive. They saw Gard. In her face, for the first time in his life, he read open, undisguised, and devouring fear.

"Watch closely–I'm going to crack her wide open, it's easy when the fruit's so rotted and stinking. Maybe you'll learn something you can use later."

Gard saw the thing somehow slide its claws, arms, into her. *Under* her flesh. Gard saw the shape of talon outlines visible under her skin, caressing her. No. No no no no no.

Wait.

"You wanna help?" The thing cackled.

I want to . . .

"Now. First we turn her over. See? Next . . ."

Joints still aching, mind mired in the monstrousness before him, he heard himself speak the words. "I want to sing to her."

A great blazing roar of laughter billowed in the greenish light. *"First, you can't sing. You never could. You can't now. You sound like a toad with a throat full of flyblown entrails. The clumsy no-talent shit-kicker from Travis County, Texas."* More laughter.

The Voice had, unknown to itself, gone too far. And Gard was brought to his stand. The proverbial now or never laid itself out before him. Clumsy? Yeah. Shit-kicker? Once he was. But no talent? The Prince of Darkness might be the King of Lies, but even Gard knew better than that one. His talent, perhaps actual genius, was not of his own making, nor of his own bestowing. He could and would take no credit for it. But it *was* his, and he knew it because when he opened up his vocal cords and let them fly, then–and only then–he knew there must be God. Now he knew the Opposition, too, and it had overplayed its hand.

245

He moved his eyes away from the horror pervading Deesh, turned his head from the spot for movies made in Hell, and fixed his gaze on its chief tenant.

"And second," the Voice continued, *"you don't listen, motherfuck. I told you that steaming pile of snacking shit does not play here."*

"It will. I do. I will. YOU watch." His voice was real, now. He heard the echoes.

The thing let go of Deesh's ghost, dropped her midturn with a sound like leaves burning.

"Always more. Got you here, and it'll keep you here, you dick-licking faggot. Okay. Sing if you can, because you can't. Here's a new deal: You sing, you can take her. You can't sing, you stay–forever–and watch me demonstrate on her what humanity's most brilliant perverts could never hope to imagine. Take it or leave her. Now."

There was more cackling, and the evil joy in it almost caught Gard; he was hurting, he was weakened, and fatigue suddenly immersed him; one more moment and he would surrender.

"Well?" A newly foul odor began to emit from the Voice, a smell striking Gard like a physical blow. No West Coast smog could begin to approach this. His throat was a burned and bleeding column. He could get no air into his diaphragm. His hands felt weighted in boxing gloves.

Let her out of here. I'll stay. You couldn't keep her forever, you said so. But I would be trapped, wouldn't I? Wanting to die for the next eight eternities, and staying alive. His voice was gone again. (It's what he wants, ignore him, don't argue, it's what he wants.)

"Big hero," the Voice jeered. *"I'm so touched by your sacrifice I'll just send her–maybe along with you– back?"* More laughter. *"You are no bargain for trade, you filthy coward. Now sing–if you can–or be damned."*

For a moment something changed.

There was silence in Hell.

And in its interlude, he remembered something else.

"It's a matter of faith," she had told him, sitting in

246

her white overalls with the light refracting from her hair. And he had rejected the truth of it because he didn't know the meaning of the most misused word in the language.

Oh, Deesh–can I ever look into your face again? Even if I do get you out, I'll have lost you.

"*It's a matter of faith.*" Too late he'd come to understand. "*It's a matter of faith.*" She had told him she could not come here. He knew better than to pray for it. But there must be something she could do. *If you can't send me you, send me something, anything. I know you can do that. Anything you would give me, I'll owe you forever. For. Ever. Anything you would give me. Anything anything anything. Forever.*

The Gibson was in his hands. He felt it, he saw it, he wasted no time in astonishment. His time was running out, his one chance, his choice nearly at an end. He flexed his fingers. It felt awful, but at least the boxing gloves were gone. He picked at the strings. Not a good sound. He tried to tune up.

The thing of the Voice held Deesh up by her neck, shook her like a dishrag. Her eyes seemed to focus again. She looked straight at Gard. Locking on her eyes, his voice low and loaded with memory and desire, encompassing only the two of them, he said to her in the drawl of old,

"'Lo, darlin'."

There was no answer, but she had heard. He knew it.

The Voice shrieked with screaming laughter. "*You know it? You know so much, don't you? You know enough to . . .*" The holograph screen opened again. "*Party on, Gard! Did you know that little girl killed herself? Know how she did it? All because of you? You know who found her? Oh, let's watch.*"

Ignore him don't argue with him don't look back whatever you do don't look back it's a matter of faith you can get her out and there's no guarantee of a happy ending, but don't look back.

No, I won't. I won't look back. I swear, I won't look back.

"Or, how about this? Take a look at the world as it will be. Sooner or later. Inevitably. THIS is how it is going to be, and there's nothing you can do to stop it."

Only a glimpse, but it nearly derailed him. No, he thought, no. No NO NO NO. That cannot happen! Not ever! NO NO NO.

Something passed through him then; he had no frame of reference, but he could have sworn his soul had just drained out of his body. There were no words to describe it, but he knew, no matter what had passed, or what was to come, this was the worst, the most hopeless moment he would ever know. To the end of his days, he would never be able to forget. And he would want to. Every day that remained to him he would wish he had never seen what he was seeing now.

Ignore him. Gard could feel the words *ignore him* as if they boomed in the hollows of his head. *If you do not ignore him, you let him in. You let him in, she's lost. You let him in,* you're *lost.*

Gard closed his eyes. He found himself somehow closed away from everything but Deesh. Confounded by, despite his transporting humility, the fatal loneliness and absolute despair emptying his spirit at so rapid a rate, he wondered how in all of hell he would do the thing that he had come for.

He tried again. He could not do this. *Oh, get off it, Gard. If you managed to write a song, you can sing one, can't you?* His own voice pulsed in his head. Who else had he expected to hear? The Road Rescue van didn't drive this highway. Any ninth hour denouements were his. *Choose.*

He opened his mouth.

Fixed his eyes on the Gibson.

Went to the private place he'd kept himself singing in all his life. So private there was room only for him. The beguiling Voice, so saturated with lies, goading him into casting himself off another hellish building, was shut out. For a moment he thought of doing "Praise the Lord and Pass the Ammunition" because Deesh would get the joke. If she could hear him still.

Before he could begin, one more savagery was visited on him.

All the physical and emotional agony just . . . stopped. His fingers flexed again, easily now. He drew in clear, breathable air. The muscles between his shoulder blades untwisted themselves, and his eyes no longer burned. *All righty, now,* he thought, *the guitar* and *relief from all the squeeze?* He hadn't even asked for more and he had gotten it. The veins in his neck ceased throbbing and he nearly grinned. *That's it. Don't ask for more and they'll give it to you. Ha.* This was going to be easy now.

But something had left with the pain, confusion, and fear. Something else gone from him. No time to wonder what. Later, he could think about it later. He cleared his voice. Still there. He'd be out of here soon enough. Out and never looking back. Easy. *Now, let's see, what are we doing? Playing, yeah. Uh, but what for? Why waste precious time?* He knew the exit; he should just cash it in and leave all this . . . this . . . *hell* . . . behind. Kicking up dustless dust and leaving it smaller and smaller and smaller until it disappeared. If he got out now, he could forget it all, never remember a thing, return to being himself untouched by the day's events.

Packing up and checking out. This gig was over.

There was silence; yeah, the bastard had given up, no tricks left. No copperheads to pull from a hat, no magic horror movies that wouldn't end, no guilt to lay across him like a poisonous wand. He'd won.

Deesh.

Deesh. She was fading, coming apart, disappearing like smoke. No, not Deesh exactly, but his urgency for her, for himself to save her. The freedom was relief more massive than the chains had been. He felt nothing. Whatever they had once meant to each other was no longer any concern of his, and he could have shouted for joy. Freeeeedom! There was nothing but liberation in him. No hate, no fear, no pain, no guilt, no love. That he had loved her amused him slightly.

249

Such a big goddamned deal for half his life. He'd broken out, escaped in enough time to have the rest of his life before him. Yes! He turned back toward the black chambered nautilus disguised as stairs, put one boot in front of him, then another.

Deesh.

He stopped. But what for? Keep going. Deesh. Keep going.

Deesh.

Get your ass out of this place, he ordered himself. But. Wasn't he supposed to take her with him? Wasn't that the plan? He couldn't remember why he'd made such a plan to begin with. She was nothing to him, and he gloried in the feeling that he had no concern at all of what he meant to her. *Shit. All those wasted years worrying. Go.*

You're supposed to take her. It's what you came for. Maybe so, but the plan had changed. He'd come because her life had meant more than his own, but thank God or the Devil, he was over it. No reason to stay. No reason *at all.*

Except to simply choose to stay. For no reason. Choose to save her when he'd get nothing from it or for it, and might be giving himself over to the terrible dangers here if he stayed one more minute.

He stopped again, and the full meaning of the truth was before him. He could take it or leave it. This fucking free will was worse than he thought. Now it was easy to go and the greatest risk to stay, and something was suggesting he remain, regardless. For no reason, except perhaps that Deesh would be left in a fatal coma for another forty years or more. He didn't care. It was simply a matter of self-preservation. Still, he hesitated. When had Deesh come to mean nothing to him? He strained to recall, but there was nothing. It was simply a matter of taking her out or leaving her here. Period. Free will had nothing to do with love or goodness or bodily ascension into heaven. It was purely an intellectual exercise. Do the thing or do not do it. What was in it for him? Not one frigging thing. So that was the deal, that's all there was to it. You have to choose, and you have to choose with no reward tipping the balance. His anger smoldered, ignited. What kind of games were they playing with him? Who the hell did Blonde Overalls think she was? All that bullshit, making him think he was on some noble mission, that he was some knight errant regaining his lost honor, that heroics were not lost to him. Bullshit, bullshit, *bullshit.* It was all just a fucking game, just to see what he would do. What he would choose for the sake of choice alone. Well, fine. Fine, and dandy. The game was over, and he had won. The decision was easily defined, and ought to be easy to make. He should run while the running was good. Good-bye, one and all.

He sat down on something too short for him–better not to know what. Rested the Gibson on one knee, and made his choice.

The Gibson, think on that. His celebrated J-200, low action, natural blond finish. Deesh had once said this guitar was the only natural blonde he'd ever nursed any passion for. Had a big sound, but it played like silk. He realized the Voice tormenting him had ceased flashing swamp light, or that he no longer was aware of it, or of his own, either. Without another word in his head, he cleared his throat, and opened it up.

He sang.

The loss of love was worse than Death and Hell, he sang. His only woman would never forgive him–he had looked back, and his mistrust of the gods had cost him all.

"One mortal man, not two.
One chance in the Underworld,
Or she's lost to you."

He went into the bridge, and the vile thing that was the Voice began changing shape. Gard's late sense of well-being drained away suddenly, without warning, leaving him as he was before. By force of will, he focused on the music. He trembled to the edge of his eyelashes, but his voice did not falter.

He was amazed at his own sounds. His throat cleared completely, air rushed in, and he began to let it out. His love did forgive him, before he'd finished asking. Falling back into the Land of Shades, nothing crossed her face but sorrow. Now she would wait. "How long?" he sang. "How long?" and his tenor drew itself out farther and farther, diminishing slowly into memory.

The Voice was a vague, sandstone sculpture. Ugliness of form and face so terrible no poet could ever have described it in words understandable to the human ear. And many had tried. Their failure was perfectly understandable.

Into a chorus.

Despite his efforts not to, Gard stared at the huge, wrecked statue. As he sang on, its blurred lines sharpened a bit. Became animate. Shifting, settling, shifting again.

Gard slid into a verse.

Mutable as sand, the rock pile in front of him swept itself back from one nightmarish figure to another, as if it had lost control of its own pack of wolfish mendacities. Perhaps the Voice had taken shape so obscene, so evil, so grasping toward him that his mind had no words to put to it. He felt his tongue swell in his mouth. The sight in front of him was too unspeakable to know and go on living. Just let him die now. Oblivion was the only heaven. Die, he begged himself. Please die. Let me be dead. He kept singing.

The Voice becoming thing becoming horror show now showed itself in lines Gard recognized without remembering why. Hairline cracks ran length, width, depth, as if the figure would fall apart at a touch. A face became discernible where a face ought to have been, faint, almost suggested more than formed. Sandstone arms and sandstone legs folded close to what was perhaps the body. A scrapulous face, made all the more so by what was barely visible underneath it. It seemed that layer upon layer of time was erasing itself, revealing something ancient and infinite and terrible. The worst revelation of all.

Once, this thing had been beautiful.

The poets all had said so. And the poets were right. What had been lost was there in the creature's face. Gard was staggered. He nearly lost his place. Perhaps this sea change had been forced upon the thing. Or maybe it had chosen to reveal itself to stop the singer in his tracks.

Whatever the cause, Gard saw the darkest shadow of what once had been. And if fear were the objective of the show, fear had won. He felt white-hot pliers twisting his heart. He sang.

Under the ruined angel, he saw that even Evil is not born of itself, but of Good. And someday it would have to return to Good or cease to exist. Now he recognized in a flash what he had never believed. The matter of faith, he saw, was about forgiveness. The basic element in every form of love. Not only giving it, but taking it. All you have to do is ask. To want it. So easy. So hard. The wonder of it raced through him, though he kept on singing.

Forgive me, Deesh. Have mercy on my soul.

He was approaching the end, the coda he had added since she had been taken from him, a part she would know instantly and would never tell anyone else that she did know. The sacred part. A fade-out he would have to manage without faltering. He might not make it. He was overcome with a sorrow so old, so killing, so endless it made everything else he'd known seem without significance. It was if his own voice had brought the thing, the Voice, to a heap pathetic on the floor of Hell, and it had taken him with it. Facing a naked desert or surveying an empty kingdom of polar ice. Better fire and pitchforks than infinite nothingness made worse by the memory of glory.

How could you have stood it? How can you stand it now?

A rumbling began from the shifting shape. Gard felt its hatred trying to shut down his voice. He thought of Deesh and of her beloved poet Pope, sang the coda.

"But soon, too soon the lover turns his eyes;
Again she falls, again she dies!
Yet even in death Eurydice he sung,
Eurydice *still trembled on his tongue:*
Eurydice *the woods*

Eurydice *the floods*

Eurydice *the rocks and hollow mountains rung!"*

He slowly repeated the final line, took the chords down to single notes, held the last one, and came to the end.

Impossibly, the music had played in Hell.

Gard had not taken his eyes off the mutating Voice, and he did not now. *How can you stand it?* he wondered for the second time. *To never know music again, or love, or joy so fierce it never leaves you, no matter what, and the peace within the fierceness?* How could the Host of Hell continue its own existence without wings and guitars? *Incomprehensible.* Yet he had, dreamlike and distracted, comprehended. There was nothing to know here but pity. And pity him Gard did.

To dare the temerity to feel sorry for the Devil was to bring the full extent of its cruelty and power down upon him. Sensations tore through Gard that hollowed out his belly and left him faint. He seemed to be experiencing every grief, every sorrow and loss of hope, every pain and every death since the beginning of time. It brought him to his knees, and physical pain was nothing, nothing at all, compared to a forced knowledge no sane mortal, in the unlikely event he survived, would ever be able to escape or explain. Then the feeling passed, but its after image burned, remained, clutching at him, talons bound to sink through him wherever he went for the rest of his life. Before his eyes was the ruin of his future. He flung it aside, and forced himself to rise.

The image of beauty bleeding into hideousness let out a crashing roar. It began to crack, run to sand, reform, shifting again, faster and faster.

"GET OUT!" it screamed, its loathing of Gard beginning to avalanche. In the place where music never reached, he had played, and he had pitied, and it was not to be borne.

"GET OUT!"

Not unless she goes with me. A thought intruded on his concentration. *I* would *be the man who got thrown out of town, tour schedule, record contract, half the bars in Germany, and Hell.* The momentary irony was wasted. He couldn't find Deesh to read his thought and puncture whatever balloons of grandiosity might float through the joke.

"GET OUT!" The words were like the noise of a falling building.

Where is she? I'm not going without her.

The rock fall of sound took on a quality Gard wasn't sure he heard correctly–weeping.

"Just go. Take the cunt and GO. JUST GO! TAKE HER, BUT GO!"

The cavern, or whatever it was, shook. The crying coarsened back into a roar. Gard shouldered the Gibson and stumbled in the direction of the stairs. He heard nothing behind him. Darkness came upon him again, so complete that he guided himself with the sound of his own boot heels. Rise one. Two. Three. Four. Was she there? *Don't look back.* But why not? What was the point? He knew with certainty he wouldn't fall back into Hell–he'd been ejected, hadn't he? Like an arrow through the apple, the words flew through him one last time; *"it's a matter of faith,"* she had said. A matter of his own–that he would believe what was true or be left with nothing worth living for. A matter of faith–not in something apart, but in himself. That was what she'd told him, he realized at last. Faith in himself meant faith in everything else worth the effort.

Like Deesh. In whom he'd never had sufficient trust to believe she wouldn't leave him. The Gibson, slung on his back, thumped slightly. He put his arm behind him. Felt nothing. Not even the tips of her fingers. The stairs wound greasily upward in continuing blackness, and he had lost count. If he could just hold her hand to take her out of here.

No! Don't ask for more. Do not need. Don't need more. This is Chicago and it's both of us, and me drunk and disoriented, and we're both crouched outside a hotel room twenty floors up, and we're way too near the edge.

So. He'd either bring them back in through the window, or he wouldn't. He heard nothing but the loudness of his own thoughts and the tap of his boots on the stairs. One hand against a suppurating wall he could not see. *You will not look back. You have no need for more.* Why think at all? Keep climbing. *Good title for a tune. Gotta tell Cleve; see if he can write something for it. Him and his stupid blackout aviator sunglasses. Twenty-four/seven, that's Cleve, likes it dark as—*

He didn't finish the thought. He heard himself laugh, though no sound issued from his throat. *He takes 'em off for Deesh, though. Likes her lookin' straight into his eyes; she does that with everybody, but he don't know. Thinks he's the only one. Yeah. Makes me think so about me, too. But she means it with me. I knew that. I knew that, so why didn't I believe it? What more did I want her to do? More. Don't know more what, but more something. Like it can't be safe to have everything. You gotta want more so maybe you'll have enough left when you start losin' it. Or they start taking it away. Maybe.*

Maybe more *is voodoo, the lie to the masters that you're not getting enough so they won't decide you have too much. They'll be happy watching you ruin what you have 'cause you wreck yourself trying to guard it. For crying out loud, Gard, just keep walking. Walking, walking, she's got to be there. Lady Overalls wouldn't have told me I could get her out if I couldn't.*

Couldn't. Wouldn't. Haven't. I'm dragging ass, keep moving, don't look back.

Don't look back. One of his and Deesh's non-negotiable laws of living. They neither one looked back. Nothing any good to look back to, before the last thirty years of their lives apart and then together. *If she's there, she'd say* 'I see you're dragging yourself out of hell again. Do make a faster trip of it this time.' *Wouldn't say a thing about herself in hell, the hell of her life before she'd left home, before she left, left and didn't look back, and hers was worse than mine. I must be the only one now who knows that. The only one left. Deesh. Always stronger than me. Had to be, I guess. She saved me from Chicago. Where was I when she needed saving? Somewhere in Texas, most likely, trying like hell to break out. Funny how I know exactly what that means. I'm trying like hell to get out of Hell and I've been circling these stairs for so long. So long.*

Don't look back. Be tired, be a whineyass, feel sorry for yourself–you're good at that, leastways you used to be, give up already, but don't look back. His mind shut down for a few minutes. Then,

But that's it, isn't it? Looking back is *giving up. And giving up is the unforgivable sin. Why didn't I ever know that? For God's sake, why couldn't I ever know that?* No answer.

Keep climbing. There should be some light by now; why isn't there? Been climbing these stairs for a month at least, why can't I see some light?

It was a longer climb still, but at last, the stairs ended. He was out. It was night. He looked up, saw the sky cluttered with a luster of glimmering stars.

Look now.

He found himself lying next to Deesh, in the middle of the sheets, like children huddled on a bed too big for them.

His hand ached. He looked down. His hand was wrapped so tightly around Deesh's that her fingers had gone white. He carefully disintwined. Nothing had changed. She lay still, breathing evenly and independently, but except for the signs of pressure on her hand, there was no change.

He sat up, swung his legs to the side. Feet on the floor, he dropped his head into his hands. What had he expected? That a dream so sharply real would actually have been real?

He looked up a second time. Through the glass of the cupola, the revolving spirals of stars seemed so low he could almost hear them scratching at the glass. Scratching, as if trying to make themselves audible. Scratching that sounded for all the world like rustling sheets. He froze. A voice like a rusty blade whispered,

"Gard?"

He turned to see her blinking at him, puzzled and questioning.

Coffin Fodder

He sat at the window gazing into nothing. He lay on the floor looking up blankly. He moved without animation, as if he were a failed experiment in bringing back the dead. And he was dead, or parts of him were. He walked among the living, ate and slept, breathing and blinking as if it were his obligation to fulfill.

The old rage was gone, taking with it the fuel that sparked his need to live. In its place was a sadness cloaking his soul such that he had never known. Had not imagined it was possible to know. He withdrew; rumors ignited: he was in rehab, he was in a psych ward, he was drugging in a Paris hotel room back to the bad old days, he was dead. In truth, he remained in Deesh's house. His own he could not bear. Where once the rear walls of glass were access to the water, now they were windows to a vast and perpetual emptiness. Sea waves in their endless rolling roar made him ill. His house sat in stale silence, a void. Deesh went there sometimes, or Lily, for what care-taking they could do for a house now corpse.

She intruded on his grief, trying to shake it loose. Tell me, she said, tell me. He shook his head. I can't. I don't know. He half-believed if he could tell her, he could escape himself, and he tried. But no words were yet come into the language to define anguish brought home from Hell.

She remembered nothing. She awoke as if it were the same day and hour she had last lived. Without tangible information, he assumed—he hoped—she would never know it or see it or feel it. But now and then, some shadow fluttered in her, and then flapped away if she turned her head to look.

In time, he would leave it behind him, he thought. Or it would leave him behind. There was, however, no energy to hope.

She would come upon him, staring into her wrecked garden, finding in herself a despair she was certain had long been lost to her. How to bring him back? He was broken; she knew it. And king's horses and king's men were, as always, useless.

*   *   *

His voice is gone. Perhaps permanently. When he speaks–occasions few and far between–she hears the old tones flexing easily under the remaining trace of Texas. But when he tried to sing, even a little, nothing rose from him but air. Never mind, he says, kissing her hand. It hardly matters, he says.

It's all that matters, she thinks, worry gnawing slowly, inexorably.

There is nothing now to do but wait. And read to him, as if she were the singer, poetry in D flat major. She reads Keats, she reads Yeats and Eliot, but not Pope, and he nods, sometimes.

She would find him staring through the panes, without expectation that the landscape beyond her windows would be the same as it had been yesterday, the same as it would be tomorrow. He was a stranger in his own life.

There was no measuring his sorrow; it was if having looked upon the shores of an entire world caught in black and ancient pitch, he could not rid himself of it. And the bleeding grief that had Shrike as its source continued to hemorrhage from him, despite invisible scar tissue he could actually feel. If it is possible for a soul to scar, then his was a latticework of shoddily healed wounds.

She cannot remember; he cannot forget.

Like cracked glass, his face was crisscrossed with lines laid into him apparently overnight.

When she is near him, he longs for her. She can see it beneath the desolation in his eyes–but he can barely speak to her.

How to traverse the ice field between them? She

catches the image of herself building a pyre on the edge, keeping it burning. But she cannot make it real.

In the mornings she would wake to find her hand trapped in his; there was often difficulty in prying it loose.

The brown of his hair had given way to wide tracks of silver; Deesh colors it for him in her bathroom sink. He does not object. If she can make him look a little like he used to, then maybe he will be a little like he used to. Dirty water runs down the porcelain, circles the drain, drips into oblivion. His hair is brown again, but he knows that won't last.

She cannot remember, and he cannot forget.

One night deep into the winter, she dreams of him a year in the future. He was fifty years old and a cardio-vascular detonation tore his heart apart. She rode his Harley to the funeral and returned home to a house she now–with all the passion she could muster–hated.

She awakens, shaken. He sleeps silently beside her.

When morning comes, he slowly rises to it, and lumbers into the library. Takes his place by the window and stares. From behind him she slides her arms around his neck. "Tell me," she says.

"What?" he asks, not looking around.

"Anything." Her voice is void of desperation, but it always sounded that way.

Absently he rubs her arm.

"Good day today."

Carefully, she says, "Oh?"

"Yeah." Now he does turn his face to her, halfway. In his inflection are starless nights and sunless days. "It's Beethoven's birthday."

He does not speak again for a week.

The year withered, and another came to take its place.

Resurrection

"I know how you did it."

He glances up from the magazine he is pretending to read. "Did what?"

"Got me out of it."

The little color in his face leaches away. He cannot forget. If she knows anything, she *must* forget. He will have to see to it. Somehow. Executing deals with the Devil was its own, apparently life-long, reward. But it was his reward and his alone.

"What are you talking about?"

She looks at him as if he were stupid. "Two years ago? I was in an inexplicable coma? You pulled me out of it. And I know how you did it."

He relaxes imperceptibly. "You do?" He turns to face her, his face rising higher over the back of the sofa.

"You sang to me, didn't you?"

He rolls the magazine, twists it between his fingers. "Yes," he whispers. "But how do you know?"

She props her elbows on her desk, rests her chin on her hands. "Ohio."

He drops the magazine; it lands with a flap behind the sofa. "I don't know what you mean."

She sighs. "Yes, you do. Mrs. Betty Hudson contacts your management company. They in turn relay a message to you. Her eleven-year-old son is in the hospital, comatose as the result of–a car crash?–and when she plays your music to him, his vital signs stabilize. She wonders if you could take the time, would you make a tape of yourself speaking directly to him? It might help, and she is out of options. You, in turn, take a plane out there, take a taxi to the hospital, sing to the child for an hour, and–holy legerdemain!–he comes out of it. The mother is hysterical. She wants to nominate you for sainthood, but you're embarrassed, thinks it's coincidence that Tommy Hudson is revived from a coma while you're there. You insist she must never, EVER tell anyone you've been there. The doctor has to know, doesn't he? Okay, but the doctor has to promise he will never, EVER reveal you visited his patient. Then you fly right home, back into the recording studio, feigning you went out for a really long coffee."

"How do you know?" The words emerge slowly.

"Small article in the *New England Journal of Medicine*. You weren't named, of course, but I knew it was you. Who else?" She shrugs slightly, but the gravity with which she's posed the question alerts him to the futility of attempting to argue with her. He is caught and that is that.

"You read the *New England Journal of Medicine*?"

"I read everything."

He knew that. Where is his mind, or what's left of it? "That must have been ten years ago. All this time you've known, and you never said a word?"

She rises, crosses the library floor, assumes her usual perch at the fireplace. "You didn't want anyone to know. Why would I give you unnecessary pause?"

"You mean why would you tell me something that might upset me?"

"I mean."

They have not had so long a conversation in two years.

"I'm telling you now to convince you I did hear you sing to me, and you rescued me from–well, whatever."

He shakes his head once. "What did I sing?" She cocks her head in question of the question. He shrugs. "Do you remember?" Unconsciously, he holds his breath.

She closes her eyes and squinches up her face in the common human misconception that wrinkling her features will facilitate memory. "I *think* I remember."

In the silence following, the mantle clock ticks audibly, as if her mind is counting off recollections. Finally she says, "'Eurydice.' You sang 'Eurydice' to me. That was the

262

last time I heard it."

He slumps forward on the sofa. She unwinds herself from the hearth, slides in carefully next to him. Lifts his head gently in her hands, smoothes the pads of her fingers against the ravages of his face. "What?" she asks.

He leans his face into her fingers, as if her touch would erase the fissures in his skin. "I didn't sing that."

She looks puzzled. "No? I could swear–I hear it in my sleep sometimes, even yet. Still, you brought me back. You need to know that."

"Why?" His dejection is apparent, but there is something else in his voice that rings faintly of fear.

What is wrong? Should she have remained silent? But she has remained silent for two years, and time, she senses, is running out.

"Because you think you've done something so terrible you don't deserve to live. I can't understand it. Whenever I feel I'm just at the edge of knowing you as I once did, my mind shuts out everything. I'm blank." She lets out a sigh. "What could you possibly have done you'd work so hard to prevent me from knowing? You know there's nothing that would force me to judge you."

"Oh, Deesh." He pulls his head away, and hangs it. "I don't know. I don't know what I can't tell you." He hides his face the better to hide the lie.

She sighs again, more heavily. "I know you told me things, too. Things we–don't say."

"I'm sorry," he says, miserably.

"Why? The words were for my gain, not yours."

"But I broke the rules. Once you say the words, you can't ever take them back. So don't say 'em."

"Do you want to take them back?"

"God, no!" His own body was feeling too heavy to sustain. The killing weariness was upon him again. He was losing her, losing his connection. In a moment he would be gone again, back into the swirling nothingness his intellect had become.

They were quiet for a long time. He may have slept.

In any event, when he refocused, she was there, watching him, a look of gentle sadness settling over her.

"Deesh?"

"Hm?"

"You okay?"

"I'm just thinking."

"But you're okay?"

She reached over and rubbed his arm. "Yes. You needn't worry. I'm fine. Why wouldn't I be with you around?"

That was so out of character for her that he sat up with the shadow of his old self in the gesture.

"Lot of protection I am these days."

"More than you think."

"Less than you think. In fact," he stared away into the fire, "I'm no good to you, not anymore. Don't think I ever will be. It's time for me to move on; I'll sell my house and go–somewhere. As soon as I can."

So many words at once fatigued him to the point that he wondered how he could summon the energy to even walk across the library. He didn't look at her.

"Let's go upstairs," she said suddenly.

"Deesh, I–I can't–I mean I want to, but . . ."

"No. For something else. The other is for you to say, if and when."

He looked ashamed.

"And stop that. I'm *fine*."

He nodded dumbly, took her proffered hand, and together they hiked up to the abandoned fourth floor.

She stopped at the tiny room in which he had imprisoned himself after Chicago. He glanced at her, afraid.

"I said, stop it!" she said. "Come inside."

They sat on the floor, knees to knees. He waited, wanting to go back downstairs and sleep a few days.

"Why here?" he exhaled.

"Because this room is small enough to contain what I have to say. I don't want the words flying around like some escaped canary."

He nodded. He had learned from her the power of language. It could be dangerous, you had to take care where and when you said what to anyone.

"I don't know what happened two years ago," she began, softly, "but I know you literally saved me, and that the cost to you was just about everything."

She paused and pushed her hair off her forehead. He wanted to tell her she didn't have to do this, he knew whatever she was saying was like dragging cotton through a rake, and whatever it was, she didn't need to put herself through any more. He had put her through more than enough.

"I need to tell you something."

She stopped, and the room's narrow dimensions seemed to close further in. "Something I swore twenty-two years ago I would never tell you, no matter what. Ssh. Don't interrupt. It's not bad, at least I believe you won't think so. I hope you don't."

Somehow his fatigue receded a little, he fell into her gaze and found there what he had so many times before. Before, when he was able to see a world without end, without horror. Able. Now there was a concept good and gone.

"Gard." It was almost as if she were supplicating. But she couldn't be. He knew better. "Gard," she repeated. She drew in a long breath, as if she were about to swim a mile under water. Her lips actually trembled a little. That had to be a trick of bad lighting from the single small window high on the wall. Still there was something about her he had never seen. He didn't know what to make of it.

"I want to tell you the same thing you told me when you thought I couldn't hear you."

He raised his eyebrows in genuine puzzlement.

"You say you're no good to me, that you're in the way, that my life would be better without you." She drew in another long breath, let it out slowly. "You idiot. You ARE my life."

A spasm passed through him. Could that be true?

Maybe. But living under her dormers as the object of obligation and pity was something he could no longer do. She would see it was better without him as soon as he left.

"You don't get it, do you?" she asked, sharply.

He seemed paralyzed, unable to comprehend her shift in tone.

"I don't feel sorry for you. Not in the way you think. I do feel compassion for everything you've lost, and sorrow that you've lost it. But that doesn't change one single molecule of everything else."

"Everything else?" He spoke slowly, with difficulty.

"Oh, Gard. Don't you know?"

He shook his head. He had no idea what she was getting at, and rather wished she'd just get at it. He felt like a block of concrete, a gargoyle hunched there on the floor.

She took his head in her hands again, straightened it until their eyes locked. He was too tired to drop it again. She refolded her hands around her knees; her voice moved into a music he'd never heard from her before. He could that be? His weariness blurred the question.

"Don't you know that I love you? Don't you know that I have loved you until my soul ached with it?"

Words he never dreamed he'd hear, the very words he was wanting to say to her from the beginning of it all, somewhere in Europe he can hardly remember and hardly forget. His throat has tightened and he can barely breathe.

"Don't you know," she whispered fiercely, "that *you* are everything? Father I should have had, brother I almost had, son I will never have?

"Don't you know, John Gard? What will make you know how it is, how it has always been? Don't you know that if you were damned, then I would want to be damned with you?"

He froze. "Don't say it," he choked out.

"It's just an expression," she said gently, more gently than he has ever heard. "But even if it were not, even if it were true, I would mean it. I do mean it."

He was speechless.

"Don't you know," her voice was shaking, "that I have loved you, almost from the hour that we met? I didn't want to, I couldn't understand why I did, but there was something in your face that day, underneath all the layers of assumed outrage. Something that I recognized, something I never expected to see again. It was–me. No, not that exactly. More like . . ."

She stopped and he vaguely knew she was actually having trouble gathering words. His head was still ringing from her first sentence. She loved him, and she'd said that she did.

"It was a person I knew, that I *could* know, that I wanted to know. That's what I saw, and I was mixed in there with it. With you. And I was right."

Her words began to come haltingly again. "I suppose–I guess–" She shook her head, as if to straighten the jumble within. "It was–I was caught in a moment that nearly never happens. To anyone. And I didn't know what in hell to do with it. A refurbished life in a field full of the dead?"

He knew she was not talking only of the inhabitants of the cemetery. But she was speaking of them, too, and he remembered the wind in her hat. The sun on the gates of Heloise and Abelard. For the first time in two years he managed a memory untinged by damnation.

"I love you, Gard. I love you more than I could ever let you know. You were used to women clinging to you, dropping into your bed, thinking they knew the rock god Gard well enough to crave you to distraction, mostly their own. I didn't know you–the earthbound Gard–not enough to recognize whether you really were caught in that moment, that five minutes where the earth actually stood still, or you were cruising an odd neighborhood for living, and momentary, flesh."

His face, usually inanimate, took on a look of hard amazement.

"I thought I was taking a big chance, a non-calculable risk, in spending any time with you, much less taking my clothes off with you. But by the time we got around to that, I had to know if it was real. You might disappear the next day, having scored at last, but it almost didn't matter. I wanted to see if I could make love, if *we* could, rather than engaging in nothing more than what I believe is known as a celebrity fuck."

"Celebrity fuck? That's what you called me?"

She shrugged.

"I know you've had other men. Before me. What did you call them?"

"Mistakes."

She heard a gurgling in his throat, as if he were trying to laugh.

It was her turn for amazement. "Gard?" He shook his head, but the gurgle rose to his mouth, and she could have sworn he came very near a smile. The light was quite bad in the room, however; perhaps she had only imagined it.

"So, you see. You mustn't go unless you no longer want to live with me. Otherwise, you should live here as long as you can, as long as you need to. If you leave, and disappear, I'll survive. But surviving isn't living, it isn't joy, and it isn't worth it. Oh, Gard. I've loved you for so long. I don't know how to live without you."

He leaned forward, kissed her mouth, and some small spark of his old self came back to him. He had no confidence it would last. His hope of home was just another bad bargain he had made at the back of the devil's bin.

And yet . . .

Life Everlasting

He had wrapped it himself, and tucked it under the pile of pillows on his side of the bed. Between earphones, he was listening to those tracks laid down before, to put it bluntly, the shit had hit the fan. No voice was left him, but he could produce this album, save what recorded vocals he could, bring Evermore back into the studio to finish the rest, and salvage their latest–and last–album. He wasn't eager to do it, but he had to for the band. He had to.

He heard his own voice as a stranger's, and for the first time in his life he could judge it as a stranger's. Surprise had him sitting straight up in bed. This was what they heard, those many audiences over the years? This? He must have been speaking aloud, because Deesh had laid her book on its pages and was looking at him quizzically. He took off the phones. "Did I say something?"

She nodded.

"Oh. Didn't mean to." She made no move to retrieve the book. "Uh, it's different thinking like a producer." She nodded again. "I mean, well–jeez, Deesh! I really had a voice."

"Like you didn't know," she said, wryly.

"I didn't know like this. I was always on the inside of it. Hearing it from the outside is a whole 'nother thing. Did I *really* sound–like that?"

"You did," she said, quietly. "And I still think you could again, if you wanted."

He sighed. "I know you think that. What can I tell you? I'm an old man. I look like one, I feel like one, I must be one. Better to just accept the inevitable."

Laying her reading glasses aside, she rubbed the soft sleeve of his nightshirt. "I wasn't trying to talk you into anything."

A flash of a smile crossed his face. "Yes, you were."

"Yes, I was. I tremble with shame."

"Sure you do. You hussy." He was making an effort, and so much so she could see it.

"You think? I see my reputation is rising."

"I don't see you writing much these days."

"I don't want to write," she lied. "At least not at present. I want to read, all I want, anything I want without keeping one eye on what I can use, what I can analyze, what I can dissect for the glory of cultural history. Since you insist on paying the light and grocery bills, and every other bill that finds its way here–oh, you think I didn't know about the others? What do you take me for?–anyway, I don't use much money these days, so I'm not so driven as I used to be."

"I thought you wrote because you were a writer. Because you love it. No filthy commercialism involved."

She wiggled down into the mound of sheets beneath the comforter, pulled it around them both, and turned on her side. "Dr. Johnson said no man but a blockhead ever wrote for anything but money."

"You don't believe that." He slid down facing her, propped himself up with his elbow.

"Not usually. But at the moment I think he's got a point."

He reached over with his free hand and stroked her hair. "You silly. Bet you flowers and candy you change your mind by next week."

"Possibly. In the meantime, I plan to read for no good reason until I go blind." She looked at him carefully. "Looks like it's time to do your hair again."

He grimaced. "At least it's easier now that it's shorter. I wonder why I keep doing it."

"Because it's something tangible to maintain your dignity. Which you think you've lost."

"Mm."

"You are better, you know."

"Yeah. Some. But not, as you would put it, *significantly*." He sighed. "At least I can speak in more than monosyllables again."

"Then why don't you line up your multi-syllabic thoughts and tell me what's on your mind? I know something is wandering around in there looking to get out."

What can he reply? That he would come back if he could? If he could want to? But he wishes nothing; there is no human apparatus left with which to do otherwise. *Wishes are fishes all drowned in the sea.* He feels her fingers tighten around his wrist. "Deesh." Her name emerges as a croak.

"Tell me," she says.

"I–." The sentence dies in his breath.

Her grip tightens again, as if she would squeeze words through his fingertips. He feels himself growing very tired; he wants to give her a present, not the hollowness in his heart.

"Would you let me give you something I know you don't want?" Confusion compresses her face. "Please."

"Yes. If it's so important. Though I can't imagine you giving me anything I wouldn't want. Why is it so urgent?"

"It just is."

"All right, then. But I'm in the mood for a deal."

"What kind of deal?" He tries to pretend to be suspicious.

"I'll take your present, and use it however you want, but you have to tell me."

"Tell you what?"

"You know what."

"Deesh."

"Gard. You know I've never asked you for anything of yourself. It isn't right." She pauses a moment, as if she would begin again. "I would never intrude on your mind; I wish there were another way, but whatever has fractured your soul is still present, and I don't like being afraid for you."

The night was very black and cold. And nauseatingly infinite. All the heavy draperies around her greenhouse bedroom were closed against it. Except above. Through the cupola, light from a few faint stars strained toward him. He imagined the room as a fantastically luxurious, velvet-lined casket. With Egyptian precision, everything he might need in it forever. It would be just like Deesh to get in there with him, check it out, make sure he wanted for nothing. But he would literally return to Hell before he'd let the mortuary man bury her with him. Perhaps if he finally explained, in whatever way he could, she would understand, know why every year felt like twenty to him. Maybe. Maybe so. Could he leave her and leave her never knowing why? Were their positions reversed, he would be insane with worry by now. That might be worse than the truth. Time once again–maybe the last time–to choose.

He sat up again, wrapped the covers tighter around them both. She laid her head against his shoulder. He wouldn't want her looking right at him, she thought, while he considered what to do. He adjusted his arm around her shoulders, and for a moment it seemed the old Gard, the one with huge physical strength, had come back. She felt the relief that arrives after terrible pain.

"Your igloo needs a fireplace," he said.

"Do you want to move upstairs?"

"No. I want a fireplace in here."

"Fine with me. But how could it be done? To your exacting standards, I mean. All this glass?"

"It's not that hard. Just has to be engineered right. I've thought about it. See, what needs to happen is . . ." He trailed away. "What I can do is . . ." He gazed into the distance, seeing nothing. She waited.

"I–I can't tell you everything. I just can't." She nodded beneath his arm. "But I'll try to make your deal; it's fair enough." He felt the slight weight of her leaning into him, like a child waiting for a bedtime story. One to gleefully send her into nightmares.

"I. I saw something. I can't tell you how I saw it, or where, or why. I can't even find words for all that."

He rubbed his face with his free hand. "Before anything else, though, I want to give you something. So I know if you take it, you'll take it because you want to and not because you think you need to help me, or make me feel better, or anything like that. Okay?"

"Yes," she said in a low tone, nearly a whisper.

He reached around her, buried his hand under the pillows, groped around. When he withdrew, there was a small lump of a package. There was no ribbon and no card. "Open it," he said.

She was smiling at his inexpertise in gift wrapping. The paper looked old and rather worn. She gently undid it, opened the box within.

She said nothing for a long time.

"You could wear it on your right hand," he said. "I know you don't want it on the other one."

"How long have you had this?" she asked slowly.

He nearly smiled again. "Since the hotel in Paris. I bought it right after we left. Didn't know if I'd ever give it to you, and when I did know, you said you wouldn't take it or anything like it, so I just kept it."

"Until now," she murmured.

"Until now." He took it out of the box and offered it to her. In the lamplight, the narrow circle of diamonds seemed to shimmer, the platinum to glint. She held out her left hand.

"No, the other one," he said.

"No, this one."

"Really? You mean really?"

"I mean really."

None too steadily, he slid the ring onto her finger, and she held out her hand for them to watch the room's muted light catch fire at the facets.

"I wish I had a more romantic place to do this," he said, sadly.

She brought her hand to her face, rubbed it gently against the stones. "Now who's being a silly? Think, my boy. We've done everything else in bed. We might as well get married in it."

His surprise and relief gave way to something else; gratitude? Could be. But he knew better than to thank her.

"You don't have to change your name or anything,"

he tried to tease.

"I don't plan to. 'Deesh Gard'? No music to it."

He took her hand and kissed it, then held it against his lips for a while. "Is this legal, do you think?"

"Yes," she said, greatly amused. "By common law we've been stuck with each other about seventeen years."

"I didn't know that!"

"I know you didn't. The finer points of the cohabitation statutes have got to be so boring, why even go into it?"

"I think we've been married twenty-two years."

She looked closely at the ring again. "If you bought this in Paris, you may have a point."

"The first one I've ever made."

"Uh huh. I must tell you, I've never seen anything quite like this. Stones cut like–laurel leaves?" They spilled over the band, a flashing wreath. "It's–it's . . ."

"What?"

"It's heavier than it looks."

"Bothersome?"

"No, indeed." She reached up and kissed him. Carefully. He held her tightly; she could nearly feel his heart pumping through his skin. They sat together that way for some time. Then, musing, she said "The union of Rocker and Recluse. Will you say something?"

"It's about damn time."

"I don't mean about us. Husband."

"All right." His voice changed, back into the croaking of a man so old his vocal cords were worn thin. "I said I saw something. Didn't I?"

She nodded.

"You'll have to believe it was real, or that it might could become real. But that would be . . . "

He broke off in a fit of coughing, and 'wracking' barely described it. She reached over him, poured some water into a small glass from the decanter on the night table. He drank it. He coughed again, but the sound of it was diminished. She waited. At length, he began again.

"I saw the world, the whole world, as if I were God

looking down, seeing every detail of it, every thought in it, every word spoken by every person alive. It looked just the same as it does now. Everything normal. Except, it was changed. No wars, or plagues, or famine, or floods, or anything like that. And also, there was . . . "

His whole being clenched at the thought, but he continued. "There was no music. Anywhere. But worse, the worst was that there was no–love. Anywhere. None. Nobody loved no one. Three billion people–men, women, children living, working, playing, sleeping, and for what? Nothing. They lived, and died, and it was all the same. The Kingdom of Emptiness. And watching it, I became–empty. I am empty. I can't forget. It might as well be there every day, that world, and I have to look at it, every day. I can't explain why it was so terrible, so–godforsaken. I only know that seeing it, knowing what it would be like has–killed me."

His voice was almost inaudible by the last two words. He was shaking. He hoped he wouldn't vomit in the bed, because he had no strength to run to the bathroom.

"Dear God," she whispered. Exclamation, not prayer. She held him, rocked him, made shushing sounds as if he were a child still caught in a nightmare.

"Do you believe me?" he choked.

"Yes."

"You don't think I'm crazy?"

"No."

"Sometimes I think I'm going crazy."

"That's understandable."

"It is?"

"Gard. I don't know how you saw what you did. I don't know how it was made possible for you. I wish it never had been. But it was, and you are a heroic human being that you've been able to survive in any form. I don't think I would have."

His shaking slowed. He heard an impossible sound, and turned to look at her.

"Are you crying?" he asked, astonished.

"I don't know. Am I?"

He ran his thumb softly down her cheek, showed it to her, dripping. His amazement was confounded when she did nothing. Neither did she hide her face, nor dash tears from it, nor insist she was incapable of weeping. She merely held herself very still, hands in her lap, and waited until it was over. When she came to herself, she said to him,

"Perhaps you will never recover. But with enough time, you might."

He shook his head.

"You wanted me to have this," she raised her left hand, "because you think you're dying."

"I am," he said simply.

"Don't."

She did not tell him he looked less like dying than decomposing. The whitefalls appearing again in his hair absorbed what little color was left in his complexion. The crackled lines pressed into his face were deepening.

It had begun to rain, slowly, spattering big pear-shaped drops on the glass-domed roof. "Pathetic fallacy," she murmured automatically.

"I actually know what that is," he said.

"You know a lot."

"You don't sound very sarcastic."

"I am not being sarcastic. You know too much. But it does not have to kill you." Desperation underlined her words. "Come back, Gard."

"I will," he said faintly, feeling himself a kite in a high wind, "if I can."

She made a gesture; he thought she was going to shake him. "Don't sing, or leave this house, or make love, or escape this melancholy. All right. But don't let it make you dead. Don't let it win."

"No singing, no touring, no yappidygaga, no happiness. No point."

"You don't know that it's forever."

"That's true. It ends when I do."

"No." Her voice hardened. "I have never told you what to do. Or what to think. Or what to say. And most particularly I have never told you what to feel. Again, I'm breaking my own rules. Listen to me. Do not surrender. Whatever this thing is that has so horrible a hold on you, don't give up. You've never given up, even at times anyone else would have."

The rain increased, falling noisily against the glass. Thunder erupted, and a flash of lightning illuminated the shingled clouds, then disappeared.

"See? God agrees with me."

He smiled sadly. "You don't believe in a God that's so personal."

"Not to me. But maybe, right now, to you."

"Aren't you the one that thinks discussing theology is an invasion of privacy?" He looked directly at her, and she said, "Yes. Under normal circumstances. Do you think that's what we have here? Normal circumstances?"

Well, no, he didn't. Something tugged at his memory.

"What?" she said. "Tell me."

"I don't remember like I used to. Not the things I want to remember. I think my brain is taking the train before the rest of me does." He smiled almost sheepishly. "But there is one thing." He hesitated.

"Tell me. After these last two years, after tonight, what could you possibly say to me that I wouldn't believe?"

"The last thing. Before. Before you woke up. I–uh. I think I gave her, I think I gave the Holy Ghost a ride on my motorcycle."

"The Holy Ghost is a woman?" she asked, startled.

"Uh huh."

"Really? Well, don't alert the Vatican," she said. "Whoever's the Pope now would surely collapse."

Despite himself, a dwarfed and faint chuckle escaped.

The rain suddenly let up, a little.

"What else? Was she beautiful?"

"Oh, man," he said without thinking, "like nothing I've ever seen before, or will again." He realized, then. "Oh. I don't mean more than you, I meant . . ."

"Stop it. Do you think I'm going to be jealous of the

Holy Ghost? As in Father, Son, and?" She laughed quietly.

"I don't know what I'm saying."

"Yes, you do. And I know what you're saying. It is unbelievable. But I believe you. And by the way, this is the first time in a very long time I've seen you with any genuine pleasure on your face."

"Yeah," he said haltingly. "I don't feel quite so bad. For now."

"Maybe you'll feel that way later, too."

He thought about it for awhile. The rain crescendoed. Without meaning to, they slept. Sometime in the very early hours of morning, with the sky still black and cloud-smothered, he awoke abruptly. As soon as he moved, she came awake, and reached for him. "It's okay," he murmured. In surprise. "It is okay."

She stared, as if taking inventory of his face. "Yes?"

"Yeah. I mean, just a little. I can't understand it."

"You don't have to."

"Guess not," he spoke wonderingly. "But it's just a little. I'm still so far away from myself that I can't seem to care what happens."

She closed her arms around him and said quietly, "Perhaps just a little is enough. For now."

He dropped his head to her shoulder, took a long whiff of it. "Enough," he repeated. "Enough. You sure smell good."

"See? That's progress."

"Yeah." He gazed around the room as if looking for some miraculous appearance. The room remained as it always was, the draperies cloaking the emptiness without. "I don't know why you think I can–get better."

"I saw you sing," she said.

He drew back from her. Confusion washed down his face. "Huh uh."

"Uh huh. That's how I came to know you, as completely as is possible. To understand what sort of man you are."

He seemed to be weighing the worth of the investment if he pursued this. Finally,

"And what," he asked hoarsely, "sort am I?"

"The kind that I could love for better for worse so long as we both should live, and after that, too. The kind who gave me something to trust when it was certain I could love no one. No," she repeated, "one."

"No one," he said mechanically.

"But you made it different. I could love you. And I did. And I do."

Silence infused the room. Finally, he said as if he still didn't believe it. "Tell me again."

"Haven't I already told you far too much?"

"Jeepers, Deesh. No."

"Then haven't I said enough?"

"Almost." His voice gave a lightning flash of its old self.

"What, then?"

"Tell me, that day in Paris, when we first met . . ." his voice dropped away.

"Uh huh?"

"Did you know me? Did you know who I was?"

She laid her head against his heart; it was beating without signs of irregularity. Tears began to slip out again. Perhaps he might win, after all. It was possible.

"Oh, John Gard," she said, wiping her eyes with the backs of her hands, and laughing a little. "Don't you know, no matter what, I will never tell you *that*?"

He should have known better, but still, he was disappointed. However, here they both were, and, for half a lifetime, here they had been. Maybe they would continue; maybe he would live another year. And another year after that. Maybe they could still love each other after he was dead.

Maybe it could be that at last–finally and forever– whatever was left was enough.

Acknowledgment

MLA

"You alone could make my song take flight."

Gratitude and Credit to

Valerie Martin: *Mary Reilly*
Dorothy Parker: biographies
Edith Wharton: *The Valley of Decision*
Jim Steinman: "Surf's Up"
Bernhard Schlink: *The Reader*
Dante Alighieri: *Inferno*
A. Hamilton: "Cry Me A River"
Stephen Stills: "Helplessly Hoping"
Victor Hugo: *Notre Dame de Paris*
Don McLean: "American Pie"
Samuel Clemens: *The Adventures of Huckleberry Finn*
John Milton: *Paradise Lost*
William Shakespeare: *Othello*
William Shakespeare: *Hamlet*
Tim Rice (lyrics): "The Music of the Night"